The Night People

JACK FINNEY

DOUBLEDAY & COMPANY, INC.
GARDEN CITY, NEW YORK
1977

All of the characters in this book are fictitious, and any resemblance to actual persons, living or dead, is purely coincidental.

Grateful acknowledgment is made for the use of random lines of lyrics from the following copyrighted material:

Maraville Music Corporation: "All the Way," words and music by Sammy Cahn and Jimmy Van Heusen. Copyright © Maraville Music Corp., 1957. Reprinted by permission of Maraville Music Corporation.

ISBN: 0-385-13029-5
Library of Congress Catalog Card Number 77-74269
Copyright © 1977 by Jack Finney
Printed in the United States of America
All Rights Reserved
First Edition

For Don Congdon

THE NIGHT PEOPLE

The great bridge, arched across the blackness of San Francisco Bay, seemed like a stage set now. Empty of cars in the middle of the night, its narrow, orange-lighted length hung wrapped in darkness, motionless and artificial. At its center, where the enormous support cables dipped down into the light to almost touch the bridge, two men stood at the railing staring out at the black Pacific, preparing themselves for what they had come here to do. They wore denims, sneakers, dark nylon jackets, knit caps, and each wore a daypack. Because this had been his idea, Lew Joliffe, the smaller of the two, felt he had to go first, and now he gripped the red-painted bridge railing and swung a leg over, trying not to think of what came next. He drew his other leg over, sat balanced on the rail momentarily, then pushed himself off, out and away from the bridge.

His feet stepped onto the bottom two rungs, his hands seizing the railings of the small steel ladder that is mounted at midpoint of the ocean side of Golden Gate Bridge. Its dozen rungs angle outward away from the side of the bridge to lead up to a small railed platform level with the top of the great support cable. Ladder and platform are open, a spiderwork of thin metal, and Lew's eyes looked out between the rungs at a black void he knew stretched on to China. Focusing his mind on the need to hurry, willing himself never to look down, he climbed, feeling through his rubber soles the terrible thinness of the steel-rod rungs suspended over what, on this side of the bridge, was the open sea, two hundred feet directly below. He moved with tense care; if he stumbled even slightly he was afraid he would be unable to continue with this.

Behind him he heard the small sounds of Harry following him over the bridge rail, then he stepped up onto the little railed platform, turning away from the black emptiness, and felt a rush of relief at sight of the warmly lighted roadway some fifteen feet below him. It looked wonderfully inviting; he longed to be on it. But Harry sat on the bridge railing, a foot moving out toward the ladder, and now, finally, nothing more stood between Lew and what he had to do.

Waist-high handholds run the lengths of the support cables of Golden Gate Bridge. They are of thin wire cable stretched tautly between support stanchions mounted at intervals along the big cables. Lew bent cautiously forward, reaching with his left hand, and gripped the nearer of these handholds. It felt cold in his palm and damp, and he wondered if they should have worn gloves. He extended his right foot, and set it carefully down on the huge swell of the cable, gratefully feeling his rubber sole grip. Ducking head and shoulders under the handhold wire in his left hand, he eased his torso and center of balance forward onto the big cable, and stood upright between the waist-high wires, facing north toward Marin County.

Standing on the cable, Lew looked ahead along its incredible length stretching off orange-red and almost level, it seemed; then curving up and up, leaving the bridge lighting and turning black; and beyond that, thinning to a thread, then fading from sight high in the night-time sky. Under his feet he felt the awful roundness of the cable, slightly and uncomfortably bowing his ankles, and the thought of a foot slipping off it clenched his stomach. On the platform Harry stood in the yellow light from the bridge, waiting: a big man, inches taller than Lew and many pounds heavier.

Lew had to move, and he took the first step forward, then another, and—hands gripping and regripping the taut wire handholds in unison with his moving feet—he was walking the enormous cable; slowly, hardly daring to lift his feet from the great round surface; then more rapidly, beginning to stride, chin lifting. *And then they were doing it!* The talk finally over, he and Harry were climbing up through the night toward the distant winking red beacons at the top of the long, long arc of the great ocean-side support cable of Golden Gate Bridge.

His motions were fluid, the steady stride of an athlete, it seemed to Lew, and suddenly he felt exuberantly alive. The air from the ocean pressed his left cheek coolly, and he tried to imagine how they must look from below. The evenly spaced vertical suspension cables, touched by the yellow-orange lights of the bridge, would stand like graph lines against the ocean-side blackness. The heavier line of the main cable curving smoothly across their tops would chart their steady rise; and plodding upward along it, their two tiny figures must seem like symbols in a newspaper cartoon. He liked this image and thought about telling Harry, but didn't quite want to turn his head, and he walked on.

Two minutes passed, and three; they moved swiftly, mechanically, hardly thinking. Then Harry said, "God damn," and Lew stopped, gripping the handrails, firmly setting his feet. Slowly he turned his head, and saw Harry staring back over his right shoulder and down, then Lew saw it, too. Reduced in size, a model of the van that had brought them to the bridge, he saw it standing on what had turned into a concrete ribbon, saw the doll-like heads of the two women in the roof opening, their orange-tinted faces staring up. "Move, Jo, *move*," Harry was muttering. "You'll have the god-damn highway patrol on our ass!" As though hearing him, a head ducked down into the van, then the other, and a moment later the van rolled on.

Lew turned to resume his climb but did not; all was changed. The thick roundness under his feet—he'd hardly noticed in the easy rhythm of the climb—was no longer lighted: now the bridge lamps stood far below, their light shaded toward the roadway. And because the upward climb had been so gradual, only now steepening and beginning to be felt in his calves, they'd climbed higher than he'd understood until he looked back and down onto the diminished roof of the van. They were up now, really *up*: What if one of the handhold wires ahead had broken? He saw his hand sliding off it before he saw the break, feet stumbling, body plunging . . . He stopped this thought, switched it off, then made a mistake.

The temptation had always been there, nagging at him: now unthinkingly he glanced down past his left side and in the blackness saw a fleck of grayed whiteness appear, expand shapelessly, then fracture and vanish. For an instant he didn't understand, then did: that fleck, silently expanding to thumbnail size, had been a breaking whitecap, and he said, "Jesus," then, "Oh, *Jesus*," and could not move. Eyes squeezing shut, he clung motionless and frozen to the handholds; and high in the darkness four hundred feet above the black ocean he stood wondering in bewildered panic at the impossible remoteness of this moment from the evening the Night People began.

CHAPTER 1

On the evening the Night People began, Lew was in Jo's apartment; she had to work. He lay on the chesterfield in Levi's and a green-checked shirt, leafing through *The New Yorker*, looking at the cartoons, and she sat at her draftsman's table, ruling in shapes on a sheet of bristol board.

Lew turned the last page, then closed the magazine on his chest, and lay watching Jo: her brown hair hung before her face like a curtain, brushing the white cardboard, her hands moving deftly in the circle of hard white light from the cantilevered lamp head. Lew tossed the magazine into the air, pages fluttering, and Jo looked up, swinging her hair aside. His arms straight overhead, one hand behind the other, he began rhythmically pumping them up and down, fingers opening and closing. Jo said, "Okay, I'll ask: What are you doing?"

"Hypnotizing God."

"I'll inquire still further: Why?"

"It's worth a try." He lowered his arms, hands clasping on his chest. "It could solve all my problems."

"What problems, you don't have any problems." She resumed her rapid, precise drawing. "Your work's going all right. At least you said."

"Sure. It is. Splendidly, nay, brilliantly." Eyes lazy, he watched her hand slide a needle-pointed pencil along the metal edge of her ruler. His hair was black, his brown eyes almost black, and he wore a mustache and trimmed sideburns to just above his ear lobes. Glancing up again as she spoke, Jo liked the way he looked in just this moment.

She said, "And we're okay. I think." A folded architectural drawing hung tacked to a corner of her board, and Jo read a measurement from it, scaling it down in her mind on a mental blackboard. She murmured, "Don't say, 'Yes, we're fine, Jo.' Lightning would strike."

"We're fine, except for a few of your sickening habits such as constantly picking your nose."

"Well, okay, then let God alone."

"Right-oh!" Lew snapped his fingers at the ceiling. "Sir! Come out of it now!" He rolled off the chesterfield onto his feet, and stood looking around the room. A yard-wide strip along this wall contained Jo's one-dimensional living room, her "espaliered living room," Lew said. In this strip stood an uphol-stered chair, a standing lamp, the chesterfield and a glass-topped table beside it, the rest of the room being work space. On the opposite wall her olive-drab supply cabinet stood pushed against the fireplace; her long paste-up table stood in the center of the room; the tilt-top table at which she now sat stood directly be-side the glass doors to the outside balcony.

Lew walked to the supply cabinet. Lined up in three rows on its top stood some fifteen or so miniature buildings, each no larger than the palm of a hand: some awninged stores and turn-of-the-century small-town houses, a collapsing shed and old barn, a bridge of weathered wood, a stone-fronted brick-sided lit-tle bank building. These were the beginnings of what in time was to become "Jo's Town," new buildings added at long inter-vals. Lew stood touching the perfect little cardboard structures, cautiously admiring them with his fingertips. Each took hours of work, and Jo wasn't sure she'd ever finish the town. What pur-pose it was eventually to have or where it could be laid out complete with streets, back alleys, a stream, and outskirts, she didn't know; it was to have as many as a hundred buildings.

Lew turned to the built-in book shelves beside the balcony doors. Jo's cassette player and recorder stood on the bottom shelf, cassettes lying tumbled in a green shoe box beside it, and he squatted to poke through them, glancing at titles.

But he picked up none of the cassettes, and stood again to sidle through the partly opened balcony doors out onto the narrow wooden balcony. This overlooked a strip of planted earth and, beyond that, a winding two-lane road greenly lighted at long intervals by street lamps. Forearms on the railing, hands clasping, he stared out at the empty street, and after a moment said, "Well, there it is: Strawberry Drive. Silent. Motionless. And of no god-damn interest whatsoever." A pause. "Of no interest to *us*, that is. Those of us who live here now. In 1976." This was the bottom floor of a two-story gabled redwood building of four apartments in suburban Marin County just across the Bay from San Francisco; several similar buildings lay on each side. Ahead, beyond the far curb, stood an irregular row of tall eucalyptus trees. In the darkness beyond these, and down a slope, lay the tennis courts and swimming pool which were one reason they lived here. Beyond them, the blackness of the Bay.

"But to someone of the future, a sociologist a hundred years from now, what a stunning, nay, priceless moment. To actually *be* here! Back in 1976! To look out at this long-vanished, forgotten street and see"—the headlights of a car appeared at a bend to Lew's right—"yes, here comes one now, a *car!*" Head turning, he followed its approach. "Something of which he has only read, seen only in old photographs, remote as a Roman chariot. But now here it *is*, in solid actuality, rolling along the street . . . passing under the quaint street lamps of the period . . . following the curious markings down the center of the 'road.' What was that painted line for, do you suppose?"

"Lew, what are you *doing?*"

He turned to face Jo, leaning back against the rail. "Opening up my senses. Responding to my environment. The way us modern folk is s'posed to do. I am the eye of the future." He pushed

15

forward from the railing, side-stepped through the narrow opening, and turned to Jo's casette player again. "Where's your microphone?"

"There somewhere."

He found it behind the shoe box and plugged it in. "You got a cassette you don't want?"

"Any of them behind the recorder."

He took one, snapped it in, pressed the rewind button, and watched the tape whir back to its beginning. He pressed the recording buttons and, microphone at his lips, stood thinking for a moment. "To you of the distant future," he said, then, "greetings! From us of the remote lost past. I speak to you from a time, a date, whose very sound will be antique to your ears: August the twenty-sixth . . . 1976! As I speak these words, you are unborn. But as you hear them, I am long dead. Who am I? Lewis Joliffe is my handle, pardner, and I am . . . nobody. Buried. Long gone. Forgotten."

"Jesus," Jo murmured.

"And with me in this distant time is the lovely Josephine Dunne: sloe-eyed, lustrous-haired, soft of skin. As I speak, that is. Back in 1976. But as you listen, she, too, is dust. Long since passed into wrinkle-skinned, trembling old age. Then buried deep. And now even the granite that once marked her final resting place is cracked, fallen, and crumbling into nothingness."

"Hey, cut it out!"

That was her very own voice! From a century ago! We are still gloriously alive now, vibrant with youth. I am a—well, not so tall, maybe, but a spectacularly handsome fellow of twenty-nine: charming, witty, incredibly attractive to women, and master of foil and épée. Jo is magnificent, the eyes of a blue-eyed fawn, fine brown hair, big-titted and high-assed, a good-looking kid. Claims to be several years younger than I am, though she doesn't look it. Also claims to be half an inch taller, which is a lie, a tricky optical illusion achieved by deceit, about which I expect to make a public announcement soon, perhaps a major address. I am a lawyer, an attorney, and if you don't know what that is, congratulations two-thousand-and-seventy-six, and I hope your tricentennial is better than our bi-. Jo is a free-lance architectural-model maker; makes terrific little models of our quaint old buildings, and if one has survived to your time, as paper so often survives frail flesh, it may be in your attic right now. If her signature is on the bottom, you're rich!

"But what of you? Who *are* you, and what are you like? Do you really wear those funny-looking pajamas they have in 'Star Trek'? Alas, we can never know. And so from a century ago we say . . . farewell!" He held the microphone at arm's length, and repeated softly as though from a great distance, "Farewell . . ." Then he thrust the microphone at Jo. "Say good-by to the folks in the twenty-first century."

She leaned across her table. "So long. Hope things improve in the next hundred years."

Leaving the tape winding, steadily erasing whatever else had been on it, Lew pulled the microphone cord, and stepped out onto the balcony to walk quickly along it to his own apartment next door. At Jo's insistence—she had to have a workroom, she said—they had rented these side-by-side apartments, although Lew had argued: in San Francisco they'd shared the top-floor apartment of a large Victorian. But there she'd had an entirely separate workroom. Here, she said, they couldn't both live in the small space left over. Besides, it might be a good idea, she thought, for each to have a place whenever one of them wanted, needed, or ought to be alone.

Lew was back, dropping onto the chesterfield, a wide-mouthed metal thermos bottle under one arm. He sat thumbing quickly through a packet of white-paper squares, then said, "Yeah, this one," holding it up.

It was a color photograph: Jo and Lew in tennis clothes, standing at the net holding their rackets high. She said, "Yes, I've seen it; Harry took it. It's good of us both. But what—"

She stopped: Lew had lifted off the wide screw top of the thermos, and dropped the photo into the jug. "Time capsule. Stainless steel; it'll last forever."

"Are you *serious?*"

He hopped up, walked to the recorder with the thermos, and

stood watching the winding tape. "Why not? We made the tape, why waste it? Soon as it's ready I'll bury it outside somewhere, with the photo; they'll want to know what we looked like." He smiled. "God knows who'll find it, or when. It could *be* a hundred years; really. Two hundred. What a find. Imagine the excitement. You'll be immortal, kiddo." The machine clicked, the reels stopped, and Lew punched the STOP key, and lifted out the cassette. "Anything on the other side?" Jo shook her head, and Lew held the cassette between thumb and forefinger over the mouth of the jug. "Anything you want to add? Your justly famous rendition of 'Ave Maria'? Your recitation of 'Gunga Din'?" She shook her head, and he let the cassette fall, clinking, into the jug. "Now you belong to the ages." He began screwing on the cap. "One of the tiny handful of names remembered down the long corridors of time: Shakespeare, Einstein . . . Washington and Lincoln . . . Agnew and Nixon . . . Joliffe and Dunne. I hope you're grateful." He tightened the lid, twisting hard.

"Where you going to bury it?"

"I don't know, where do you think? By the tennis courts?"

She shook her head. "They'll be building more apartments there eventually, you know they will."

"How about next to the road by the curb? No, they'll be widening the road, too: damn it, I don't want the thing dug up in the next fifteen minutes. Where's a good place?" He stood frowning, then looked up at Jo. "You know something? There isn't a single place—not the beaches, not a cemetery, not out in what's left of the country, and not home plate in Candlestick Park—that you can really be certain won't be all screwed up in the next few years, let alone a hundred. We ain't gonna be immortal at all."

"I always suspected it." Jo resumed her work.

Lew shook the cassette out of the thermos and put it back on the shelf. "Well, I'll go on back to my place—you're working, and I don't want to disturb you." He smiled at that, and so did Jo, without looking up. "Hope I sleep tonight."

"Why shouldn't you?"

"I don't know." He turned to the balcony doors and stood sideways in the opening. "I've been waking up every once in a while. For no reason. Mostly when I'm at my place. Middle of the night, and my eyes pop open. Then I lie there."

"Why don't you come over?"

"No, this is like two or three o'clock; you don't wake up so good then."

"Get up anyway." With an X-acto knife she began cutting out one of the shapes she had drawn. "My father says that if you can't sleep you should hop right up and read or something. Till you get chilled."

"He also says, 'Another day, another dollar.'"

"That's right." This was an old routine. "And, 'If it were a snake, it would bite you.'"

"A wise man. I've noticed that many of his pithy observations have been widely copied. Well, if this happens again, may what's-his-name forbid, I'll try it."

It happened again six hours later, in the way Lew was almost used to lately. At one moment he lay quietly asleep; in the next, his eyelids opened. For several seconds he lay blinking, looking across the room at the night shape of his bedroom window, the glass yellowed by the moon. Then he got up.

Barefoot and in pajamas, he sat at the living-room television, waiting. A bar of white light shot across the screen, and he watched it expand, his mustached face pale and black-stubbled in the livid light. But no sound began, no picture appeared. Through click after click of the dial the screen remained white, the set humming, all stations off the air for the night.

Lew turned off the set, and sat watching the little diamond of light shrink down. When it was nearly gone, a silver speck, he did it again; turned the set on, then off, to watch the needle point of light slide away. He reached out, turned on his desk lamp, and looked at the several piles of paperback books stacked on the shelves helter-skelter, just as he'd lifted them from the mover's carton months before. But he didn't want to read at this time of night, and he got up, rolled back the glass doors to the balcony, and stepped out.

The air slightly chilly, he stood, forearms on the railing, hands clasped, looking out at the silent street. This was the same street, the same scene, he'd stood here looking at six hours earlier, yet now it seemed different. A high waxing moon shone almost straight down, the shadows of the eucalyptus branches across the road motionless on the pavement. The moon-washed asphalt looked white, and he could see pebbles and their shadows. A mist of green light from the street lamp tinted the branches beside it a stagy green.

Nothing stirred, there was no sound, and something in him responded to this dead-of-night stillness. This was his own familiar street, winding along the shoreline of the Bay in the suburban area of Mill Valley called Strawberry. In the months he and Jo had lived here he'd have driven this road hundreds of times, seen every hour of its twenty-four. But always in a car, insulated from it. Now, greenly lit, motionless and silent, the road seemed a new place, mysterious and strange, and the impulse flared up in him to go out onto it and see what it was like in the deserted middle of the night.

In his bedroom he pulled denims and a blue windbreaker over his pajamas, sneakers onto bare feet, picked up a red ski cap. At his outer door, hand on knob, he turned back into the living room; and at his desk he printed a note in heavy black felt-tip letters on a sheet from the lined legal pad he kept there: *Jo— Couldn't sleep, went for walk, back soon. Amos Quackenbush.* Leaving the desk lamp on, he taped the note to the balcony door, seeing his own reflection in the glass. The tasseled cap lay jauntily on the back of his head, exposing a heavy wing of black hair across his forehead, and he thought, *Pierre, ze Canadian lumberjack.* The rolled-up cap front could be pulled down as a wind mask; he did this, and in the shiny black glass saw himself turn into a sinister figure. The expressionless parody of a face patterned with streaks of yellow at cheeks and forehead suggested an African mask, and he rolled it up again.

Out on the curb facing the street, Lew stood for a moment.

Across the road the great trees seemed bigger than in daytime, hugely silhouetted against the lighter sky, and the silence was absolute. He stepped out, turning left, hearing the faint scuff of his rubber soles on the asphalt; along the horizon across the Bay, towering banks of clouds hung white in the moonlight, a gigantic background for the winking lights of a silent plane, and a rush of exhilaration at being out here shot through him.

Passing the first of the houses beyond the row of apartment buildings, Lew looked up at their dark windows, and glanced at a row of curbside mailboxes, silvery in the moonlight. Reading the name lettered along the side of the first of them, he raised hand to mouth, and in a mock shout called, "Hey, Walter Braden! Come on out, and play!" He felt excited, gleeful, and began to jog, shadow-boxing, swiping thumb to nose. From somewhere far behind him he became aware of a sound, an infinitely remote whine barely touching the air, and he stopped to listen.

For the space of a breath he thought it was a far-off siren, then recognized it: a diesel truck tooling along the distant freeway a mile behind him beyond the intervening hills. Lonely as a train whistle, the high, insectlike drone grew, deepening, as Lew stood motionless. It held . . . receded . . . was gone . . . returned momentarily, even more remote . . . then vanished utterly, and he walked on, smiling.

On around a long bend past the dark silent houses, then the lower branches of a tree across the street suddenly brightened, he heard the approaching car, and without thought or hesitation stepped up onto the lawn beside him. The engine-mutter growing, the pavement lightening, Lew sat down quickly in the black shadow of a large pine, drawing up his knees, leaning into its trunk, his hand on the lawn coming to rest against the waxy hardness of a baseball-sized pine cone. Headlight beams abruptly rounded the curve, lean pebble shadows streaking forward, immediately shortening and vanishing, and Lew yanked down the mask front of his cap.

Following its own long beams around the curve of the quiet street, a black-and-white police car appeared. Motionless in the deep shadow of the pine, Lew read the block letters through his eye slits, MILL VALLEY POLICE, as the white door panel slid past. The hatless driver, elbow on window ledge, never glanced his way. Rounding the curve, the car's headlight beams sliced off, tail lights appearing, and Lew stood, pine cone in hand, pulled the pin with his teeth, and hurled the grenade after the car in stiff-armed World War I fashion, lofting it high. Flipping up his mask, he stepped down onto the street again, grinning.

A mile, walking, jogging, past the dark houses, then the road tipped sharply downhill, and Lew saw the great community-recreation field slide into view, lying spread out and level down on the flats—a great, grassy rectangle, city-block size, livid in the moonlight. At the near end: the big swimming pool, gable-roofed dressing rooms, a small parking lot. Most of the rest: two full-sized baseball diamonds back to back, the wire cages of their home plates in opposite corners black-etched by the moon.

Lew walked across the asphalt of the parking lot to the mesh fence surrounding the pool area, and stood looking in at the mirrorlike rectangle, thin patches of mist lying motionless on its surface. Squatting, he found a walnut-sized rock in the dirt beside the fence. He stood, and drew his arm back and far down to behind his right knee. Arcing the rock high, he threw as hard as he could, and stood waiting. A satisfying *plunk*, and he walked on.

He sat down in the stands facing the nearer, Little League field, looking around at the benches bleached white by the moon. Here on the flat he sat almost surrounded by hills, the blank windows of the many houses on their slopes staring down at him. Leaning back, elbows on the bench behind him, he looked out at the long length of the field, and in one of the distant houses high on the hills beyond it, a light came on. Watching, wondering at someone else awake now, Lew lifted an arm to wave slowly. "Hey, come on down," he called softly. "And bring your mitt!"

On impulse he stood, walked down the steep aisle to the field, and onto it. For a moment he stood wondering what to do. Then, in the far-off house ahead, the light went out, and he was alone in the night again. He walked to home plate, stopped beside it, and looked around him. No light had come on anywhere else, nothing stirred, and he gripped an imaginary bat, and tapped it against imaginary spikes, each foot in turn. Stepping into batting position, he rapped the plate with the bat, his motion easy, confident, fluidly athletic. He pawed the dirt, shuffling and rearranging it with the sides of his shoes. Then he dug in, twisting hard on the balls of his feet. Bat raised high and slightly behind him, he held it motionless except for the slight menacing circling of its tip, and stood facing the pitcher who studied him, then began his windup.

A brushoff, which he'd expected, and he leaned back fast, glancing at the umpire. But the umpire, Lew's lips nearly motionless, said only, "Ball one." In a glassed-in booth high over the field an announcer, his voice reproduced by a dozen radios audible from the stands, said, "Bases full, one and oh."

Lew stepped out of the box, lifted each foot once, stepped back, and dug in, bending lower this time, bat high and almost vertical. His head whirled to the catcher to stare down at the ball nested in his glove, awed at the impossibly fast pitch. "Strike!"

In batting position again, waiting for the pitch. As fast as he could hurl himself, he fell back, grimacing with fear and anger at the pitch to his ear that would have torn his head off. His mouth dropped open in astonishment at the umpire's call, and he repeated it aloud: "*Strike?*" He sprang forward to protest, but instead clamped his mouth shut, and faced the pitcher again. "Three and two count," said the announcer: Could that be right? "Five to two score, Giants behind, nineteen fifty-one—two?—World Series, deciding game." Then he added, "Last of the ninth."

Lew lowered his bat and stepped backward out of the box, turning to face the manager who was walking slowly toward him from the dugout. He wasn't sure this was allowed, but the manager did it anyway. He stopped before Lew and, Lew's lips hardly moving, said, "Son, you're a brand-new rookie just up from the minors, and I know that. All the same, it's up to you now." Lew nodded, swallowing. "Do my best, sir." The elderly manager stood considering him from under the famous shaggy brows, then nodded doubtfully, turning away. "All you *can* do, boy."

Lew gulped, and shook his head hard, clearing his vision. Again he faced the pitcher, tapped the plate. Suddenly he grinned, lifted his chin, all fear gone, and in the gesture that would be remembered forever, extended his bat to point far out toward right field and beyond, and the radios and stands went silent.

The pitch came, and in exaggerated slow-motion, Lew swung the bat in a shoulder-high curve, lining it straight out from the wrists and lifting it up and far past his left shoulder in a full follow-through, ankles crossing as his body revolved. He let the bat drop, grinning as he watched the obviously home-run ball rise in the remote distance. Nodding back at the stands as he began, he made the leisurely home-run trot of the bases, tipping his hat to the fans as he jogged.

Leaving third base, he began accepting the congratulatory handshakes of the entire team, coaching staff, Shirley, Jo, and several other vague, excited girls lined up beside the base path. Stepping squarely onto home plate, he lifted his arms in the prizefighter's handshake. Then he stood, cap off, hand on heart, bowing humbly—stumbling backward in pleased astonishment as the fans overwhelmed him.

Lew turned suddenly and searched the houses around the field. Nothing moved; silence everywhere. Smiling then, hands in pockets, he began walking the length of the field toward its far end, the grass whispering against his canvas sneakers: something about the small risk he had taken of being seen playing the fool pleased him. He wondered if anyone in all the many houses looking down on this field stood watching him now from a darkened room, a small figure moving down the length of the great moonlit rectangle.

At the far end of the long field, and the sidewalk there, he turned left onto the street that wound along the base of the high ridge bisecting Strawberry. The street lay still as a photograph; just ahead the leaves of a small curbside tree hung motionless under a street lamp, and no least sound came from the distant freeway. Silent on rubber soles, Lew walked on, glancing curiously up at each of the dark houses he passed.

Just ahead he saw a ground-level concrete porch with a wrought-iron railing; a swing hung over its floor, the traditional porch swing of wooden slats suspended by chains from the ceiling. Lew stopped: the porch ran across the front of the house, a door and a large rectangular window facing onto it. Swing and door were at one end of the porch and, inset in the door, a small window overlooked the swing. Lew glanced across the street; looked back toward the rec field; looked ahead as far as he could see. Nothing moved anywhere.

He hesitated, suddenly wanting to walk cravenly on. Then he took a deep slow breath, hearing it sigh through his nostrils, his heart suddenly pounding, and turned to walk up the slight curve of concrete walk to the porch. Just short of the porch he stopped, eying the big window and drapes along its sides, then the square little window in the front door; no one stood in the darkness of the house watching him, and he stepped silently onto the porch.

The trespass made, Lew stood frozen. Then he walked to the swing, turned his back, and eased himself onto the seat, a slow squeak sounding as slats and chains accepted his weight. Silence as he listened, staring up at the small square eye of the door beside him. The pane was black; he could see no blur of white face. He sat conscious that he could still stand up and walk silently away. But that was no longer true; he'd taken the dare.

Feet tucked far back under the swing, his rubber soles pressed against the concrete floor of the porch, Lew tensed his thigh muscles, gripping the chains, and slowly and not quite silently pushed the swing back as far as it could go, feeling the slatted seat tilt almost vertical. For one last moment, heart thumping, he waited in silence; then he lifted his feet and swept forward, the chains groaning, ceiling hooks squealing like an animal. It was *loud, loud*; audible, he knew, even across the street. A fractional instant of silence at the top of the forward arc, then the swing shot back, groaning and squealing again.

It could easily be heard inside the house: Was it waking someone now, covers flying, feet swinging to the floor? If so—if the white globe on the porch ceiling flashed alight in the next second, lock bolt cracking on the door beside him—what could he do? Run? Or stay and say—what?

No explanation could make sense, and he deliberately refused to think: he had to stay here for six full swings, six screeching swoops forward and back, and he sat, feet tucked up under the bench as he swung forward the second time, scared now. What the *hell* would happen if he were caught? An angry man who was big enough might beat him up, an excitable man could shoot him, a frightened man might already have phoned the cops; and if a cruising patrol car were nearby, radio crackling into life right now with a prowler call . . . Back he swung, then an instant of almost motionlessness at the top of the arc, Lew staring up at the blank square of glass waiting for the sudden white movement of face; the sweat sprang out under his cap. Forward again, the piglike squeal unbelievably loud.

Three more long squealing swoops forward and back. Then he was free—to jam his feet down, dragging across the porch floor, stopping. Just short of a run he hurried down the walk, turning on the sidewalk to look over his shoulder, and in that instant the white globe flashed on, the porch suddenly bright as a stage, the gliding black shadow of the still-moving swing suddenly appearing on the painted floor.

A small hedge separated this front lawn from the next, and without having thought what to do, Lew instantly did it. He took one giant step to the far side of this hedge, and threw himself like a man under gunfire lengthwise beside it.

Flat on the grass, cheek pressing into its night-time dampness, Lew lay looking through the lower branches of the hedge, eyes almost at ground level. His heart pounded, so hard and fast it piled blood behind his eyes; he had to blink to see. A door bolt had clunked, the door swung inward, and now a man stepped cautiously out onto the porch. He was in pajamas, about forty;

not taller but wider, heavier, bigger than Lew. Directly under the white globe his scalp showed through mussed brown hair. He stood motionless, arms hanging, fingers open and ready, looking wary, angry, mean. Only his head moving, he searched slowly through a half circle for whoever had been on his porch, knowing he was out there somewhere.

Suddenly bolder, the man stepped to the edge of his porch, and looked straight toward Lew, staring either directly at the hedge or off across it, Lew couldn't tell. Breathing shallowly through his mouth, Lew lay motionless. Could the man make out the telltale thickening along the base of the hedge?

Seconds passed, and still he stood staring. In quick panic Lew realized that he didn't know what he would do if in the next instant the man came striding down off his porch across the lawn toward him, and he began to laugh, feeling his shoulders shake, listening to whether any sound of it escaped. No: his stomach muscles tensing, he was laughing helplessly, but in silence. Another moment, then the man's head turned slowly away to search the darkness across the street.

Abruptly he turned, and walked back inside, pulling the door closed. A *chunk* as the bolt shot, then the porch light went dark. Lew didn't move: if he were the man on the other side of that door, what would he be doing now? He would be standing at the window back out of sight waiting for whoever was out there —making himself thin behind a tree or crouched beside a neighbor's porch or lying beside this hedge—to step out or stand up. Unmoving, Lew lay trying to watch the street through the eyes of the man in the house, to think his thoughts.

Half a minute passed, perhaps longer . . . then Lew felt the moment pass beyond which the man inside the house could no longer hope to see anything move out here. In his mind Lew saw him turn away into the darkness of his living room murmuring a single obscenity, and walk back through the house. He'd explain to his wife, if she'd awakened, then lie listening, ready to move fast if the porch swing sounded again.

It popped up in Lew's mind, the idea of going back to the swing again, and he laughed aloud. But he didn't dare; this time he wouldn't get away with it, and there'd be trouble. A quick pushup, feet gathering, and he stood, turning swiftly to walk on, ready to run. *What if the man had phoned the cops!*—Lew's head swung around for the fast-moving car coming up from behind, but there was nothing.

He walked home through the quiet streets; and, back in his living room, peeled the note from the glass door, started to crumple it, then stopped. In the light from the desk lamp he stood looking down at it; after a moment he folded the note carefully across, aligning the edges, and tucked it away among the books on his shelves.

CHAPTER 2

Jo said, "What'd you do last night? Watch the movie?" In a pink robe over yellow pajamas, her hair brushed back and tied, she stood waiting at the stove as Lew lifted hot, dripping bacon from pan to absorbent paper towels spread on the stove top.

"No movie," he murmured, eyes intent on the fork; he wore a kitchen towel tied under his arms to protect his shirt and tie from spattering grease. "It was too late, nothing on." As Jo took over to serve, he untied the towel, tossed it to the counter, and walked out of the little kitchen area to sit down at Jo's paste-up table. "How'd you know I was up?" He realized he'd added this to forestall more inquiry; he didn't want to say what he'd done last night.

"I woke up, and you were out on the balcony; I heard you clear your throat."

Lew nodded, pulling the news section of the *Chronicle* toward him. He felt good; a little short of sleep but not tired. Jo set their plates on the table, poured coffee, and sat down across from Lew, pulling out the third section of the paper. Lew sat eating, turning pages often. Jo read Herb Caen's column, an elbow on each side of the page, cup in hands; she liked half a cup of coffee before eating breakfast. Lew turned a page, glancing up, and saw that Jo's wide sleeves had dropped, lying in pink puddles of cloth at her elbows, exposing her forearms. *Good-looking forearms*, he thought; then: *What is a good-looking forearm?* He smiled at this, Jo looked up, saw him, and said, "What?"

He shook his head. "Too embarrassing to say. Something obscene. Involving your forearms."

"What?" She looked down at her arms.

He nodded. "You'd be shocked. I know you see the books and magazine articles, you watch the TV discussions. You try to be liberated, and on a written exam you'd get A. But you've never really made it, actually, and you'd be horrified. Too bad; it might have been fun."

"I'll bet. So what did you do last night? Read?"

"No. Stood out on the balcony. Clearing my throat."

"Lew, why are you waking up like this? What's bothering you?"

"Nothing. Nothing that isn't bothering everybody. Inflation. Corruption in high and low places. Decline in moral values. Blatant sexuality. In high and low places."

"You're pretty blatant yourself today."

"So watch out."

"You watch out; I don't have to punch a time clock."

He looked at his watch, then shook his head. "It's Friday; meeting day. I can't be late."

"Pity," she said in pseudo-British accent, and Lew smiled, and got up to walk to his apartment for his suit coat.

He backed his VW, a maroon squareback, from its space in the asphalted parking area behind the row of nearly identical low frame buildings and swung around into the driveway between his and the building next door. He tapped his horn, and almost immediately the door of the lower apartment there opened, and Harry Levy stepped out: hatless, carrying a zippered briefcase. Lew watched, but today there was no sign of Shirley in the doorway behind him. On some mornings when Lew tapped his horn, she would appear in her robe, standing in the doorway to smile and wave good-by as they drove off; cupping her elbows on chilly mornings and shivering her shoulders dramatically. Watching Harry walk over to the car, it occurred to Lew that he was seldom late. Harry said, "Unhh," as he opened the door, and Lew replied, "Yeah," in ritualized morning exchange.

Lew waited, hand on the shift lever, as Harry fitted his big body into the little car, knees wedging high, black hair almost touching the ceiling. He must be twenty pounds overweight, Lew thought, obviously well over two hundred. But he didn't seem fat, Lew acknowledged, and was probably in good shape. Waiting for Harry to pull the door closed, Lew watched the big head, jaw, and cheek in profile: thick hair cut somewhat shorter than the norm, heavy black beard shaved close, sideburns sliced unmodishly short. As Harry slammed the door his eyes narrowed slightly in a concentration that resembled belligerence: when he wasn't smiling, Harry was a formidable-looking man, and as Lew drove on down the driveway, he was remembering the temperance cards.

Walking in the sun one noon hour last spring, he and Harry had gone into an antique shop, a junk shop, just outside the financial district. Harry found and bought for a dollar a packet of unused nineteenth-century temperance pledges: postcard-size with a printed pledge, blanks for date and signature, a tiny, fork-tailed white ribbon glued beside the pledge. For several weeks he carried these in his inside suit-coat pocket, and he got eleven signatures: twice Lew had been with him. One of the men was a salesman for a law-book publisher, sitting in Harry's small office when Lew had walked in with some papers he wanted Harry to see. The other man was a junior partner of another law firm, meeting with Harry and Lew in the firm's conference room to discuss a case in which both firms had an interest.

Each time, presently, Harry had taken out his cards, exhibited the signatures he had, and begun talking impassively of the modern need for "teetotalism." Each time the other man had begun to smile anticipatorily, but Harry's face remained expressionless, and as he talked on with a low-voiced almost angry intensity, deep voice rumbling, Lew watched the other man's smile waver, become fixed, then fade. Finally Harry brought out a pen, pressing the other man to sign, insistently and with latent threat. And presently, each time, eyes bewildered, the man had reluctantly taken Harry's pen and signed, glancing away in embarrassment. Harry had examined the signature, nodded solemnly as he tucked the card away with the others, soberly congratulated the man with a handshake, and resumed the interrupted discussion.

The man from the other law firm had complained by phone to Tom Thurber, a senior partner of their firm, and Harry had been called into the office, and formally rebuked. He'd listened, offering no explanation, then pulled out his cards and asked Tom to sign, too, and Thurber had laughed.

Lew followed the shoreline road of this northern arm of the Bay; then slowed for the Ricardo Road stop sign, and turned toward the service road and freeway just ahead. Harry had taken a long-paged legal typescript from his briefcase, laid the briefcase along his slanted thighs, arranged his papers on it, and as they rode he followed the text line by line with the tip of a yellow wooden pencil. As Lew turned toward the freeway entrance, Harry glanced up, then resumed his reading, murmuring, "Goddamned legal gobbledy-gook."

"Bring it up at the meeting this morning," Lew said. "Propose that we be first in pioneering plain English," and Harry said, "Yeah."

On the crowded freeway, Harry working, they rode in silence, a part of the sluggish river of cars, moving up the long Waldo Grade, then into the Waldo tunnel which bored through a particularly high range of Marin County hills. Watching the narrow arched opening of daylight ahead, Lew waited for the moment just beyond it. It came: as they passed through the opening, there it all was—the great red towers of Golden Gate Bridge ahead, and beyond them across the blue Bay the clean white city spread out on its hills. It was a moment Lew waited for, this first, suddenly expanding look at the city, and as always he felt a little surge of anticipation at knowing he was going down into it, followed by the little anticlimax of knowing exactly where he had to go. He said, "Harry, could you give up law?"

"Give it up?"

"Yeah. And go into something else."

"Like what?"

"I don't know: I just mean is it okay with you if this turns out to be all you ever do?"

Harry turned away to look ahead through the windshield. "Well. I get something out of it. In court, anyway; sometimes you can feel your argument taking hold." He glanced at Lew. "Something about the way a judge starts to listen, and you know you're winning if you just don't blow it: I like that. Not this shit"—he rapped his knuckles on the briefcase. "But sometimes in a courtroom . . . It's a *fight*; you know? You can feel you're really a lawyer." Harry sat watching the great rust-red towers enlarge. "But I could give it up. Get into something else, and not even miss it a week later. Sometimes I see myself doing something outdoors. What about you?"

"Well, yeah; there's some fun in it. I like working up a brief; for appeal. Working it over, becoming persuasive; you can feel it when it starts getting some bite. But still; sometimes it bothers me that this could be more or less it from now on."

Ahead, traffic from the Sausalito entrance seeped onto the freeway. Well ahead, halfway across the bridge, brake lights flickered, everything before them slowing to a stop because of the toll plaza up ahead at the San Francisco end. Harry sat watching the stopped traffic, then said, "Hey, it's Friday: what're you guys doing tonight?"

"Nothing I know of."

"Come over for supper: we'll lay in some hamburger and junk, and do something. Or nothing. We could play some bridge, damn it, if Shirley'd settle down and finish learning the game. Come early, and we'll drink it up a little."

Friday or Thursday night generally meant food-shopping, and for that Jo waited for Lew. She owned a sun-faded blue Chevy

33

van, MARINWOOD FLORISTS still faintly visible lettered on its sides. She'd bought it for its floor space, using it to deliver her finished models; but it was third- or fourth-hand, the shocks nearly gone, and so cumbersome—heavy wooden bumpers projecting a foot or more front and back—that it was hard to park. So she waited for Lew and his VW.

At the Safeway, Jo inside, Lew waited in the car, angle-parked at the curb before the huge store: he wore tan wash pants and a red plaid shirt buttoned at the sleeves. The air was warm, his window open, the sun still well above the hills across the freeway behind him, Daylight Savings still on. The low, red-tiled roofs of the great shopping center extended out to the curb line, roofing the sidewalks before the store fronts; from speakers tucked up under the roof, music sounded softly. People passed steadily along the walk before Lew's bumper, and he sat watching them, studying their faces.

When Jo appeared with her loaded shopping cart—in the peach-colored cotton dress and white sandals she would wear to the Levys'—Lew got out, and helped her unload into the car. They got in, but he didn't immediately start the engine. He sat staring at the windshield for a moment, then turned to her. "You know something?" he said puzzledly. "I never see anyone I know down here. We *live* here. In Strawberry. But all I ever see here is strangers."

"Well, it's probably the biggest shopping center in the county. And right beside the freeway. So the people you see here come from everywhere."

"Yeah, I guess." He started the engine.

Driving home along the road he had walked last night, it seemed to Lew that now it was a different place. Cars passed; people moved about their yards in the late daylight; the chug of a power motor sounded somewhere. Looking out her window, Jo smiled in content, and said, "Strawberry's a pleasant area, isn't it. So green and peaceful."

They'd said this to each other before, and Lew nodded automatically. "I guess," he said, then surprised himself. "But . . ."

She looked at him. "But what?"

34

"But it's always the *same*, god damn it. All you ever see is people out mowing their lawns, trimming their hedges, painting their houses, for crysake."

"Well, what *should* they be doing?"

"I don't know." Then he laughed, shrugging. "I don't know what the hell I'm talking about."

They had supper out on the Levys' balcony, a dozen feet from Lew's, across the intervening driveway. In canvas-and-wood chairs they sat in the building's shade, but across the road and down the lightly wooded slope beyond it the pool and two of the tennis courts still lay in the last of the sunlight. Occasionally commenting, they watched a young woman in one-piece white tennis costume sweating with effort as she batted back lobs served up by a practice machine, the court littered with the yellow balls. Beyond the courts and pool, the Bay lay blue and sparkling, eight or ten sails visible.

For a considerable time, talking lazily, often silent, they sat sipping red wine, passing a gallon jug around. Then, the sun down, the Levys went into the apartment, and presently Shirley brought out hamburgers and potato chips on paper plates, trailed by Rafe, their elderly terrier, sniffing the air, tongue anticipating. Harry followed with two filled glasses and two cans of beer. "Iced tea," he said, handing Jo her glass. "Cheap beer"— he gave Lew a can, then set Shirley's glass on the floor beside her empty chair: "Hemlock." He wore frayed tan shorts, dirty, unlaced sneakers over bare feet, and a white T-shirt speckled with holes.

Shirley handed Harry his plate, and he sat down and began wolfing the fat, dripping hamburger in enormous bites, leaning forward so the squeezed-out catsup would drip down between his knees to the plate he'd set on the floor; occasional fragments of meat falling to plate or floor were snatched by Rafe. Lew sat at one end of the narrow balcony, chair tipped back against the side railing, paper plate held up under his chin, eating and watching Harry. He had noticed before that on weekends Harry liked to dress and eat as sloppily as he could; exaggeratedly so. Under the thin white material of Harry's T-shirt and curling

35

over the neckband lay a matting of black hair so dense and springy it held the light cloth away from his skin, and the hair lay black and thick across his big forearms, and curled on his immense legs. He had, not a belly, Lew said to himself, you couldn't say that, but a general thickening around the middle; he looked effortlessly strong, and Lew was conscious of envying Harry his physical strength. He was strong, too, for his size, more than people often realized, and he enjoyed chances to surprise them with the power of his arms or legs. But still he envied the size and strength of really big men.

Hamburgers distributed, Shirley was sitting, too, plate balanced on her bare knees. Now she lifted her glass from the floor, and sipped, staring absently out over the rail. As though his eyes had simply been attracted by the movement, Lew allowed himself to casually turn and look at her; he tried to be careful not to look too often or too long at Shirley.

Tonight she wore a short-sleeved light blue middy blouse with a white sailor collar, and tailored white gabardine shorts with a blue stripe up the sides. They were very short; she liked to show off her fine legs, and once more Lew noticed how without blemish they and her arms were, no least suggestion of tiny broken vein, red mark, or unevenness of texture; probably the same all over, he thought. Her hair was black, eyes dark, skin very white; she avoided the sun. Just looking at Shirley was a pleasure, and Lew made himself turn away for fear of looking too long, retaining the last visual impression of her face, relaxed and absent. It was a pretty face, intelligent, shrewd, but not aggressive; she was ready to like people, accepting them as they seemed, had liked Lew and Jo on sight.

Lew looked past her at Jo, comparing, and she smiled and winked, and he grinned. Tonight when they got home, they'd undress, turn back a bed, and lie down together for the best kind of sex, prolonged and amiable: the mutual knowledge lay in the air between them, and Lew felt consciously happy. He liked looking at Jo, knowing what was going to happen later, and he felt proud of the way she looked in her short, peach-colored dress.

Harry scooped up his can, swigged beer audibly, the can nearly vertical, then set it down, wiping his mouth with the back of his other hand. He said, "Well? Anyone want to talk about inflation, recession, or venality and incompetence in government? If so, feel free, but don't mind if I leave: this is the weekend, and I am in unholy retreat."

Lew said, "Don't we have to at least cover pollution, racism, and the rise in violence? And who wants to be first to say 'lifestyle'? You're right," he said. "Jesus, I get tired of the talk, talk, talk. Anyone says 'environment,' 'media,' or 'Women's Lib,' and I'll kill them."

"Aren't they things that *ought* to be talked about?" Shirley said.

"Sure. But after a while not unless you've got something new to add. And I haven't. And haven't met anyone lately who has."

Harry said, "What we need are some new problems."

"Well, I've got one," Lew said, and complained that no one in Strawberry was ever seen to do anything out of the ordinary, "including me."

"Well, what should they do?" Shirley said.

"Well, I'm all for lawn cutting, hedge trimming, washing the car, and other fundamentals. But just once I'd like to drive by somebody's house, and see him out painting an enormous mythical landscape on his garage door. Most of them around here are big—two-car garages with one big door painted white, like a couple hundred big, empty canvases crying out for creativity. And there are quite a few flagpoles around. Always with the American flag, if any. Well, I'd like to see a guy run up his own personal flag. Divided into quarters each bearing some symbol of his personality. Or to hell with creativity, how about a guy out in his yard just having fun, for crysake. Out on the lawn carrying his wife around piggyback, laughing and squealing."

"Hey, yeah," Shirley said. "Why don't we do that, Harry? Right now. You carry me around piggyback. Down there by the curb."

"I will if you'll make up the flag I design, no questions asked. We'll drape it over the rail here. Or, hey; this is better. We all strip, powder ourselves white, and pose. On Lew's balcony. After dark; I'll rig up a spotlight. Absolutely motionless in classical pose, the way they used to do in the circus. Living statuary. How about driving by and seeing something like that in Strawberry, Lew?"

Jo said, "We could do that famous statue of the couple, 'The Kiss.'"

Harry said, "Or a couple in even more classical pose called 'The —'"

"Never mind," Shirley said.

"You're absolutely right," Harry said. "Be hard to hold the pose motionless."

"You know what I meant."

"Yeah, but nobody's supposed to object to that word any more. Not since about nineteen sixty-three."

"Well, I don't care."

"Not, 'I don't care': What you mean is, you don't give a fuck."

"I mean I don't like casual, pointless dirty talk. And there *is* such a thing as dirty talk. It's so show-offy, this oh-so-casual dropping the words into ordinary conversation."

"Lew, how often do you punch Jo right smack in the mouth?"

"Once a week; that's my allowance. We talked it out. Reasonably, rationally, trying to understand each other's real feelings and basic needs. And that's what we agreed on; it was Jo's suggestion."

"Doesn't sound like nearly enough."

"Just try it, buddy-boy," Shirley said scornfully. "I watched the karate lessons on KQED, you know."

"Lew, is there much wife-swapping in Strawberry? I mean permanent swaps."

Shirley and Jo went to the kitchen and brought out second hamburgers, and Harry offered more beer or wine. They stayed out till the street lamps came on, then the air turned chilly, and they went inside. Shirley wouldn't play bridge, but got out a Monopoly board, and they sat at the all-purpose card table beside the kitchen, and played till nearly one o'clock.

In Jo's apartment then, Lew lay waiting in bed and, Jo calling from the bathroom, they talked, as people do when they've had a quiet good time with good friends, about how long they'd all known each other. Lew and Harry had gone to the same suburban-Chicago high school hardly aware of each other, the school a big one and Harry a class behind Lew. A dozen years later, finding themselves working in the same San Francisco law firm, the men had become friends. But the real friendship began, Lew and Jo agreed now, when the four of them met.

Lew was thinking of moving from the city, he'd told Harry one morning, and Harry nodded, standing in Lew's little office. "Well, it's not a bad commute from where I live," he said. "You might take a look." This said casually; a friendship was developing, but Harry was cautious about seeming premature.

Lew said, "I was thinking of a house." He sat tilted back in his desk chair looking up at Harry.

"Buying one?"

"Hell, no; renting."

Harry shrugged. "Well, you might find one, but its not easy, and they're expensive; I tried. I like a house, I grew up in a house."

"Me, too."

"I like the extra room, and walking around my own place any way I want, indoors or out, belching and scratching my ass."

"Yeah, we had a big yard; attic; full basement. My dad still had a sled he owned as a kid in the attic, a Flexible Flyer. And I had a twenty-two rifle range in the basement."

"I had a darkroom. We even had two spare bedrooms upstairs just for company. My father didn't make a lot of money either, but you could have a house then; everybody did. Well, maybe you'll be lucky. You got your own furniture?" Lew shook his head. "People don't generally rent their houses furnished any more, Lew; they get wrecked. But see what you can do, and then if you want, drop in and look over the apartments where we are. Meet Shirley, and we'll show you around."

"Can I bring a friend?"

"Sure, of course." Harry nodded, and turned to the door, careful to show no curiosity.

Talking of that time—Jo moving about the room putting small things away, shutting drawers, closing the closet—they agreed that the move to Marin had worked out well. The two women had liked each other on sight, though Harry took a little getting used to, she said. Lew and Harry, and often the four of them, played tennis on the apartment courts. Sierra skiing was only three hours away; they had all driven up half a dozen times this last winter. In good weather they went to the county beaches a lot, Stinson especially. The men had done some skin-diving with rented equipment; tried surfing and abandoned it, neither having started young enough to be good. Harry had gotten Lew into climbing, and they had twice scaled high, almost sheer faces, and descended. Now the two couples were talking with some seriousness of buying a small sailboat together. They borrowed each other's books, ate and drank and went to movies together. But more than what they did, Jo said—she was in bed now, and they lay with the bedside lamp on, talking—was the way each of the four enjoyed the others. "It's more than the usual two-couple friendship, where it's mostly the men or mostly the women who are friends: all four of us are friends. I wouldn't know what to do without them."

"Sure. It's a good life," Lew said, turning on his side to face Jo. "Especially right now," and Jo nodded, smiled, and said, "Yes."

CHAPTER 3

A good life, but four nights later Lew again awakened from what seemed to him like a sound sleep: for no reason he understood his eyes opened and immediately he lay fully awake. This time he was with Jo. He could just hear her slow breathing, and lying quietly, not to disturb her, it occurred to him to wonder: How long would they stay together? Months? Years? Immediately he was curious, and lay trying to think about it clearly. Was this quiet, modest, likable girl someone he could live with indefinitely? On and on? For the rest of his life? Did he want to? He couldn't say, and tried to force an answer. He liked Jo very much; more than anyone else he knew; didn't entirely know why, just did. He would miss her; he'd do a lot for her, and gladly. He admired her, and was proud of her. Was all that enough? It didn't sound like it. He tried another direction: What if she left him? Well, he didn't like that, but would survi——

What the *hell* was wrong with him? He liked his job—liked it all right, that is, but could give it up. Liked where they lived, but could leave. Could give up anything, it seemed. Really? Jo too?

41

It had to stop, he'd be awake for hours; and he got up very quietly, almost stealthily. For a moment he stood looking down at Jo, her quiet breathing still undisturbed. Then he turned away to walk to the balcony and along it, the wooden floor chill and slightly damp to his bare feet, to his own apartment. Just before he reached his doors, he glanced over the railing out at the silent lamplighted mystery of the night beyond it, and excitement rushed through his body with an intensity—relief and release—that surprised him. Quickly he got dressed, as before; found his note, stuck it onto the balcony door, and was free.

Conscious of the silence of the world asleep all around him, he walked down the driveway. For several seconds he stood at the curb of the motionless, green-lighted street, looking around him at the night, savoring the moment. Then once again he stepped out.

This time, after a mile past the blank-windowed houses he climbed up to, and walked the spine of, the great two-hundred-foot-high ridge dividing Strawberry—looking down at the motionless, miniaturized street paralleling it, half-dollar-size circles of green light lying on the pavement under tiny street lamps. Then, at the highest point of the long ridge, he stopped on impulse, and turned to look back at the freeway, far behind and below him.

He could see a two-mile, almost straight stretch of it; distant pale ribbons visible in the lights from the huge green-and-white direction signs cantilevered over them. Behind the long beams of their headlights two finger-length cars moved swiftly to the north, no sound of their motion reaching him here. A slower cluster of several cars followed, then the long twin stretches of concrete stood empty for a moment. A second cluster appeared and moved across the long length; then, incredibly, for perhaps three or even four minutes the great freeway stood utterly empty from high up the winding of Waldo Grade clear on to the crest of Corte Madera hill. Lew stood staring in astonishment. "*Empty*," he murmured aloud to himself after a few moments. "My god, look at it. The *freeway*—absolutely *empty*."

Twice each weekday, from behind his own or Harry Levy's

windshield, Lew saw this road filled with commute traffic, every lane solid with cars. And he had never seen it less than busy. Now it was a delight and a wonder to see the great lighted roadway standing as motionless as though the world had been abandoned. A final half minute passed, Lew grinning with pleasure at the strange, incredible sight. Then tiny headlights appeared up on Waldo, and an instant later two more pairs, one right behind the other on the nearly empty road, popped up over the Corte Madera crest, and Lew turned to walk on, glancing at the familiar shape of Tamalpais Mountain filling the night-time sky to the north and west.

He stopped to look down onto the rooftops of the shopping center, its huge parking lot deserted, its hash-mark parking lines like game-board markings of some sort, under the stars and a high half-moon. Here a tiny breeze pressed his face, and he could just detect the faint sound of the quiet music that flowed all day from speakers up under the roofs of the covered walkways. "Hey," he said, "who forgot to turn off the tape? You're fired! I'm sorry, I know you only had twenty minutes to go before your pension began, but rules are rules. Thank you: I knew you'd understand." Turning an ear toward the wavering distant sound, he tried to make out the tune—"As Time Goes By," he thought but wasn't sure.

Walking on, conscious of the pleasurable bite of the cool night-time air in his lungs, he enjoyed the feeling of superiority of the person awake when all others are asleep. At this thought he stopped and, turning in place, made the full circle, looking out across miles of rooftops, dim in the faint light; out at the lighted freeway and beyond it to lesser lamplit roads; at the dark, empty Marin hills and at huge Mount Tam; across the shining black surface of the Bay to the great new San Francisco towers glittering electrically beyond it. Was it possible that in all this vast area no one but he was awake? No, of course not; the police were awake, and there had to be others—yet it seemed like it. They seemed so helpless, all these thousands unconscious under the pale moonlit rooftops, and Lew stepped to the edge of the slope, facing south, and pulled down his mask-flap.

Arm straight out before him, swinging it back and forth in a slow, wide arc he said, "I . . . am the Avenger! Each night from among you I select one for sacrifice to the ancient gods of Tamalpais! Eeney, meeney, miney"—pointing here and there at random—"mo!" His arm stopped, finger pointing. "Tough luck, Harry." He pulled up his mask and, smiling at himself, walked on, descending now, toward the road and home.

Again, waking in the morning, he felt good, felt rested. Looking over at the inch-wide vertical strip of daylight between Jo's drapes—a core-sample of the day, its lower half the sunwashed green of a pine, its upper half a strong blue California sky—he felt suddenly elated, felt *lucky*. Beside him Jo moved, and he turned; she lay facing him, blinking, just awakened. He smiled, she smiled back, and—there wasn't time, but—he slipped an arm under her shoulders and, Jo still drowsy, they moved wordlessly together, a good start for a lucky day.

Lew believed, as everyone does, in lucky streaks, and he watched this one continue at the toll plaza. Harry braked, slowing toward the end of a long line, then glanced quickly at the adjoining line, inexplicably only three cars long. Harry owned a used '67 Alfa Romeo, the best and fastest sport car he could afford, and he yanked the wheel, accelerating, and shot over to the shorter line. Each of the three cars ahead had exact change ready, rolling on past the booth without quite stopping, as did Harry—in the clear within seconds. Harry yelled, "That's the way to screw the common people!" and both smiled at the small triumph.

As always, they left the car at the cheapest parking lot they knew, down at the Embarcadero, a long walk from the office. But today Lew liked it, the sun-warmed air full of promise. Which was kept: an approaching girl looked boldly and arrogantly from one to the other of their faces; then, in passing, she smiled at Lew alone. He grinned maliciously at Harry, who said, "Near-sighted bitch. Not entirely sane."

Lew began watching the sidewalk with what he felt was the certain knowledge of finding money. Half a block later a car pulled from a parking space beside them, and he stepped down from the curb to pick up a quarter that had been lying under it. "Jesus, you can't lose," Harry said. "Take the day off, and go out to the track; I'll give you my paycheck."

Lew knew these were omens pointing toward some more solid piece of good fortune ahead, which came at ten-thirty. Walking along the wide, green-carpeted corridor hung with Rowaldson prints which led past Partners' Row, he heard, "Oh, Lew, got a second?" It was Willard Briggs, smiling out at him from his desk, and Lew replied silently, *I do indeed have a second,* and turned in. Approaching the small, delicate desk, a valuable antique inlaid at front and sides with procelain ovals depicting eighteenth-century hunting scenes, he understood that Briggs had been waiting for him inevitably to pass: ordinarily this office door was kept closed. He said, "Morning, Will"—the firm was carefully informal—and sat down at Briggs's gesture.

"Friday I had lunch with Frank Teller," Briggs said immediately. "He told me you worked out a compromise for their problems with the FDA, and that he's had reliable word the FDA is going to accept it after a little noodling around about details. So he's happy, and thinks maybe you earn your money around here."

"That's good to hear." Teller was one of the important vice-presidents of the large pharmaceutical company which was among the firm's best clients, and praise from him was valuable.

Briggs slouched down in his chair, hands clasping behind his neck, the posture flattering, suggesting plenty of time for Lew Joliffe. He was tall and thin, hair parted at the side, graying in front, and he had it all. He wore gray or blue suits and generally, as today, a bow tie. He looked like an eastern-law-school graduate of the forties, although he had always lived in California, and his degree was from Stanford. He was about fifteen years older than Lew. They liked each other, a little tentatively and warily yet, mostly because each occasionally made a small, wry joke the other appreciated. He said, "What about councilman, Lew? You had time to think about it?"

"Well, I checked with City Hall, Will. Found out how you get on the ballot. Nothing to it; you get a few signatures, and pay a twenty-five-buck fee; anyone can run. So I did it." He raised a palm, warding off premature congratulations. "But only because I can always withdraw, Will, by just forfeiting the fee." He frowned, reaching forward to move a finger across the smoothness of one of the porcelain panels. "I'm still not sure. I . . ." He paused, shrugging. "It's just that I'd want to be sure before I began kissing all those germ-laden little babies."

Will nodded. "Well, you've got time to think. How many vacancies coming up on the council?"

"Three."

"Okay"—he sat up decisively. "I've lived in Mill Valley all my life. So has my family, since the town was called Eastland. And between me and some friends we can give you some pretty good help. I think you might just pick up one of those seats your first time out." Hands folded on his desk top, he sat staring at Lew, apparently appraising him. Lew had seen him do this in a court-room with a witness for as long as a minute; it could be intimidating. "I was a Mill Valley councilman myself," he said then. "As I've told you. Sixteen years ago. Two terms, and they led directly to my running for and being elected to the state assembly. Also for two terms. I didn't do a hell of a lot there, frankly, but . . ." He paused, spreading his hands, palms up. "It got me known. To some of the people who run things, to put it plainly. I hope that wasn't the only reason I got my partnership, but it sure helped. I might not have got it otherwise; I just might have missed out."

He sat forward, letting the weight of his arms sprawl loosely on the desk top, shoulders slumping so that his coat collar rose a little in back. This posture said that while there was still no hurry, that he still had plenty of time yet for Lew if Lew had something to say, the meeting was otherwise ending. "You know what I'm telling you, Lew. If it's what you want, and you work it right, I think eventually you can be something around here. You're twenty-nine, aren't you?"

"Yes, sir." It was time for a *sir* now.

"Well, that's young. If you're on the move. Not so young if

46

you aren't. So think by all means. But think hard, and think soon."

Sitting on the balcony over drinks before dinner, Lew told Jo about the conversation, watching her eyes begin to blink with excitement, seeing her smile with pleasure. Lew *had* to run for councilman, she said then, *had to*, and when he didn't reply but just smiled, she said, "Well, *don't* you?"

"I guess so; looks like it. I was just trying to think what campaigning would mean. My god!—I'd have to have bumper strips, wouldn't I."

"Of course!" She clapped her hands in excitement, and stood up to lean back against the rail, facing him. She wore an old denim skirt and a worn white blouse spotted with india ink. "Saying what? 'Jolly Lew Joliffe . . .'"

"'Jolly Lew Joliffe, Your Jolly New Pol'?"

"Too long."

"Use two cars." He stood, taking her empty glass from the rail. "How about, 'Jolly Lew Joliffe: He serves the People Right.'" He walked in with the two glasses.

After dinner Jo worked, and Lew, changed into Levi's and sport shirt, walked over to the Levys' to see what Harry was doing. Their apartment was identical with his and with Jo's; the furniture rented, like theirs; chosen in minutes from a glossy printed catalog supplied by the apartments' rental office. This was page after page of color photographs of modern furniture to be ordered by groups with names such as Studio, Design Contemporary, Nob Hill, Domani, Capri, Budget. Lew's and Jo's had arrived by truck the next day, new or seeming to be, and had been set up in both apartments in under thirty minutes. Its rental they paid monthly, part of the same check as the rents. Jo had picked Budget, also renting dishes and cooking equipment; Lew took Design Contemporary and a television set; the Levys' was Heritage.

Lew and Harry sat out on the balcony talking desultorily. Behind them, at the all-purpose card table, Shirley sat writing a letter to Harry's parents. Rafe had come out to lie between

47

Lew's and Harry's chairs and, his arm dangling, Lew scratched his ears.

Again Harry spoke of the four of them buying a sailboat, and Lew nodded and said yeah, it might be fun. "If I could just sell the stupid camper," Harry said. "Worst buy I ever made; half worn out, and underpowered to begin with. Useless for the mountains, and where else would I use it. Two hundred bucks and it's yours, Lew."

"Well, I might trade you some skin-diving equipment. Or camping stuff. Or a pair of cross-country skis or some climbing equipment. Harry, we buy this stuff, we buy the stupid equipment, get all buzzed up about it, then our interest fades. You're stuck with a no-good camper. The skin-diving's through; we know it. We still talk about climbing some more, but don't seem to get around to it. And now it's a sailboat. What are we *doing?*"

"Looking for a little excitement, I suppose. It's a pretty tame life all in all, and there's a little risk, not a lot but some, in diving, climbing, even skiing. And we'd probably find some in sailing; get outside the Gate in a small boat and it can get a little lively, I've heard. Trouble is, Lew, you have to expand. Dive, and pretty soon you want to start going deeper. Maybe get into treasure hunting. Climb, and at first it's fun just learning. Then fun getting pretty good. But after you've gone up the local cliffs and rappelled down a few times, and then the High Sierras and maybe Yosemite Valley, why, I guess it's the Himalayas next or forget it. That's how it works with me anyway. You were in on the protest stuff at Berkeley, weren't you?" Lew nodded. "Well, I was still at Illinois, and there wasn't too much doing. How'd you like it?"

"I liked it. Might have kept on, if there'd been anywhere to go with it."

"Well, some did go on; the so-called revolutionaries. But do you think they really believe the country is on the edge of revolt? Just waiting for them to push it over? With a few well-timed explosions? They know better—Lew, they're playing, too! They hide out, sneak around in disguises, plant bombs, send tapes to radio stations, have safe houses—because it's *fun.* A way to hold off the god-damn boredom of just slogging away at a job. And what we do is acquire a closet full of sports equipment. But don't let it get you; so do plenty of other people. It's why sports are so big. Everywhere in the world. Anyway, it's only money, and what good will that be in another ten years or so? So think about the boat, Lew; we'll watch the ads, and maybe pick one up cheap this winter."

Lew stayed with Jo again that night, and as he lay back against the headboard, wearing the gray pajamas in which he'd walked along the balcony from his apartment, she moved about the room in a yellow nightgown, tidying. In all she did Jo was neat: working, her tools lay arranged in order in a wide semicircle, her board kept clear of scraps. Now she folded those of her clothes which were to be washed; set her shoes onto the built-in closet rack; closed the closet door till the latch clicked; crossed to the built-in dressing table and screwed the lid onto a jar of cream. Lew sat staring ahead, and presently Jo glanced at him, and said, "What are you thinking?"

"Oh"—he turned to look at her. "Nothing. Just remembering a trip I took when I was a kid. With my folks. On a train."

After a moment she said, "Where to?"

"I don't know; I don't remember. But we spent a night in a Pullman. In a compartment or whatever it's called; three berths, and they gave me the lower so I could look out the window. In the middle of the night, maybe two or three in the morning, I woke up, and of course I raised the blind. I couldn't see much, just blackness. Then we tore through a little town—fast, racing through, the train making time at night. I had a quick flash of a little street, a row of wooden houses and big trees in the light from street lamps; and just a glimpse down a little empty main street. And heard the crossing bell: you know the sound: DING, *ding*, ding, ding, ding, fading away fast.

"Then suddenly I saw something. We zipped into and out of that little town; I don't even know what state it was in: Illinois, Iowa. And right away the houses became more and more scattered, the street lights gone, just a bare bulb hanging high over the cross roads, the corn fields beginning again. And at the very edge of town or maybe just past it, we suddenly passed the back of a house and a little yard right beside the tracks. And there up on a wire was an impossible sight. Two spotlights were angled up from the ground to the wire, and they made a little blaze of light up there in the sky, everything around it solid black night. And in that circle of light a man in white tights sat riding a bicycle across the wire. He had a long pole balanced across the handlebars, and a woman in white tights with long blond hair stood on his shoulders, balancing with a parasol.

"They saw me: watching the train flash by below them, they caught a glimpse of me staring up at them from my berth, lying on my stomach, face at the window, and they smiled, and were gone in the blink of an eye. Vanished; nothing but blackness outside my window, and I could hardly believe I'd seen what I had."

Lew turned to look at her. Jo lay in bed now, facing him, listening. "Who were they?"

"Circus people, I suppose: they have to live somewhere. And that's where these two lived. They were practicing."

"In the middle of the night?"

"Probably didn't want spectators."

"What did your parents say?"

"I didn't tell them. I was afraid they'd say I'd been dreaming. And would convince me I had been."

Jo pulled the light blanket up over her bare shoulder. "It isn't true, is it, Lew."

"No." He smiled at her. For a long time she'd recognized this trait: of occasionally spinning out a fantasy to her or others, making it as believable as he could. If it were accepted he'd let it stand, but would answer truthfully if questioned. She didn't understand why he did this, and sometimes it amused her, sometimes worried her, but she had come to associate it with some uneasiness he was feeling, perhaps now at the prospect of running for city council.

CHAPTER 4

The night of his third walk Lew slept in his own apartment. When his eyes opened at two twenty, by the green hands of his alarm, he knew that this time he'd actually been waiting for it in his sleep. Flipping the coverings aside, knowing what he was about to do, an excitement shot through him sharp as a touch of flame. Dressing, staring at his face in the mirrorlike window pane, it occurred to him, troubling him a little, that the intensity of his pleasure at again going out into the compelling mystery that drew him there was greater than at anything else that had happened to him all that week.

This time, stepping out onto the asphalt from the driveway, he turned right. Tonight a small breeze pressed his face, the leaves rattling overhead, and as he walked he consciously inhaled, pulling the cool air, medicinally touched with eucalyptus, in through his flared nostrils, feeling it as clean. Possibly the air *was* very nearly pure just now, the air moving in from the ocean, with no traffic. Arms swinging, legs striding easily, Lew looked up into the unending blackness of the sky, the stars a hard, electric blue, and was happy again. Passing each of the other apartment buildings, he glanced at their blank dark windows, listen-

51

ing to the steady scuff of his rubber soles, and felt himself alive and alone in this silent new world.

Following the Bay shore, he walked to the freeway, hearing the occasional air-rush of a fast car as he approached, usually followed by silence, the traffic at low ebb. Then, crossing the empty frontage road, stepping up onto the curb, stopping at the seven-foot wire fence, he reached it, U.S. 101. In the faint starlight, fingers hooked onto the diamonds of the fence mesh, he stood staring out at the concrete slab. Far to the north the tail lights of a car moved up the Corte Madera hill, then winked out over its crest, and now the long road stood empty; he could see possibly two miles of it from the Corte Madera crest north to the Richardson Bay bridge south.

It lay there enormously, just before him, in semi-darkness except for large brightly lighted patches under the great direction signs. In the pale even light from the stars he could see separate oil spots at the edges of the dark streaks down the centers of the lanes. In the utterly black no-man's land between the two roadways, the wooden posts and metal scrape-rails stood up sharp against the paleness of the lanes beyond them.

Lew stood fascinated at the motionlessness of the great freeway. Seconds passed, yet these two miles of concrete emptiness continued to stand without motion or sound. It seemed impossible; like staring at a frozen Niagara. Or as though, coming from another world, he stood watching a motionless, mysteriously lighted expanse whose purpose was beyond understanding.

Something moved. He heard it, and his head swung to stare north. Silence, then again the stillness broken by a small sound, a gravelly scraping. Lew searched for and found the movement: a formless, solid-black small bulk crossing the slightly lesser blackness of the shoulder fifty yards to the north—an animal of some sort. Waddling, it moved onto the pale concrete, a skunk or small raccoon, too slow for a dog or cat. Lew jammed his toe into the fence mesh, and pulled himself up onto the fence to stare over its top.

Without hurry the swaying bulk moved across the three lanes of concrete, disappeared into the blackness of the median strip.

A small sound, dull and metallic; the creature squeezing under the wide band of the scrape-rail. Silence; Lew felt his heart beat in his eardrums. Then the animal reappeared on the other roadway. Leisurely it crossed the lanes there, was absorbed into the darkness, and again the night-time world stood motionless and still.

Clinging to the fence, Lew stared after the vanished animal, astonished at the thought which had just occurred to him: that, incredibly, it was possible for him to go out there too. For a moment he hesitated, then heaved himself higher, arms straightening, elbows locking, to support his weight. Swinging a leg over, he straddled for an instant, then swung the other leg over and pushed off, landing crouched on the shoulder. There he hesitated—as though a whistle might blow or a voice shout. Then he stood erect, walked forward, and as his foot touched the concrete, he grinned.

Looking both ways, he walked cautiously to the center lane: except for road workers in fluorescent vests he had never seen anyone walk out onto a freeway, not a busy commute-route. Yet here he stood, grinning. He turned to face south, the direction of oncoming traffic if there had been any, pulled down his face mask, and thumped his chest: "Come on, you bastards, it's Superman," he said softly, the sound of his voice out here startling.

Still grinning, he walked in a great, irregular circle from edge to edge of the pavement, feeling the eerie experience of tramping this forbidden territory. He stopped, glanced around, then did it again, stamping his feet, making a loud, slapping sound. But in no matter what direction he walked, making the circle, his head slowly turned to keep his eyes to the direction of oncoming traffic: being out here was a little frightening.

Still no car appeared, the long lull continuing, and he sat down in the center lane, wrapped his arms around his knees, and sat staring down the freeway through the eyeholes of his mask; a foreshortened, strangely close view, the surface of the concrete rougher than he'd supposed. He sat back, arms behind him, palms on the pavement, supporting his weight. For what he thought must be a full minute he sat watching, ready to scramble to his feet: something *had* to come along. But nothing did. Slowly, working up his nerve, he lay back—watching ahead, straining for the first far-off intimation of an approaching car— till his shoulder blades touched the concrete behind him. But he couldn't bring himself to lower his head. Chin pressing chest, head upright, he lay on his back staring at the darkness for the first flash of headlights. Then he forced himself to lie back completely, ears intent, till the back of his cap touched the pavement. For an instant he lay staring straight up at the immense scatter of stars, then his head jerked up again.

But he knew that in this utter silence he would hear a car long before it could reach this spot, and he made himself lie back once more, clasping his hands under the back of his cap, lifting ankle to knee top in a deliberate posture of relaxation. Ears hyperalert, he stared into the infinite distance searching for the Big Dipper, and in his mind he saw himself from above, a tiny figure lying on a great paved expanse. Aloud, imitating a cop's voice, he said, *"Hey, you!* What the hell you think you're doing!" In his own voice, slightly muffled by the cap, he replied in mild surprise at the obviousness of the question: "Why . . . I'm lying on the freeway, Officer."

"What for! What's amatter with you! You some kinda creep!?"

"Why . . . I'm doing it for fun. To break the awful monotony of life; surely you understand? Why the fuck don't you climb down out of that pig van, and try it yourself?"

"You're under arrest!"

"What for, pork chop, what's the charge? Freeway-lying? *Malicious* freeway-lying? Crossing state lines with intent to lounge on the surface of an interstate free—" A sound cut his voice off, a scrape against the metal fencing beside the road, and Lew sat up fast.

A woman stood watching him from the other side of the fence; she had a small dog on a leash, his front paws up on the meshing, staring at Lew. After a moment Lew said, "Hi." She didn't answer, just stood staring, and he knew she was frightened. *As why not?* he thought. He felt certain that if he stood

54

up she'd turn and run screaming, and he slowly drew up his knees, and put his arms around them, one hand loosely clasping the other wrist in the most relaxed unthreatening posture he could find. Then he sat waiting for her to find her voice, and after another moment or two of motionless staring she did.

Voice tight with the strain of trying to sound calm, she said, "May I ask what you're doing out there?" The dog had lost interest, dropping to the ground to sniff the dirt.

"Oh," Lew said slowly, and shrugged, "I couldn't sleep, I got bored." Would this make any least sense? "And decided to take a w—"

"Lew? Lew, is that *you?*"

"Yes—*Shirley?*" He yanked up his face mask.

"Oh, for godsake. *Yes*, it's me! What in the *world* are you doing?"

He stood up quickly, and walked toward her. "Well, as any fool can see, I'm freeway-lying. Malicious freeway-lying with intent to amaze and astound." Grinning, he stopped at the fence: Shirley smiling at him through the mesh, her head slowly shaking in disbelief. She wore a red scarf tied under her chin, a belted raincoat faded almost white, and plaid wool pants. "Lew, what in heaven's name *are* you doing?"

"I don't know, Shirl." He stood, still grinning at her, pleased with the encounter. "Looking the world over, I guess, in the one time when it's a little different. *Look* at that." He flung out his arm, gesturing at the freeway.

"I know: welcome to the club. Every once in a while I've come wandering down here on a white night. But it never occurred to me to wear a mask or lie on the freeway. Do you do it often?"

"First time. I've been out a couple other times, but this is my first on the freeway. Come on and try it." He grinned. "It's fun; tie Rafe to the fence."

"You serious?"

"Sure."

"All right." Stooping, she thrust the leash end through a bottom loop of the fencing, tied it, and the dog lay down, muzzle on forepaws. Shirley seized the fence, pushing a toe into the mesh, and sprang up, arms straightening, as agilely as Lew had. But she hadn't scaled fences like this as a child and didn't know how to get over. Cautiously, she tried to lie along the fence top, an arm and a leg on each side. Lew reached up quickly, got one hand on her shoulder, the other on her hip, and held her in place. She switched both hands to the mesh on his side, and tried to lower herself with Lew's help, but a button and her belt buckle snagged on top.

Lew said, "I've got you good; you won't fall. Let go with your hands, and untangle yourself." She did; then slowly rolled off the fence top into Lew's arms. He liked it; there was a moment when she lay smiling up at him which he wanted to prolong, but he set her on her feet, and as they touched the ground the electric dots of a pair of headlights appeared on Richardson Bay bridge to the south. Her ankle twisted on a small rock and, Lew trying to support her, they both half fell, half sat down, tangled together and laughing. "Stay down." Lew nodded at the approaching car. It was coming fast, its lights now touching the roadway before them, strangely close at this level. Lew yanked down his mask, then turned up the collar of Shirley's coat. "Sit close; make one silhouette." They huddled together quickly, the car no more than a hundred yards away. "Don't move." Their eyes following the car, they sat motionless, and it flashed past in the inner fast lane, the driver never glancing their way. An instant later the wind of its passing touched their faces, and as Lew turned to grin at Shirley, yanking his face mask up, she swung to face him, eyes gleeful.

"Yow!" She jumped up, ran out to the inner lane, put a fist on one hip and, raising the other high, wrist bent, did a nimble, defiant little jig behind the diminishing red lights of the car. "I don't *believe* it," she yelled. "This is wild!" She sat down on the inner lane, facing south.

Lew walking out to her, she started to lie back as he had done. Instead, scrambling on the pavement, she changed her position to lie, not lengthwise, but across the width of the lane, head toward the center of the road, feet near the dirt of the me-

56

dian strip. She lay back on the concrete then, but her face was turned south: "I've simply *got* to see if a car's coming."

"Right." He lay down across the center lane, feet toward the mesh fence, in upside-down relation to Shirley, only their heads side by side. She turned to look back at him over her shoulder, saw his inverted face, and giggled. Lew said, "Hey, you're on watch! They come fast this time of night," and she turned quickly to face south again.

Lew rolled to his back, clasping his hands under his head, and stared up at the stars. "Well?" Shirley said. "How's your lane? Comfy?"

"Great. Yours?"

"Just dandy." She planted an elbow on the concrete, propped her head on her palm, and lay on her side, watching. Lew turned to look through the triangle formed by her bent arm, head, and neck: nothing was coming, the smudged white of the road fading into darkness far ahead to the south. Again he lay back to stare straight up, and at the movement Shirley glanced over her shoulder at him, then turned swiftly onto her stomach, smiling down at him. On impulse, glancing first to the south, she bent down and kissed him, then lifted her head again. "First time I ever kissed anyone upside down—it's weird. But nice."

Lew reached up, drew her face down, and they kissed again, this time longer, a strange and suddenly exciting experience to Lew. She drew away, and turned to her side once more, propping her head on her hand to watch the road again, her back to him. "Me, too," Lew said. "I know you won't believe this, but it's the very first time I ever kissed a girl upside down while lying on a freeway."

"You've led a sheltered life. There are all sorts of firsts we could establish if we could be sure a car wouldn't come. Imagine: right here on the freeway!"

"Be marvelous. On the freeway or anywhere else with you." In a parody voice he said, "There! I've said it at last."

"Oh, you've said it before; this is just the first time out loud." She glanced back at him, smiling. "Think of the accident report if we were run over!"

57

"I don't think my Blue Cross covers it." He sat up, swinging around to sit beside her, forearms lying on his upraised knees, hands dangling. Shirley pulled herself up, and they sat side by side, staring down the road.

She said, "I used to sit on the floor like this with my brother watching television when we were kids. 'The Mickey Mouse Club.'"

"So did I. M-i-c . . ."

"K-e-y . . ."

Then, both joining in the familiar slow, sad tune, they sang, "M-o-u-s-e, Mickey Mouse . . . Mickey Mouse . . ." Faces solemn, staring ahead, they let the last note die, then Lew yelled, "*Hey, kids!* It's 'Howdy Doody' time!" Shouting, they sang, "It's Howdy DOO-dy time! It's Howdy DOO-dy time! It's time to watch the show! Come on, let's—" Lew gripped Shirley's forearm; a far-off, high, mechanical whine had touched the air, and they turned toward the other side of the freeway to look north. Just over the crest of the Corte Madera hill far behind them, they saw the slow-moving headlights and yellow toplight pattern of a trailer truck, and Lew stood, reaching a hand down to help Shirley up. "Road's getting busy as hell. We better get off while we can."

The truck whine slowly growing, they walked hand in hand to the shoulder, and Lew glanced south: a pair of headlights had appeared there, too. Facing the road, they stood watching them grow, the car moving fast in the inner lane. When it was two hundred yards off, Lew stepped out into the slow lane, and Shirley followed.

He pulled down his mask, and Shirley turned up her coat collar, yanked her scarf off, and with clawed fingers combed her hair down over her face. Hunching her shoulders, she drew her neck and chin down below the buttoned-up top of her coat. The approaching car was less than the length of a football field away, the pavement before them brightening. Suddenly it slowed as the driver spotted them, brakes squealing slightly.

The car still slowing, the driver leaning across the seat to stare, Lew and Shirley stood utterly motionless. Then Lew swung to face the oncoming car, rising high on his toes, arms shooting straight up, hands dangling, in classical Dracula pose. Only a hair-covered knob rising above Shirley's coat collar, she extended both arms out at her sides, elbows loose, forearms and hands hanging limp, and began stumping about in a small circle, bent-kneed, as though blind. A dozen yards off now, the face of the staring driver a white blur behind his windshield, the car accelerated, its front end rising, and shot past them.

Shirley screamed, a wild, cackling, banshee laugh, and Lew slowly revolved on the balls of his feet to continue facing the car, arms high. He held the pose, Shirley continuing her mindless stumping—and safely up ahead now the car's brake lights glowed, the car slowing, then it stopped. Through its rear window they saw the white shape of the driver's face looking back at them. Lew ran down the freeway toward the car as hard as he could go, arms still raised, angling over to the fast lane, rubber soles slapping the pavement. The brake lights went out, the car bucked forward, and sped on, and Lew turned to walk back to Shirley, laughing, pulling his face mask up.

He helped Shirley up onto the fence, her foot in his linked hands. When she got part way up, a toe in the mesh, his hands gripped her waist to lift her higher. Directly across the freeway behind him he heard the truck's diesel, and as he shifted one hand from Shirley's waist to her rump, boosting her to the top, he glanced over his shoulder. Leaning far out of his cab, the driver was watching them, and he reached forward, grabbed his air-horn rope, and blasted it twice. Balanced on top of the fence, Shirley turned her head, saw him, and waved. The driver waved back wildly, then reached forward again to give them a final toot.

They walked home, Rafe off his leash, sometimes following, sometimes ahead; sniffing, wetting the bushes. Following the shoreline, passing between the two- and three-story wooden apartment buildings on each side of the road here, Lew said, "Do you realize we're surrounded by dozens of unconscious bodies? Except for a few thin walls we could see them—lying motionless, some of them twenty feet up in the air, eyes closed, slowly breathing, not five yards away on either side of the road."

"That's spooky."

"I know."

Sighing, she said, "Oh, Lord, this has been silly. And fun; such fun."

For a time they walked on in silence, around the bend beside the black Bay. Then Shirley said, "Lew, what else have you done? On your walks." He told her; she listened, occasionally nodding as though in agreement; and when presently the curved line of their own apartment buildings came into view, she stopped and gripped his forearm. "Lew, let's *all* of us do this! Harry'd love it. I know he would! The Night People! So would Jo. Let's! Okay?"

He felt a sudden pang of loss, deepening as he stood searching for something to reply that would restore it. Then he knew it was too late, the solitariness of his night-time walks already gone. "Sure," he said slowly. "I guess so."

"Great." They walked on. "Maybe a few nights from now: okay? We'll get together, and figure it out."

At the driveway between their two buildings Shirley snapped her fingers for Rafe, and they turned to walk up it. "I'll never sleep," she murmured quietly, then smiled. "I'm going to wake Harry up, and tell him! All about this! I can't possibly wait till morning."

Lew grinned. "Be sure to—wake him up right away. Shake him if you have to. And tell him I said to. G'night, Shirl."

" 'Night, Lew. Such fun. So much fun. Come on, Rafe."

CHAPTER 5

Jo listened at breakfast as Lew told her about his night-time walks; of meeting Shirley last night; and of what Shirley had proposed—listened, eyes and hands busy, buttering toast, rearranging dishes and plates. "Well," she said when he'd finished, not looking at him, hands still busy, "that's fascinating. Secret walks. In the dead of night. And I didn't even know!" she said brightly, finally looking up at him.

He made his voice mild. "They weren't exactly secret, Jo; I'd have told you soon enough. And if you'd ever happened to wake up, and come over to my place, you'd have seen the note on my door."

"Of course. More coffee?" Without waiting for an answer she began to pour. Eyes on the hot black stream, she said, "But I *could* wish I'd known before Shirley."

"Running into Shirley was an accident."

"Yes, I know." Holding his eyes, she leaned toward him over the table. "Listen: any time you get bored with me, in or out of bed, you mustn't be bashful. Just mention it, and with a quick handshake and a twisted little smile I'll be out of your life before you can say 'Jo, it's been great.'"

"I will, I'll do that. But that's hard to imagine. Not quite possible, in fact."

She looked down instantly, finding a crumb that needed flicking. "You're what my father calls a 'bullshit artist.'"

"I'll just bet he does. What a phrasemaker."

"The only time you'd miss me is maybe at breakfast." She handed him a piece of toast. "When you had to butter your own toast."

"You're crazy: I worship you."

She nodded.

"That cynical quirk of the mouth isn't justified. The fact is—you know those big religious paintings? Where the saints all wear—not halos: those big golden discs around their heads."

"Nimbuses. Nimbi."

"Thank you. Well, when I imagine you naked, as I often do—sitting around at work or right now, for example—I see you wearing not one but several golden nimbuses. Not around your head—"

"All right."

"Three of them. Gold, and beautifully polished."

"And you?"

"Just one for me. And only silver. Sterling, though. And hallmarked."

"Sounds pretty cumbersome."

"Not at all. Be like cymbals. Clashing musically while a choir of angels sings 'The Hallelujah Chorus.'"

"Is that what they mean by making beautiful—"

"Exactly, as I'll be glad to demonstrate. Right now."

"No, you won't, bullshit artist. And maybe never again, either. I'd hate to scratch my nimbi."

They finished breakfast, Lew reading the news section of the *Chronicle* while Jo read Herb Caen. As Lew walked toward the balcony doors to return to his apartment for his suit coat, Jo called to him, and he turned. She said, "They *were* secret, weren't they? The walks."

He puffed out his cheeks with a breath, held it a moment,

then released a little sighing pop of air. "I guess so. Yeah, I guess so, Jo, I don't know. But I'd have told you eventually."

"I know. But meanwhile I'm curious: why so secret?"

"Well." He began walking back toward the table. "I've always liked the notion of some secret way to walk off into another world: I was a natural for *Lost Horizon*. I've got a paperback copy, and every once in a while I reread the Shangri La parts." He stood looking down at her. "And when I was a kid I ate up the Oz books, though I can't say I enjoyed them: I didn't like it that there really wasn't any such place. But I couldn't stop reading them. I think the closest I ever actually came to whatever the hell I thought I wanted, was in Illinois when it would snow at night. You'd wake up and you'd know the moment you opened your eyes, because the ceiling was different: the light reflected up onto it from the new snow outside. And it moved; shimmered like water reflections. The sounds from the street would be changed, too, and you'd get up and look out, and for once it was true: the world *had* changed. Into something different and better, or it seemed like it."

"Were you unhappy?"

"No! Hell, no; I had a good time as a kid. I miss snow. I like California all right, but I still feel a little alien out here. Probably always would. There aren't any falls or springs, and even winter isn't much different from summer except that it rains. A few years ago I got so hungry for snow—real snow, not Sierra snow—it was during the Christmas *holidays*, for godsake, yet it was warm and sunny—that I flew back to Chicago. Just bought a ticket, and went. It was great. It was snowing when I got off the plane. Few hours later it turned colder, and I wasn't really dressed for it, and the slush froze, but it was still good to see things covered with white. I got a cab, and went out to my parents' house; I thought I'd ask whoever lived in it if I could come in, and look around, but I didn't; just sat in the cab across the street, and looked."

"Why not?"

"It was the wrong color." He smiled. "It was a frame house, and we always painted it brown, but now it was peach. And the yard was different. They'd put in some ornamental fencing, iron pipes with low chains slung between them; and there was a new concrete walk around the side, and a new front door. It wasn't our house any more. Anyway, I was satisfied. I'd seen snow, and I flew back next morning. I met you not long after." He looked at his watch. "What the hell, Jo; some people are just never satisfied with the way things are, that's all. They're a boring bunch; they talk about snow a lot." He shrugged. "You just keep hoping for the big *difference* some day. And that's about as close as I can come to what I liked about the walks at night."

"When I was a girl I always liked the idea of a summerhouse. I'd seen pictures: the little lath and scrollwork places you'd go off to by yourself on a long 1890 kind of summer afternoon. I'd still like one. Maybe I'll make one when I get time. For The Town." She stood up, kissed him quickly, a little peck, and said, "You'll be late for work."

Harry Levy sat waiting at the wheel of his Alfa as Lew settled himself into the bucket seat beside him. Lew slammed the door, Harry turned onto the driveway, onto the road, then he glanced at Lew, face expressionless. "I hear you've been fooling around with my wife. In the middle of the night. In the middle of the freeway."

"That's right." Lew kept his face equally expressionless, not wanting to anticipate a joke Harry might not be making. "I didn't think you'd mind." He looked at Harry, intentionally meeting his eyes, then looked past him at Richardson Bay: they were moving along its edge.

"Oh, I don't. It was *hearing* about it in the middle of the night that I objected to. I'm told you were all for breaking the news to me at 3 A.M." He smiled, and Lew did, too, relieved.

"Right. Usually the husband is the last to know, but I wanted you to be first."

"Damn white of you. Lew, what the hell *is* this? Shirl says you run around Strawberry night after night in some kind of clown suit, and that we're all supposed to join in the fun. That right?"

"More or less."

Harry nodded. "Well, okay. Try anything once."

Sitting on Jo's balcony Saturday afternoon drinking lemonade after tennis, they agreed to go out on Monday night: too many people were out late on weekends, Lew said—the women nodding, Harry listening skeptically—and the essence of this was the deserted quality of the night. "Play hell with sleep on a work night," Harry said, but shrugged and agreed.

Their alarms having run in the darkness of their bedrooms some minutes before, the two couples met on the driveway between their buildings at two thirty. Glancing doubtfully around in the dim light from the stars and a partial moon, they exchanged semiwhispered greetings. Then Harry, Jo, and even Shirley stood waiting apathetically, shoulders hunched against the lingering pull of interrupted sleep. Jo wore her white Irish knit sweater and tasseled cap, Lew's red daypack containing a thermos of coffee strapped to her back; Shirley again in bleached raincoat, and pants, though without a scarf tonight; Lew in the clothes he'd worn on other nights; Harry wore a black baseball cap and green nylon jacket, fists tucked up into the slanted breast pockets of his jacket. Their interest, Lew saw, was minimal now, and he felt resentful: these walks at night had been his alone, he hadn't asked them to join him. "Well, come on," he muttered, and walked down the driveway. Turning right, toward the shoreline road, he led them straggling down the silent street past the dark apartments.

It wasn't the same: Lew knew it the moment his foot touched the street. The blank-windowed buildings beside them offered no suggestion now of the mystery he had felt out here alone, but looked only as they ought to, the people inside them sensibly and enviably asleep. Plodding along, heads down, the others didn't even glance up at them, and Lew felt tired, wishing he were home, and thought irritably of stopping right here to call it all off.

But Jo tucked her arm under his, and he smiled at her. And

after a mile, climbing and descending the hilly shoreline road winding along beside Richardson Bay, they warmed up, awakened, and when Lew abruptly turned off the road onto a level stretch of empty ground at the left, Shirley said, "What? Hey, where we going?" and he felt the interest in her voice.

"You'll see."

As they crossed the leveled stretch, there loomed up ahead the tree-covered dark bulk of Silva Island, facing a cove of this far north end of Richardson Bay. Harry said, "Hey, nice work, fuehrer; I've never been over there." They stopped. At their feet between them and the island shore lay an eight-foot ditch shaded by the overhanging branches of a large tree on the island shore. Through this ditch a shallow tide-water pond, a bird sanctuary just to the north at their right, drained and refilled; four storklike white birds stood in its shallows, stick-legged, heads tucked under their wings. "What now?" said Shirley. "Wait for the ferry?" But Harry stood leaning forward over the ditch, reaching. Then his hand found the rope suspended over the water from a tree limb; used, as he and Lew had often seen driving home from work, by boys of the neighborhood.

Rope in hand, Harry walked back a dozen feet, then turned and tugged on it hard, leaning far back, testing his weight against it. He stood erect, regripped the rope as far up as he could, then leaped high, drawing his legs up, and swung forward toward them, past them, and out over the ditch. He landed running, paying the rope out, braking with his feet. He shoved the rope back, and Lew caught it.

The women swung across, Jo as agile and skilled as Shirley, Lew was pleased to see. He followed, lifting his legs almost straight overhead to cross hanging upside down, landing with the short run and graceful bowing stop of a circus acrobat, and Shirley said, "Toss him a fish."

"All set?" Lew murmured. They stood under the tree, deep in its shadows, trespassers now, the island privately owned by the four or five families who lived on it, the uninvited not welcome. A few feet ahead, dim in the starlight, lay the narrow road which ran the length of the whalebacked little island. They walked to its edge, and stood listening. As Lew was about to step out, Harry stepped out first, and they followed, feet carefully noiseless, looking curiously at the few widely scattered old houses. The island thick with old trees, the ground under them lay sparsely grown, heavily leaf-covered. The old houses, individually oriented, stood at various ground levels, and with outbuildings. It was a country landscape in miniature, remote and rural seeming although the freeway lay only a few hundred yards ahead. "Love to live here," Jo whispered over Shirley's shoulder, and Shirley turned eagerly: "Oh, yes!"

Ascending the whaleback, they watched apprehensively but no dog came racing toward them, no light flashed on, no shout sounded. Silva was no longer truly an island: when the old highway had been expanded into the present multiple-lane freeway, the strip of bay water between island and shore had been filled in to expand the roadway. Now, a hundred yards ahead, at the end of the island road, lay the service road beside the freeway, and having seen Silva undetected, they were free to walk off it. Instead, hardly knowing in advance that he was going to, Lew turned abruptly to his left, down toward the houses. "Hey!" one of the women called in a whisper, but he walked on, downhill toward the shore. Behind him, feet scuffling the fallen leaves, he heard the others follow.

Passing between two of the houses in straggling single file, they reached the shore, stepping out onto a tiny beach. Far ahead across the long reach of black water lay night-time Sausalito, a few scattered lights on the dark slope of its hills. "What're we *doing* here?" Jo whispered urgently, and Lew turned, smiling in the faint light, and reaching to the pack on her back. "Exploring a newly discovered island. Sit down."

Embedded on the rocky little beach, a bleached log lay half exposed, and as Lew passed out Styrofoam cups and unscrewed the thermos lid, they sat alternately looking out at the view, and glancing behind them. But no sound or movement came from the dark houses up the slope to the rear, the nearest of them fifty yards off; and presently, sipping coffee, they sat in a row looking far ahead across the shining dark water. A new view for them, they identified the black shape of Alcatraz beyond Sausalito, and beyond it the shoreline lights of San Francisco's Embarcadero. Shooting out ruler-straight from the Embarcadero, the glowing yellow beads of the Bay Bridge lay across the blackness, red pinpricks blinking above them. "This is fun," Jo said, and Shirley nodded above the white of her cup: they sat side by side between the men. "I know. But a little scary." She glanced behind her.

Harry pointed ahead and, voice low, said, "Those are the drydocks, right?"

Lew followed Harry's point; far out on the Bay he saw the tiny, slightly blacker rectangle near the Sausalito shore. "Yeah." They all knew the drydocks, standing in four identical open-ended sections stranded in the shallow water before the town: they'd been a part of the scene for years, a landmark of southern Marin. Small though they looked from here, the docks were enormous; four pairs of towering wooden walls rising up out of the Bay from their rotted-out bottoms sunk in the mud.

"Quiet night like this you could row out there easy," Harry murmured. "Wouldn't be far from Sausalito." Lew nodded. In his mind he saw the scene movie-style, externally and from above the rowboat looking down at its pointed silhouette on the night-time water, two dim figures pulling at the oars. "Climb up the damn things," Harry said, and in Lew's mind the scene cut, and he watched himself climbing the wooden slats he knew were nailed to the sides of the docks. "Get a hell of a view from the top," Harry went on, and again the picture in Lew's mind abruptly cut, and now he saw himself high on the top of the great wooden wall, sharply defined against the lights of San Francisco. His arms moved alternately, rapidly: he seemed to be hauling up a weight from the boat by a rope, then it came into view, and he set it by his feet. It was a cluster of explosives, vaguely defined; he didn't know what they ought to look like.

Lew blinked, startled at himself. "Damnedest thing," he said, leaning forward to look past the women at Harry on the other end of the log. "I wasn't even thinking about it, and all of a sud-

den I start imagining rowing out to the drydocks. At night."
Voice wondering, he said, "To blow them up . . ."

"Be something, wouldn't it." Harry nodded. "*Whammo.*"

"Blow things up," Shirley murmured. "You guys are in tune
with the times, all right."

"You couldn't do it, though," Harry said, staring out at the
tiny distant blackness on the Bay. "Take tons of stuff to send
those things up. And you'd have to plant it under the bottoms
somehow; they're *built.* I was out on them once."

"When?" Shirley said.

"That time with Floyd Weatherill. In his FJ. We tied up to
one of them. The bottoms are rotted out, but the inner floors
were still above water, just barely. We walked around in one,
and they're immense." He turned to Lew, grinning, his face dim
in the wan starlight. "What you want to do, Lew, is burn them.
Forget explosives: use gasoline; that you can get. Take plenty of
gas, and really soak them down. All four sections. Then row off
a few feet, and heave up a torch or something."

"Flares," Lew murmured. "Half a dozen road flares." He sat
staring out at the distant drydocks, seeing the film again—the sudden smoky red light flaring up. "Light one, then hold it under the
others and light them all at once. Stand up. Crouched low so
you don't tip the boat. All the flares bunched in one hand.
Heave them up hard—"

"Sidearm; sidearm would be best."

Jo murmured, "Honestly . . ."

"Yeah. Sidearm and arched high. So they'd clear the top with
room to spare. On the way down they'd separate a little before
they hit bottom. But road flares wouldn't go out."

"Take a while to catch, though. For a while you wouldn't see
anything."

"Give you time to row away," Lew said. "Fast as hell."

"Yeah. Then a little way from shore—rowing, you'd be facing
the things—you'd see just a tip of flame, maybe. Sort of flickering up over the side for a second."

"Yeah. You'd reach shore, tie up, get back out of sight somewhere, and—"

69

"*Whoosh!* All of a sudden up she goes. Then all four of them catch. Jesus: you'd see the god-damn things all over the Bay."

"Sure would." Lew nodded. "Four pair of those walls; high and completely surrounded by air; and there'd probably be a breeze, they'd get all the oxygen they could use. They been soaking out there in the sun for years; the wood's bone dry. Loaded with tar. And then soaked with gas—my god, the flames'd shoot up two hundred feet. And against the darkness, on a night like this, the fire reflected in the water . . ." He sat staring.

"Well?" Harry leaned forward to grin at him. "When do we do it? Tonight?"

"Not tonight or any other," said Shirley.

Harry shrugged. "Wouldn't do any harm. They're well out in the Bay, nothing else anywhere near them. And they're no fucking good; the county's been after the owner for years to get rid of them. They're abandoned, actually. We'd be doing the world a favor. Right, Lew?"

"Absolutely. Let's ditch this pair of deadheads, and go find us a siphon."

They finished their coffee. Jo took their cups and put them into her pack, then they walked silently back to the road, and turned toward the freeway just beyond its other end.

The freeway pulled at Lew: he wanted the others to see the eerie sight of the great lighted road lying empty and motionless in the middle of the night. But they reached the service road, lying dark and empty, turned onto it, and almost immediately a car passed on the freeway beside them. As they walked, they watched its tail lights shrink, but just before they winked out over the Corte Madera rise, the blazing eyes of another pair of headlights popped up over the crest. They grew fast, lengthening into beams, then the car shot past on the southbound side of the freeway. Shirley's head turned, following it, and as she looked back over her shoulder, her eyes met Lew's, they read each other's mind, and both smiled at the memory of the night last week when they'd lain together out there on the empty concrete.

Exasperatingly, the road would not clear. Reaching the concrete overpass, they turned by common impulse onto the cork-screw ramp, then walked along the overpass, and always, at least one car and occasionally a clump of two, three, or four moved along the two-mile stretch below them.

By tacit agreement, they stopped over the southbound lanes to lean, chins on wrists, on the concrete rail and stare out over the long reach of concrete, dim and livid in the even starlight. Headlights approached from the north, and they watched them rapidly grow into brilliance, the car behind them indistinct. Fifty yards off, the windshield was a blank black sheet of reflected sky, then suddenly it cleared as the car shot toward and under them, and they saw the driver's startled face staring up at them, open-mouthed.

Smiling, they walked on, and after a dozen steps Lew realized that now once again the world lay silent all around them. He checked both ways: as far off as he could see nothing moved, no headlights appeared. As they turned onto the downward ramp Harry realized it, too. "Hey, look"—he gestured at it—"look at that *road!* My god, it's empty! It's *empty;* look at it!" He began running around and around the ramp, the others breaking into a trot to follow, and at the bottom he ran directly onto the free-way-entrance curve, the one he and Lew took every weekday morning, and out onto the freeway itself.

The others followed, then they all stood in the center lane, heads turning, looking one way, then the other. The lull held; nothing appeared, and Harry looked at Lew, grinning. "This freaks me out, old buddy, it really does," he said, and Jo nodded happily. "I can't believe this," she murmured. "It's wonderful." And Lew felt himself nodding modestly, as though he'd made a big promise he'd managed to keep.

Harry snatched off his cap, wadding it up, tucking the bill in, compacting it. "Yours, Lew!" he yelled, running backward, arm upraised, the quarterback hunting a receiver. He threw it hard in a pass, Jo leaping to intercept, Lew running for it, but the light cloth fell too quickly to catch. Yelling, "Fumble!" he scooped it up anyway, and ran toward the women, folded cap under one arm, the other out in an old-fashioned straight-arm. They shrieked, partly real, partly faking, and separated, Lew running between them, and Harry grabbed him around the waist in a mock tackle. *"Car!"* Lew yelled, pointing; they all whirled, saw the headlights far to the north, and trotted off the road, Lew tossing Harry his cap in a short pass.

Off the road and behind the mesh fence they lay in a row on their stomachs facing the freeway; waiting, grinning. As the car approached they lay motionless, heads low, watching, and saw first the red-white-and-blue lighting strip across the roof; then, as it moved past at moderate speed in the far lane, the lettering across the white door: MILL VALLEY POLICE. The hatless driver never glanced their way, and they watched the two broad tail-light strips move slowly up and then dip over the crest of the Richardson Bay bridge to the south.

They walked back across the overpass, and at the Standard station along the service road on the other side turned in and walked past the pump islands of the dark locked-up blue-and-white little building to the drinking fountain beside the wash-room doors at the side: Shirley was thirsty. Each in turn drank, then as Lew bent over the fountain, reaching for the handle, he froze, they all did, at a small sound from the front of the station, the slight but unmistakable scrape of a bumper-guard on concrete. A faint brake squeal, a muttering engine abruptly switched off, then silence.

Lew and Harry crept toward the front corner, and stopped short of it. Through two windows, across a corner of the dark office, they saw the length of the car stopped beside the nearest pump island, MILL VALLEY POLICE, across the front-door panel. Its lights were off, and behind his windshield the cop sat facing their direction but looking away, off across the freeway, watching.

He *had* seen them; running about the freeway, probably, and seen them run off. Keeping his eyes straight ahead then, giving no sign—knowing they could run off into the darkness before he could stop, get out, and reach them—he'd driven slowly past, aware of them watching him undoubtedly, on the other side of the fence.

On over the bridge, and then—out of their sight just beyond the bridge's other end—he'd have driven across the freeway through the bus-lane gap in the divider fence, and full speed back on the other side. Lights out, probably, as he came over the bridge, he'd swung immediately onto the off-ramp at the bridge's foot, and down into the station. Now, screened by the pumps, he sat waiting for them to reveal themselves somewhere.

Well, here we are, old buddy. Right beside you, Lew said in his mind, aware of a thrill of—what? Excitement: sudden, intense and deeply pleasurable. He turned to grin at Jo and Shirley behind him; but their eyes on his were apprehensive and questioning. Possibly a minute passed, then another, the cop waiting, watching across the freeway, occasionally looking slowly all around him; behind the windshield, his face was indistinct. Then he leaned forward, started his engine, and an amplified metallic click sounded from the car roof as the speaker there came to life.

Lew thought he'd drive off; instead his door opened, and they edged back out of sight. Footsteps sounded, leather on concrete. Almost immediately they stopped. A pause, then the locked front door of the station rattled in its casement. Startlingly loud, a woman's bored and distant voice squawked three unintelligible words from the speaker on the car roof. Silence, then distantly from the other side of the building, the rattling chain of a rising garage door.

They ran swiftly back to the rear of the station, then Lew and Harry walked to the opposite corner. Slowly Lew moved an eye around it, Harry beside him. White fluorescent light filled the roof-high square of the garage entrance, spilling out onto the concrete. From inside they heard the distinctive dead clunk and then the small clatter of a coin rattling down a slot. A metallic click, a soft pop, a gurgle. Slow approaching footsteps, and they drew back their heads. A light switch clicked, the garage door rolled down. The tiny metallic clickings of a key finding its lock. Slow footsteps again, receding now, and they looked around the corner. His blue-shirted back toward them, feet shuffling, the cop moved slowly back toward his car holding a steaming Styro-

73

foam cup out to the side, apparently full almost to sloshing over.

Again they watched at the front corner: the car door stood open and the cop sat sideways on the seat facing the station, heels hooked to the narrow sill, the cooling cup in his hands. Through his door window they could see his face in three-quarter view: narrow, wedge-shaped; hair dead black, straight, and cropped short; wide, close-trimmed pistol-grip sideburns to below his ear lobes. Back in his car with no further need to activate the roof speaker, he'd turned off the engine—they could hear the small pings and cracklings of cooling metal—and he sat staring absently at nothing, waiting for his coffee to cool.

For minutes then, behind the station, they waited; sitting on the asphalt leaning back against the wall. Just beyond the little asphalted area lay the wide expanse of the bird sanctuary, no exit that way. Presently Lew said, "Well, Go'father, what do we do? Shoot our way out?"

Harry smiled but he said, "You know what annoys me? No reason we shouldn't just walk out of here. Instead we sit here because we know he'd stop us: What were we *doing* back here? What're we out for this time of night?"

Jo said, "Well, it *is* kind of suspicious, don't you think? Four people lurking around the back of a gas station. It's only reasonable to stop us. Especially if he saw us on the freeway earlier."

"Maybe. But I don't like the choice! Either go out, and we're stopped: answer questions; produce *identification*, for crysake. All that shit—I hate it. You don't *have* to produce identification, you know. All you have to do is identify yourself orally. But the dumb cops never know that. So you either do it or make a fucking court case out of it. Or sit back here hiding."

Another minute passed, then Harry got up suddenly, and walked restlessly to the back edge of the asphalted area. A fifty-gallon open-topped oil drum stood there, discarded grease rags draped over its rim, empty cartons and a discolored fluorescent tube protruding from the debris heaped inside it. Harry walked over to it, stared into it, then reached in, moving something aside, metal clinking on glass, and Shirley called, "Shhh!"

Harry brought out his hand, something in it, and shook it vigorously. He tipped it toward the open drum, they heard a soft hiss, and saw a whitish glob piling up on one of the rags. He turned quickly to walk back, holding up the tall can. Standing, leaning close as Harry stopped before them, Lew could read the larger label type: ACEWAYS METAL CLEANER/ SPRAY ON, WIPE OFF!/ DISSOLVES GREASE INSTANTLY! He looked at Harry who grinned and said, "There's some left."

Lew didn't know what to reply. "Well, good: you can clean my nail clip."

Harry shook his head, still grinning. "If I could sneak out there, back of the cop car, I could write something on it. Spray it on the back."

"Like what?"

"I don't know. 'Greetings!' 'Hello, there!' 'Fuck you!' Anything—just so he'd drive off with a mysterious little souvenir. What do you think?"

Shirley said, "I think you've lost your mind."

He didn't look at her, just stood waiting, smiling, eyes on Lew's.

Lew said, "I don't think so, Harry. Not a sound out there, nothing stirring, he'd be bound to see some movement or hear any little sound. And he's facing the station: how would you walk past him?"

"Clear out at the side, a long way from the car. Then I could—"

Lew said, "Listen! Say I *walk* out. Just come walking out by myself! I don't know he's there, see, and I walk out, see the car, and do some kind of surprised take. He calls me over: What am I doing here, all that. I just shrug: I'm walking around, couldn't sleep. I often do this, and so on, and so on. Was I on the other side of the road earlier? No, I came from another direction. His eyes are on me standing there by his door blabbing away. And you're in back of the car spraying away!"

"What'll I write?"

"Harry, I won't *have* it," Shirley said. "That's not why we came out tonight!"

A car door slammed. Almost running, Harry and Lew walked

swiftly to the front corner again, but as they reached it, looking through the windows of the office, the car's headlights were swinging away, sweeping through a quarter-circle as the car turned down toward the driveway. It bounced onto the service road, straightening, accelerating, heading north, then they watched it swing up into the driveway of the car wash next door. There the cop tested the office door, then shaded his eyes to peer inside as he shone a flashlight. He drove on to the next in line, McDonald's, and Lew said, "Well, boss, we scared him off."

"Yeah." Harry idly streaked the concrete with a long spatter of white, then tossed the can into the small open drum between the pumps.

Walking home, back around the shoreline, they were quiet, and Lew felt with a host's chagrin that the outing had failed. But passing the little bird sanctuary, Jo murmured, "Look," pointing, and they stopped to stare out at the four motionless sleeping white birds, each standing on one astonishingly thin, sticklike leg, head under wing. "Isn't that wonderful," she said softly, then looked slowly around at the silent darkness, and up at the remoteness of the stars. "There's something about being out here like this that's—I don't know—magical. I'll think about it all day while I'm working tomorrow."

"I knew you'd love it," Shirley said complacently, and Lew smiled. They walked on: Harry and Shirley, Lew and Jo. "Next week, then?" Shirley said, turning to look back at Lew. He shrugged, and she said, "Harry?"

"Well. It's weird. You're a real freak, Lew. But I think maybe you're onto something. Sure. Next Monday again?"

"If you want," Lew said. "But why don't you lead, Harry? I've about shot my wad."

Before he could answer Jo said, "Let me!" And—surprised—the others nodded and agreed.

CHAPTER 6

It was Lew's week to drive, and in the morning the two men drove around the shoreline they had walked last night, then onto the service road: passing McDonald's, where a boy stood beside a steaming bucket, squeejeeing the windows; past the car wash, a blue Volvo just emerging, front bumper dripping; past the Standard station, four cars at the pumps; past the pedestrian overpass, three men crossing toward the bus stop. They stared curiously at each of these places, then turned to glance at each other and smile.

As they entered the freeway, sliding into an empty space in the slow lane, Harry shook his head in disbelief that they could ever have run and cavorted on this traffic-clogged road. He said, "I'll admit it, Lew: there *is* something to nutsing around like that in the middle of the night. But what?"

"Well"—Lew nodded toward the windshield—"take a look at this frigging freeway; you can hardly see the concrete. And look at us, sitting here breathing this stuff; you can smell it today. I hate the freeways, but who doesn't, and what can you do? We're on it again, we'll be back on it tonight, tomorrow morning, and for the rest of our lives—you know it." He smiled. "But

77

last night, at least, we defied it. Played on it, pranced around on it, thumbed our noses at it."

"Yeah, maybe." Harry waited as Lew, checking his rear-view, sped up slightly to slide over into the center lane, braking immediately. Then he said, "Something like that, anyway, but . . ."

"But what?" Lew said after a moment.

"But we didn't defy anything, did we, Lew? We just sneaked onto it when it was safe. Looking both ways first. We were like kids making faces at Daddy when he's taking a nap. The time to do it would be now." He smiled, interested at the thought. "Seven-thirty in the morning. You and I climb the fence, and just bulldoze our way out into the middle of the god-damn road, cars hitting their brakes. We face the traffic, straddling the markers, and block all three lanes. The cars behind us move on, the road clears, and we turn around and start running all over the fucking freeway. Bring a real ball, and pass it, kick it, run with it, tackle. Cars backed up to San Rafael, every horn blasting, guys leaning out yelling blue murder."

"Be something," Lew murmured, eyes on the rear-view, waiting a chance to move into the next lane, and Harry nodded, then slumped down to try and nap.

The week passed. On Wednesday night Lew and Jo saw a double-bill Hitchcock at the Surf, in San Francisco, one of them being *The Lady Vanishes*, which they'd never seen. In the ticket line just ahead of them stood a college friend, Leonard Beekey, whom Lew hadn't seen since Berkeley, and the two couples sat together, and had coffee in the little place next door.

During the last half of the week he worked hard and well, finding citations for a memorandum, in the company library and on two afternoons in the law library at Hastings. He added an invented citation, *City of San Francisco vs. Josephine Dunne*, as explicitly described as the real ones; but before handing it over for typing, he crossed it out.

Thursday evening, with Jo's help, he worked on devising a bumper strip for when it should be time to begin campaigning: JOLIFFE FOR CITY COUNCIL, they decided it should read, and in

78

smaller letters underneath, TO KEEP MILL VALLEY MILL VALLEY. On Friday they bowled with the Levys. On Saturday evening, in Lew's apartment, they watched "The Mary Tyler Moore Show," lying on the chesterfield together; presently, the television still on, they made love, then watched it some more till they fell asleep. It rained Sunday, the Levys were away visiting Shirley's parents on the Peninsula, and they spent the day in one apartment or the other with the Sunday paper, books, magazines, television, and Jo's worry because she'd thought of nothing interesting to do for tomorrow's Night People Walk. "Don't worry about it," Lew said. "Just improvise as you go; I'll help you." But Jo said, "That's your nature, not mine. Oh, I hope it rains tomorrow!"

It did. When the alarm rang at two fifteen, Lew shut it off, snapped on the little bedside lamp, then swung his feet to the floor to sit on the edge of the bed, holding his eyes open. Jo had gotten up instantly, and now the kitchen light came on, then the small sounds of Jo starting the coffee maker, which she'd left filled and ready to plug in. The phone rang, he picked it up from the little table, and as he put it to his ear he heard Jo's voice on the kitchen extension: "Hello . . . ?"

"Jo!" Shirley's voice wailed. "It's *raining!*" Lew lay the phone on his pillow, walked to the windows, and parted the drapes: the glass was streaked and, stooping to look up at the white mist of the sky, he could see the slant of a soundless fine rain.

"Lew!" He heard Jo's actual voice from the kitchen duplicated in the phone on his pillow. "Shirley says it's raining, and we're to come over! To their place. For coffee, a drink, *anything,* she says."

"No!" He was going back to bed and to sleep, but he tried to temper the blunt refusal. "Tell them to come over here! And don't take yes for an answer!" He sat down on the bed, yawned enormously, then got under the covers again. From the kitchen Jo called, "Harry's on the extension: wants to know why we won't come over!"

Lew got comfortable, lying on his back, then picked up the

79

phone, and spoke into it quietly. "Because it is raining. And I not only know enough to come in out of it, I know better than to go out into it in the first place. But apparently Harry doesn't. So cut out the argument, Harry, and get your ass over here. Shirley's, too. Shirley's especially."

"Love to, Lew, love to," Harry's voice in the phone said. "Except that it would not only mean getting out of this comfy bed and getting dressed. It would also mean getting soaked to the skin on the way over: we don't own umbrellas or raincoats."

"Teddibly unfortunate; hard cheese," Lew said. "I believe you, of course. And we'd be on our way over there this very moment, me trudging through the torrential downpour on my crutches, with Jo's kindly assistance. My old wound, you know; acts up whenever it rains."

In the phone Shirley's voice said, "Listen. I am *not* just going back to bed; I'd never get to sleep. My alarm rang, I woke up all set for the Walk, and I am now stark wide awake and ready to do *some*thing. I don't mean all night, for heaven sakes. Just a drink, a cup of coffee, tea, or a tall glass of water. It would actually help us to get back to sleep that much faster. So let's! Here or at your place, I don't care."

Lew said, "Damn it, Harry, I was just sinking back into the blessed Nirvana of sleep, when your crack-brained wife brings up this fantastic notion of venturing out into a typhoon. So the only honorable thing for you to do—"

"Listen, it was Jo, panicked by the thought that you might seize this moment of idle wakefulness to wreak your sordid will upon her, who instantly accepted that fantastic notion instead of squelching it. So if you have an ounce of decency—"

"I agree with Shirley," Jo said firmly. "To just go right back to bed would be—"

"Anticlimactic," said Shirley.

"Right. So one of you is going to have to make the supreme sacrifice of getting a few clothes on, and walking twenty yards. It'll only be for half an hour!"

Lew said, "Listen, ladies." Under the covers he crossed an ankle over his upraised knee. "As I understand the problem, you two, feeling an understandable sense of letdown, would like a brief get-together. At which Harry and I dispel your ennui with swift repartee and inimitable antics. Right?"

"Well, I'd never have thought of putting it quite that way: would you, Jo? But, sure."

"Well, fine," Lew said reasonably. "Because that happens to be exactly what Harry and I would like, too: we just think pneumonia is a little too high a price to pay. But the problem is already solved: through the miracle of science, if we will but realize it, we are *already* gathered together. What are we doing right now but happily chattering, gaily laughing, each with his own phone in hand, in the blessed comfort of our own homes? And beds. No one has to stick a foot out in the god-damned rain, and I can talk to Harry without seeing his face, a definite plus."

"Wonderful!" Harry yelled into his phone. "Lying in bed seems to have immeasurably sharpened your wits. That's as brilliant—"

"No," said Shirley. "You two aren't going to talk us—"

"Get into the mood, Shirl!" Lew said. "The party's already started! Yippee! You dressed for a party, Harry?"

"Yep. Something told me to put on dinner clothes when I went to bed tonight."

"I'm in mufti myself: white gloves and matching tennis shoes. But I'm sorry to report that Jo is still in her Dr. Dentons. What're you wearing, Shirl?"

"My old drum majorette's outfit. The one I wore to the State Finals. Listen, we can't tie up the phones like this."

"Why not?" said Harry. "Who's going to call at 2:30 A.M. with a better idea? Yippee, to quote Lew, we're having a party! What're we serving, Lew?"

"Beer, I guess. Haven't got any wine, have we, Jo?"

"Just for cooking."

"Okay," Harry said, "I'll put away this pre-Restoration chartreuse, and switch to beer for the sake of the party. Lew, take that lampshade off your head!"

Smiling, Lew put down the phone, got up, and walked to the

kitchen. Jo stood in her nightgown, phone at her ear, leaning back against the little sink, nodding as she listened. She said, "I know; but at least you can reason with children." Lew opened the refrigerator, brought out two cans of Schlitz, yanked off the tabs, handed Jo a can, and started out the door. Then he turned back. Just below the formica-covered work space beside the sink was a drawer filled with old string, a broken flashlight, nails, screws, a souvenir ash tray: junk of all sorts. Stooped before it, Lew poked through this mass for something he remembered seeing, and found it, a small cellophane package imprinted with ringing bells and HAPPY NEW YEAR. From it he pulled two folded paper hats. Opening a blue one, he walked over to Jo, and pulled it onto her head. Working a red one onto his own head with one hand, he walked to the door, then turned on the threshold to look back at Jo. "Yippee," he said, saluting her with his beer, and walked on back to the bedroom.

He took a swallow of beer, sitting on the edge of the bed, then got under the covers, and picked up the phone. "—ever remember drinking beer this time of night before," Shirley's voice was saying.

Lew said, "Harry, you got your beer?"

"Yeah. All set."

"Shirley?"

"Yes. It tastes pretty good; I was surprised."

Jo said, "Shirley, is Harry in bed?"

"Of course. While I have the living-room phone. Sitting in that straight-backed chair at the desk. With the heat off."

"No suggestion that *you* take the more comfortable place? For this alleged party?"

"Certainly not. And I gather that you—"

"Well, here's to the party!" Lew said quickly, and clicked his beer can on the mouthpiece of his phone. He heard the others do the same, and he took a swallow of beer. It *was* good, very cold, just what he'd wanted.

A silence of several seconds, then Shirley said, "Some party. Beats having fun, doesn't it, Jo?"

"Well, wait a second," Lew said. "This is the early quiet stage that all parties go through at first: later on we get wild. But now it's just quiet, sophisticated conversation. Harry, toss off an epigram."

"What *is* an epigram, exactly?" Shirley said.

"One of those things that begins, 'A woman is like . . .' *You* tell her, Harry."

"Well, let's see: A woman is like . . ." They heard him take a swallow of beer, then silence.

After a moment Lew said, "Wrong pose, Harry: you can't think of epigrams lying down. Stand up by your dresser. Can you reach it?"

A pause, then Harry said, "Yeah."

Shirley said, "Incredible: you made him stand."

"Now drape one arm negligently along the top of the dresser as though it were a fireplace mantel. Lucky you're wearing evening clothes."

"There's no top to this dresser; it's built-in flush to the wall."

"Well, just hold your arm out, then."

A momentary silence, and Shirley said, "Jo, no fooling; I think he's *doing* it."

"You bet I am. All set, Lew. My eyes are heavy-lidded with *Weltschmerz*."

"Good. Your drink in hand?"

"No, how would I hold the phone? A yard from my ear at the end of this negligently draped arm?"

"Wedge the phone between your shoulder and ear. Like a senior partner in a big-time law firm. And hold your drink sort of high up against your chest. Too bad it's not a martini. Or chilled white chablis. I believe they're the natural drink of the sophisticate; beer and epigrams seem a little unlikely. But try. All set?"

"Yeah, but my neck hurts."

"Honestly," Jo murmured.

"Pitiful, isn't it?" said Shirley.

"A woman is like the winning horse of a race," said Harry. "Impossible to ever predict with certainty . . . forever just beyond the reach of logic and reason . . ."

"He's not just a male chauvinist pig, he's a whole herd," said Shirley. "Is it herd?"

". . . and yet," Harry continued, "with a seeming inevitableness of result once it has occurred."

"Splendid!" Lew yelled. "Capital!"

"It doesn't even make sense," said Jo.

"Naturally," Lew said. "That's the test of your true epigram. The best ones, anyway: they *sound* as though they mean something, only you're just not quite clever enough to figure out what. And you're afraid to ask for fear of revealing your total lack of sophistication."

"I'm not afraid. Are you, Shirley?"

"Not in this league."

"A woman," Lew began, then interrupted himself. "I am standing with one elbow on a portable mantel I had in the closet, staring moodily down into my glass, absently swirling its contents. Now, then: A woman is like a pretzel, smooth and glossy on the outside . . . brittle underneath . . . creating and sustaining an unquenchable thirst for ever more . . . and holding within her preordained form the eternal symbols of Yang and Ying."

"Hot dog!" Harry shouted. "Man, that's cool!"

"Thank you, Noel." Lew clicked his beer can against the mouthpiece.

"Women's Lib, *wait for me*," said Jo.

"A man is like a bad television comic and straight man combined," said Shirley. "Roaring at his own jokes. Grinning like an ape. And puffed up . . ." She stopped.

"Like a popover," said Jo, "and just as full of hot air."

"That's right, and hollow underneath!" Shirley said, and snickered.

"That's not an epigram," said Harry.

"More like minestrone soup."

"Shirley, can't you just see them? Lying flat on their backs grinning like happy idiots. Alternate straight men and comics just like you said."

"Right. Their own best friends and kindest critics."

84

"Noel," said Lew, "we seem to have blundered into the wrong drawing room."

"Afraid so, George Bernard."

"All right, wise guys," Shirley said. "You're so good, what're you going to do to entertain us, this is supposed to be a party?"

"Enter*tain* you?" said Harry.

"That's right, Noel. This scintillating company has us tingling with anticipation. Right, Jo?"

"Tingling or numb."

"Lew, now is the time for all good men to come to the aid of the party."

"What about a little bridge? I'll phone Mr. Loeffler in the next building, get him to shuffle a deck, and deal out four hands. Each of us phones him, one by one, and he reads off your hand. Write it down, then get a deck, and pick out your hand. All get back on the phone, and we call out our cards as we play them. Finish a hand, wake up Mr. Loeffler—"

"Come on now, George Bernard," Jo said.

Harry said, "Lew: time out for a conference. Jo and Shirley off the phone for a minute." They heard the sounds of Shirley's phone placed on the desk top, and Jo's on the kitchen counter. Harry said, "Lew?"

"Yeah."

"Listen." He lowered his voice, and spoke quietly.

"Okay, fine," Lew said. "*Jo!* You can pick up."

Shirley picked up her phone and Harry said, "Ready?"

"Yeah," said Lew.

Harry tapped three times on the mouthpiece of his phone, then to the tune of "On, Wisconsin," Harry and Lew sang:

> "On Proviso, on Proviso,
> Fling your colors high!
> Our whole school is backing you,
> Let's pass all others by!"

"Their high school song," Shirley murmured. "Can you tie that?"

"On Proviso, on Proviso,
Ever loyal beee . . . !"

"God help us," said Jo.

"FIGHT! For Proviso High,
and Vic! Tor! Reeee!"

"I've reconsidered that offer of cards," said Jo. "Right now a round of old maid would sound pretty good."

"Or slapjack," said Shirley. "Jo, I'll phone you in the morning during my coffee break."

"Wait!" Lew yelled. "The fun's just starting! Jo: Shirley and Harry will hang up for a minute. Then you dial the all-night drugstore in the St. Francis Hotel. When they answer, you say, 'Have you got Prince Albert in a can?'"

"I don't *believe* this," said Shirley.

"And when they say yes, you say, 'Well, let him out!'" Both men howled with laughter.

"Fifth grade," Jo murmured. "That was the peak of wit in the fifth grade: remember?"

"You must be wrong; it couldn't have been higher than third."

Harry said, "Lew, is your father a mailman?"

"Nope."

"What is he then"—Harry could hardly finish for laughing—"a *female* man?" The men roared, vibrating the ear pieces of the women's phones.

"Okay, phone me in the morning, Shirl. When the fun's died down."

"Well, too bad," Harry said. "Always a shame to end a great party."

"Best party I've ever been to," Lew said. "Lying flat on my back in bed."

"Well, that's life, G.B.: at every party there's a party killer. And in this case two. See you in the morning." Harry hung up.

The women talked for a minute or so longer, then Jo turned off the kitchen light, and returned to the bedroom. In the light

86

from the little bedside lamp Lew lay nearly asleep, but he smiled slightly and made a small gesture without opening his eyes. His paper hat lay on his pillow, and Jo removed it. She reached up to find her own still on, and took it off. The light out, she lay for half a minute listening to the rain, heavier now, then slipped into sleep.

As often in this particular Bay Area fall, the slight rain soon subsided, and seemed to go away forever. For the rest of the week summer returned as though for good. On Monday after dinner, Lew at the sink washing dishes, Jo still at the long paste-up table finishing her coffee, she said, "Tonight's the Night People, and I'm still leader. I don't like this just waiting to see what'll happen. Maybe nothing will, maybe I won't be able to think of anything."

"Jo, so what? Maybe in that case we've had the Night People Walks. There's only so much you can do, wandering around at night, and maybe we've done it."

"Wouldn't you miss them?"

He nodded, smiling, and began rinsing dishes under the faucet. "Yeah. I count on them now. It's weird."

"We all do: we're hooked; Shirley and I have talked about it." She stood up with her empty cup, gave it to Lew, then stood looking around the tiny kitchen area, her thumb and forefinger rising to her chin, and Lew smiled inwardly, knowing what was coming. Jo liked to organize her next day aloud, and now he heard her murmur. "Eggs yesterday. And bacon Friday." She kept track of the cholesterol in their diet. "Should have cereal tomorrow. With fruit." She glanced at the aluminum bowl on top of the refrigerator, and Lew looked, too: it was like being able to read someone's mind. There were two bananas in it, and he watched her open a cupboard, take out a box of Special-K, and rattle it. There seemed to be plenty, and she put it back. "Milk," she said, and turned back to the refrigerator. She opened it, peered in, then stooped and began shoving things aside. "Damn." She turned to Lew: "I have to go down to the shopping center. For milk."

"Want me to?"

"No, you're busy." To herself she murmured, "Better go now or they'll be closed."

An angled parking space stood empty directly before the Safeway, and Jo turned the VW into it, feeling pleased; there was seldom an empty space this close. She walked briskly toward the big store to the beat of "Tea for Two" tinkling from the little overhead speakers spaced along the underside of the walkway roof: as always the store just ahead was whitely and shadowlessly lighted. She stepped onto the green rubber mat with the big Safeway emblem, heard the clunk of the automatic door-opening mechanism and barely stopped herself from walking into the glass of the locked door which had moved only a fraction of an inch. Angrily she stood looking into the vast interior, aisle after aisle in an area as big as two basketball courts, all of it now empty of people except for a man in green uniform shirt and pants shoving an enormous dry mop. She glanced up at the clock on the back wall, and saw that the store had been closed for six minutes.

At the 7-Eleven half a mile back down the service road at the foot of Ricardo, Jo walked to the refrigerator to get her milk, irritated at herself for having to shop here and pay fifteen cents more than she'd have paid at Safeway for the same quart of milk. At the counter the clerk reluctantly put aside the *TV Guide* he'd been reading to punch out the price on the register while Jo stood finding her wallet in her purse. Beside her stood a cardboard display basket filled with green bottles, their necks wrapped in gold plastic foil. MISSION CHAMPAGNE, SPECIAL $2.29 QT., a printed sign read, and Jo picked up a bottle, and stood staring down at the label as though reading it. Actually, her eyes half closed in concentration, she was calculating in the only way she was able to without a pencil. On an imaginary blackboard she printed $2.30 in white chalk, rounding off the price. Under the zero she wrote 6, and drew a line under that. Compulsively she said it to herself as she'd been taught in grade school: *Six times zero is zero;* and drew a zero below the line. *Six times*

88

three is eighteen, write the eight and carry the one. Six times two is twelve, and one are (not *is*) *thirteen.* She wrote the thirteen, drew the dollar sign, and read the result from the blackboard. Six bottles of even cheap California champagne, with sales tax, would cost more than fourteen dollars. But the idea that had come into her mind was too good to pass up. Accepting her change from the milk, she checked her wallet to be sure she had enough money, then began lifting bottles from display basket to counter. At home, the kitchen empty, Lew in his own apartment at the moment, Jo walked to the refrigerator, and laid the six tall green bottles on their sides in the vegetable compartment.

Seven hours later, at two thirty in the morning, Lew and Jo walked toward the driveway, each carrying a Styrofoam cup of coffee steaming in the chill air: instant coffee because Jo had forgotten to prepare the percolator. She wore red plaid slacks, her Irish sweater and tasseled cap; Lew his usual dark blue nylon jacket, blue denims and sneakers, red cap. His other hand gripped the straps of a canvas shopping bag filled to the top with newspaper-wrapped packages which Jo had irritatingly refused to identify, the load heavy enough to pull his arm straight. At the driveway, seeing Harry and Shirley sitting out front on the curb, they turned down it.

Huddled together just outside the light from a street lamp, they looked up as Lew and Jo stopped before them: Harry in his black baseball cap and green nylon jacket, Shirley in a denim suit, no hat or scarf. "Jesus, it's early," Harry said. "And cold. Is that coffee? Or cyanide? I would gratefully accept a sip of either."

"Take it all, I've had enough." Jo handed him the cup. "Hi, Shirl."

Shirley made her voice and body shiver. "Hiii. What's on tonight, Jo? If you still haven't got an idea, I have." She gestured with her chin at the dark buildings behind them. "Let's all go in, get into one bed, and turn the blanket on high. Harry, save me a swallow."

Lew handed Shirley his cup. "Here, take mine. Two things

you can always count on with instant coffee in Styrofoam cups: it's always lousy and always too hot."

Sipping carefully, Harry slowly stood up. "This is good," he said to Shirley. "It's called coffee. We ought to get some."

Quickly, brightly, the anxious hostess, Jo said, "You'll all feel better soon: that's a promise! Come on, now." She extended a hand to help Shirley up, who groaned and said, "Careful; I'll break."

The winding road silent except for the scuff of their sneakers and shoes, dark except for the greenish patches under the widely spaced street lamps, they moved, straggling, along the shoreline. It had been warm during the day, but at sunset the thick white fog had rolled in, the temperature dropping swiftly, and now the air was sharp, and Lew wished he'd brought his sweater. He felt hollow, metabolism barely ticking over. It was one thing to be up because you're restless and can't sleep, he thought, but something very different to be yanked out of sleep by an alarm. The loaded sack was heavier now, and with each step it brushed his leg annoyingly. Yet, looking out across the dark still water beside them, and up at the black, star-flecked sky, he was content and happy.

"What's in the bag?" Harry said presently.

"A big surprise, Jo won't say what. But it's heavy; heft this damn thing." He held the bag out to Harry beside him, who took it, hefted it, then nodded and offered it to Lew again. But Lew's fists were shoved into the side pockets of his jacket now, and he was grinning. "Your turn, sport."

"Anyone can dupe me at two forty-five on a raw, bitter morning. What are we *doing* out here? Jo," he called to the women ahead, "this better be good."

At the foot of Ricardo Road they passed the 7-Eleven, dark now except for the night light, and turned onto the service road, heading north. Beside them the great lighted freeway stood virtually empty again, only an occasional car flashing past as they walked beside it. Half a mile ahead the large, unlighted, shell-shaped sign of a gas station stood outlined against the lavender-tinged lighting of the shopping-center parking lot.

They reached the lot, empty now except for a huddle, near the center, of four or five cars and the delivery van of the TV-repair shop. Jo turned in, and, their faces strange in the violet mist of light from the parking-lot lights high overhead, they straggled across the white-lined asphalt, their multishadows branching out from their feet, wheeling as they walked.

The shopping center was three huge, low buildings of varied shapes, covering acres; under its low red-tiled roofs some eighty-odd store fronts faced a maze of concrete walkways. The roofs continued on down across these walks, covering them; and at intervals along the outer edges of the walks, great square pillars of aged wood supported the roof at the eaves. These massive pillars were entwined with ivy, and Jo thought, approaching it, that this was actually a handsome place, the low roofs and covered walkways reminiscent of early California missions. As they walked across the wide lot toward it, the daytime blatancy of the shop windows now lost in darkness, the place seemed mysterious, inviting, and she felt a surge of hope that her impulsive plan for this night had been a good one. But to Lew, this place, before always busy with movement but shadowed and still now, the low roofline ahead black against a dark sky, seemed forbidding and almost menacing as though aware of their approach.

Then the silence was gently broken, their heads tilting as the first hint of sound touched their ears. Each step across the asphalt brought it clearer though it remained subdued: a quiet orchestral background to a softly tinkling piano. Her voice pleased with the coincidence, Jo said, " 'Tea for Two.' It was playing when I came down for milk tonight, and now the tape's come around again."

Harry said, "Music. Playing here all by itself. In the godforsaken middle of the night. Some sort of symbolism here, Lew, if I was awake enough to figure it out."

"It's the way the world will end, Harry. Recorded cocktail music nuclear-powered to play on for centuries after all life has been destroyed. Selections from *No, No, Nanette*, throughout eternity. That do you for 2:55 A.M.?"

"I want to go *home*," Shirley said, but smiling.

They stepped up onto the covered walkway, Jo stopping beside a backless wooden bench, turning for her shopping bag as Harry set it down before her. The others stood waiting beside her, facing the bench and parking lot, faces ghastly in the lavender light. They saw a brown-paper sack lying on top of whatever else the canvas bag contained, and Jo opened it and brought out a newspaper-wrapped something, which she handed to Shirley. As Shirley unwrapped hers, Jo handed out others to Harry and Lew, taking the last one herself, crumpling the paper sack, thrusting it down into the side of the shopping bag. Her hand trembled slightly; this whole idea suddenly seemed to her embarrassingly absurd.

"A *glass?*" Shirley said wonderingly: she raised it to her face, holding it to the light from the parking lot, twirling it by the stem.

Jo nodded shortly. She stood unrolling a foot-long newspaper-wrapped cylinder she'd taken from the canvas sack; then they saw it was a bottle. "Open it." She thrust it abruptly at Lew.

"Champagne," Harry murmured. "It is. It really is."

Lew peeled off the imitation foil, then squeaked out the plastic cork with his thumbs: a soft pop, and a sliver of lavender smoke curled from the bottle-neck.

"Marvelous," Shirley said. "Champagne right now may kill me, but I don't care: I think it's marvelous. Gimmee." She held out her glass.

Lew poured, filling their glasses and his own. Then, standing at the little bench in the strange light just under the eaves of this great dark place, they waited, glasses in hand, looking to Jo for a cue. "Well, *drink* it," she said, embarrassed, and lifted her glass in an awkward little toasting motion. She tasted hers, then they all sipped: tentatively, glancing at each other to smile, conscious of the oddity of what they were doing. Then Lew drank again: it was very good, very cold, and he realized he'd been thirsty. "Good," he murmured, and grinned at Jo. "Damned good after that walk."

Harry stood sipping thoughtfully, testing both the taste and the idea of champagne out here at three in the morning. Then he nodded abruptly, and drained his glass. Holding it out to Lew for more, he said, "First prize, Jo. Permanent possession of the silver trophy for leadership," and Jo looked suddenly relieved and pleased. Lew filled Harry's glass, he tasted it, nodded again, then glanced up and down the long length of the covered walkway stretching off into darkness at either end. "But . . . is this the idea for tonight, Jo? Drinking champagne at the shopping center?"

"No, of course not," she said firmly, sure of herself now. "You'll see. Lew"—she was hostess—"Shirley's ready for more."

All had second glasses, emptying the bottle, which Lew shoved into the shopping bag, neck down. He unwrapped another, the others watching, grinning. This time he pushed the cork loose quickly, deliberately making it pop. It struck the ceiling, bouncing out of sight, the champagne frothing from the neck, and he poured quickly, topping off their glasses.

Pleased with the novelty, they stood glancing around them; down the long walkway into the darkness; up at the invisible loudspeaker now softly playing, "Willow Weep for Me" in a guitar arrangement; smiling at each other and at the absurdity of sipping champagne here at this place at this moment in the deep of the night.

Once again Lew refilled their glasses, then Shirley and Jo sat down on the bench, two lavender-edged silhouettes against the parking lot. Lew lifted a foot to an end of the bench, and Harry turned to sit down on the walk, leaning back against the store front of The Record Shop. "Well?" Jo said. "How's everyone feel?"

"Idiotic," said Shirley. "Wonderfully idiotic. I'll never be able to walk by here in the daytime again without giggling."

They couldn't see Harry's face, but the glass in his hand held a wavering glint as he spoke. "Twenty-odd minutes ago sitting out on the curb I felt like a burned-out dry cell. But sitting here with my third snort of this stuff"—the glass lifted, saluting Jo— "well, here's to the Night People!"

They all drank, and Lew said, "Amazing. The first glass was obviously dollar-seventy-nine-cent imitation champagne. Number two was fair; about like Korbell's." He raised his glass to twirl it by its stem. "But this is Piper-Heidsieck."

"And a vintage year," said Harry. "It's a"—he tried to give it a French pronunciation—"*formidable* little wine."

"A *charmant*, laughing little wine," Lew said.

"A snickering, giggling, grab-ass little wine."

"Well, then," Jo said, the hostess still, and she nodded at Shirley beside her, "I think Shirley wants to dance, Lew. Because that's what this is: a dance. We're having a party! Complete with music."

"My god, of course." Lew was delighted. "That's what it is— a party!" He bowed at Shirley. "Ma'am?" Grinning, she stood up; they both set their glasses on the bench and began to dance. This was shopping-center, doctor's-office music, "classics" from the forties and fifties and earlier, and they danced appropriately, old style, cheek-to-cheek.

For a dozen seconds, moving within a space of only a square yard or so, they danced slowly. Then as "Willow Weep for Me" gave way to a big-orchestra "Begin the Beguine," they moved faster, and after a moment or so began to twirl, feet shuffling swiftly, and Harry had to draw in his legs. Down the walkway they whirled for a dozen yards; here a transverse passageway between two store fronts led to the other side of the building and the shops there. Now it was a black tunnel, its other end a lighted square of roadway. They danced to the opening, glancing in, then Lew led them back toward the others. Jo sat watching, smiling, one leg crossed over the other, a foot keeping time. Lew began to feel dizzy, and he stopped the twirling, dancing them back toward the tunnel again, and this time, slightly pressuring Shirley's back, he led them into it; he'd wanted to the first time, and now he did. Shirley felt good in his arms, he was acutely aware of the light pressure of her cheek against his, and he wanted to kiss her; to move through the dance holding her close, his lips hard on hers. Then, deep into the darkness, well out of sight, and the opportunity at hand, he felt that to do this just here and now would be a small betrayal of why the four of them were all here together. Leading them out to the walkway again, he felt his face flush; he was certain Shirley knew why he'd brought them in.

They emerged, Harry's face toward them, and Harry turned to set his glass on the narrow window ledge of the store front behind him. He stood, and made the suggestion of an invitational bow to Jo. "Lovely party," he said formally.

"So glad you could come." Jo stood up from the bench, lifting her arms, and they began to dance sedately. Then Harry stepped back, and began a slow jitterbug. Surprised, Lew saw that he was very very good, his movements slightly exaggerated, parodying it. Dancing in place, Lew and Shirley watched. Jo began jitterbugging too, a little cautiously but doing pretty well, Lew thought. Harry began singing fragments of the verse, pausing during forgotten phrases or for breath. "Begin the Beguine, . . . tropical splendor! . . . Begin the *Beguine*, terrific mind-bender . . . Oh, let them beginnnn . . . the Beguine!" Then in normal speaking voice, "Yeah, quit horsing around, you guys, and let 'em begin!" Feet shuff-shuffling, jitterbugging in slow, expert rhythm, he sang words and phrases when he knew them, invented others, murmured to and amused Jo whenever he approached her. Shirley and Lew began to jitterbug, but neither really could, and Lew moved them to the bench, and stopped to pick up their glasses, handing hers to Shirley. They drained them, then resumed their old-style dancing.

The music stopped, and in the short pause they stood grinning at each other, Harry's and Jo's breathing audible. Then softly, softly, in the very gentlest of transitions from silence to sound, the music resumed with a slow, orchestral "All the Way." In the moment before they could resume, Jo said, "Change partners," turning to Lew, her arms lifting, and Shirley turned away toward Harry.

To this all danced old style, feet hardly moving. Drifting past the bench, Harry stooped to fill three glasses, swaying in place, and handed them around. Bottle in hand, he danced on with Shirley to the store-front ledge, and filled his own. Then, each couple moving in hardly more than a square foot of space, they swayed to the soft, sweet music, glasses held at partners' backs, occasionally lifting them to sip over the other's shoulder.

Quietly Shirley began to sing the words: "'When somebody loves you, it's no good unless he loves you, all-l . . . the way.'" Jo and Lew began to hum, and Harry whistled softly. "'Happy to be near you,'" Shirley continued, her voice true and slightly husky, "'when you need someone to cheer you . . . all the way.'" Her voice, the humming, and Harry's soft whistle joined, they moved to the quiet music in what seemed like a single moment held and prolonged. "'Taller . . . than the tallest tree is,'" Shirley sang, "'that's how it's got to be. Deeper . . . than the deep blue sea is, that's how deep it goes if it's real.'" And now at the chorus—glasses in hand, bodies swaying, violet-tinged faces bemused, the prolonged moment magical—they joined in the words. "'When somebody needs you, it's no good unless she needs you, all-l . . . the w—'"

The moment was shockingly destroyed, ripped apart like an explosion by a voice: "What the *hell* you think you're doin'!"— it was harsh with ill-will. An achingly bright layer of new white light clung to Shirley's face like another skin: blinking, squinting, backing away, she tried to swing her astonished, frightened face out of it, but it followed maliciously. As Harry swung around to face the voice behind the glare, the beam swept off Shirley's face onto his, but he didn't move to step out of it. Staring into it without blinking, his voice suddenly gone hoarse and deep, Harry said, "Take that god-damned light out of my face or I'll *knock* it out," but it continued to hang waveringly to his face and shoulders, and Harry turned to set his glass on the store-front ledge. As he swung back, his face set, the light dropped to his chest, the voice behind it simultaneous: "All right, I said whatd'you think you're doin' here!"

Harry's hands moved to his hips, fingers splaying, elbows belligerently out-thrust. "I *know* what I'm doing. What do *you* think we're doing!?"

The flashlight reflecting from the dark store window behind Harry, Lew could see that this was a cop in insigniaed blue cap and silver-badged, short-sleeved uniform shirt. A black-and-white plastic name plate pinned to his shirt read FLOYD PEARLEY. He was tall, extremely thin, his forearms skinny but muscularly corded. His uniform pants were too large, cinched in with a belt, and strangely short, a good several inches of bony ankles in white socks showing. Under the shiny peak of his uniform cap his face—and now Lew recognized the coffee-drinking cop at the Standard station two weeks earlier—was hostile, thin and wedge-shaped, black pistol-grip sideburns to below his ears. The flash-light flicked nervously from one to another of them but, Lew noted, at waist level now: the man had lost some nerve.

For a moment of mutual assessment they stood, the cop's eyes darting angrily from one face to another as they stared back at him. It was too chill to be out on foot in a short-sleeved shirt: he'd been trying store doors, Lew decided, in nightly routine, his patrol car somewhere. And—Lew was conscious of a reluctant attempt to be fair—he had turned a corner to come upon something so strange and out-of-routine he'd had no prepared reaction. Without it he was blustering, and before Harry could continue Lew came in as peacemaker.

"No harm intended, Officer." He smiled, waggling a palm placatingly, but no response appeared in the black hostile eyes. The beam of the flashlight swung to the bench, played along it, froze on the shopping bag with the upended bottle protruding greenly, then swung to Lew's chest, a question in itself, and Lew tried to answer it. "We just had this . . . idea, is all," he began, voice carefully slow and easy; for a moment it seemed possible to explain. "You know: with the music playing, no one else around, we thought . . ." His voice trailed off. What they had been doing here could not be explained to this mind: the man stood in narrow-eyed impatience listening without compre-hension. No words of Lew's would bring a sudden smile of un-derstanding to this face, but out of sheer momentum Lew con-tinued, "Didn't realize you were here, but all we were doing—"

The cop cut him off, and Lew understood that to this man a conciliatory tone meant weakness, had restored his feeling of having the upper hand. "I don't give a good god-damn *what* you were doin'; this ain't no playground! Now, you just haul ass out of here"—his light brushed the bench—"and take this here crap with you!"

Harry said, "I'm afraid I don't allow men I don't know to say 'ass' in front of my wife. I can say it. So can my friends. So can she: say, 'ass,' Shirley. But you can't, Floyd." His face dead serious still, he was clowning now, amusing himself and the others, the Western gunslinger facing down the sheriff. In deliberate parody, Harry hooked his thumbs into the top of his pants, fingers tensely splayed, knees bent in a slight crouch—ready to go for the nonexistent gun on his hip. Slowly, menacingly, he began walking toward the cop.

"*You want trouble!*" The man's skinny rear shot backward as he bent forward and began to retreat, hand flying to the butt of his holstered revolver, the beam of his light hard on Harry's chest.

"Harry, for godsake," Shirley murmured, but Harry continued to walk slowly after him, and in the man's face Lew could see the effort to make himself stand still. But his feet wouldn't obey. For each slow step forward of Harry's, the other could not prevent a synchronized backward step. "That what you want! You want trouble! Because you'll get it! I'm tellin' you, mister, and that's the Pure-D truth!"

Lew wanted to grin but did not: this was an angry, worried man and a cop, his hand on a gun he was licensed to use. Lew reached out, and took Harry's elbow, saying, "All right," trying to give his voice a touch of authority and quiet common sense, "there's no need for the gun: we're going, we're going." He demonstrated this immediately, turning to the bench, deliberately presenting his defenseless back, taking their glasses from the women's hands, thrusting them into the canvas bag. Stooped over the bench, face hidden from the cop, he released his bottled-up smile; from the corner of his eye he saw Jo watching him, and winked.

But then, bag in hand, turning to cross the walk to the store front for Harry's glass, Lew's smile faded and he felt the heat swiftly rising in his face. He took Harry's glass from the window ledge, ready to shove it into the bag, but suddenly there wasn't even time for that, and he swung around from the store front to face the cop. "But some time, old buddy, when you're contemplating your shriveled-up little soul, ask yourself what harm we were doing. And why you couldn't have just asked your questions, smiled, and walked on. Or stopped for a drink with us; you'd have been welcome. Because if we were here to rob the place, this isn't quite the way we'd go about it!" He swung angrily back to the store front before he could say too much, and snatched up the empty bottle from the walk where Harry had left it. Still he wasn't quite finished, had to turn back. "Or if you *had* to run us off, what exactly would have happened if you'd made it an ordinary, decent request? Would they kick you off the force for unauthorized courtesy? Is there some rule that when you put on that uniform you have to act like a shit?"

"Watch your mouth! Don't talk to *me* like that or I'll put you under arrest! The whole damn lot of you!"

Lew turned angrily to the curb. "Come on," he said to the others, "let's get the hell out of here."

They walked off, angling across the big lot toward the cluster of parked cars and the service road beyond them, Lew half a step behind Jo, then Shirley, with Harry last. Eight or ten steps, no other sound but the scuffle of their shoes, the soft sweet music fading behind them: it astonished Lew; it was still "All the Way." A step or two more, then he had to glance back, and as he turned, so did Harry. Continuing to walk on, they stared back over their shoulders. The cop stood just under the eaves of the walkway, watching them, his flashlight gone now, stuck in a back pocket probably. They began angling between the cluster of parked cars out in the middle, and Lew turned away, the episode over, when he heard Harry call softly, and turned. His hand on a fender, Harry stood facing the walkway: "Hey, stupid," he called pleasantly, "your pants are too short," and that did it.

"You're under arrest!" His hand flew to his gun butt. "*All* of you!"

Lew felt his face drain white. "Go *fuck* yourself," he yelled, voice shaking, and he walked on after Jo between the cars.

99

The gun yanked out. "Stop! Right there! *Freeze or I'll shoot!* *You're under arrest!*"

But Harry had shoved Shirley hard, on between the cars, instantly ducking low and hurrying in after her. Then they stopped beside Lew and Jo, turning to face the walkway, the metal bulks of several cars between them and the angry violent man with the gun.

Through the glass of the cars they watched him step out onto the asphalt of the parking lot, gun pointing. "Come out of there, I'm warning you, god damn it! *You're under arrest!*"

Lew called, "No. We're not. What's the charge? What do you think has *happened* to be arrested? You can't arrest for personal spite! We're not *taking* an arrest. Now, put that gun away: I'm a lawyer, and I—"

"*Fuck you, lawyer!* I'll put *nothin'* away! Come on out of there, or I'm comin' in after you!"

"You do that," Harry called. "Come on in here, Floyd; that's a personal invitation. And I'll take that fucking gun and shove it up your ass."

The man stood in classic TV pose, feet wide apart, bent slightly forward, pistol in hand at waist level, his other hand behind him and out to the side as though to maintain a delicate balance: Lew wondered if he'd ever before drawn a pistol in threat. Several seconds passed; no one moved. "Come out of there! I'm warning you!" But the voice had lost authority; he had to decide now that he would walk into the narrow dark aisles between the cars, Lew thought, but he didn't know what would happen if he did. They waited motionless, protected by the car bodies, and Lew wondered if the absurd situation seemed as unreal to Floyd Pearley as it did to him. Four or five more seconds, then the man whirled, and ran hard along the covered walkway, holstering his gun; they could hear the leathery scuff of his shoes on the concrete. They stared puzzledly out at him, then Lew said, "He's going for the phone! Let's move!" They turned and ran hard toward the service road, leaped the foot-high hedge onto the road, and ran straight down it into the darkness, the women first, Harry jogging beside Lew. In Lew's sack the glassware jingled musically, and he thought momentarily of abandoning it—the sack brushed his leg at every step—but was angrily unwilling to.

"Lawsy, lawsy, ah heahs de bloodhounds!" Shirley said.

Over her shoulder Jo said, "I planned all this, you know; I do hope you're enjoying it."

They were at the Shell station, running past it, their breathing audible. Stretching ahead into the dark lay a half-mile of straight road lying between the freeway fence beside them and, at their left after a ten-yard width of weed-grown flatness, the abrupt rise of the ridge paralleling the road. It occurred to Lew that they were running into a long, narrow trap, if headlights should suddenly appear ahead or behind them. "Harry! He could have help here in two minutes; let's get off the god-damn road." Lew took Jo's elbow, and veered sharply off to the left.

Harry following with Shirley, they ran through the high weeds beside the dark station. The building stood between them and the Safeway pay phones; the cop couldn't see them.

Harry said, "Son-of-a-bitch, I hate to run from that shit. He hasn't got a charge he can make stick: we didn't *do* anything, damn it!"

"He'd lie," Lew said. "Say we spit on the flag."

Shirley said sweetly, "If the sheriff comes, Harry, just take his gun away."

Reaching the abrupt rise of the slope, they began clambering up it, women first, then the men, and as they climbed laughed semihelplessly, hilarious with the excitement of what they found themselves so unexpectedly doing. The slope was rocky and steep; almost immediately they had to climb on all fours, finding footholds, grasping handfuls of weeds to pull themselves higher. These sometimes ripped loose and someone would slide back, cursing or snickering. Each time Lew managed a step upward he had to find a place overhead to set his bag.

Here on the slanted face of the ridge it was almost but not quite completely dark; they were still just within range of the freeway lighting. From the service road Lew knew they'd be moving shadows on the slope, and he glanced back over his shoulder to scan the road. *"Freeze,"* he called softly.

Instantly motionless, they lay sprawled on the rocky face: Lew had seen headlight beams begin to lighten the road. Staring back over their shoulders, they watched the asphalt brighten waveringly as a fast-moving car rocked toward them. It flashed past, then brake lights flared, tires squealing, and the headlights jounced as the car shot up the shopping-center driveway. Staring across the low roof of the Shell station, they watched it, accelerating, flash across the angled white lines, the unlighted dome light winking red as it passed under the overhead lights. A side of the car momentarily illuminated, they recognized the green body and white door of a Marin County deputy sheriff car. Its brake lights flashed, the front end dipping as it abruptly stopped: from around a far corner of the long row of store fronts a Mill Valley patrol car had appeared. It drove over to the sheriff's car, swung in beside it, and stopped, the drivers' doors side by side.

Jo said, "I'd love to know what they're saying."

Shirley said, "That we resisted arrest—"

"Hell he will," said Harry. "The last thing he'll ever tell another cop is that he couldn't arrest us. He'll say he saw us at a distance or something, and that we ran off into the shadows and he lost us. Probably sorry now that he called for help, the dumb son-of-a-bitch."

A sudden tire squeal: off to their left and now well below them, the Mill Valley police car shot forward toward the service road, the sheriff's swinging in a tight, rubber-screeching half circle toward a side entrance of the big lot, headlights whitening the store fronts as it turned. Onto the service road, fishtailing dramatically, headlights jouncing, came the first car; instantly it slowed, and a spotlight shot out. Slowly the car moved toward them, the hard narrow beam of intense white light steadily crisscrossing, searching both sides of the road. "Don't move, don't move," Lew murmured.

"Hide your faces," said Harry, "he could take a notion to flash it up here."

But he did not. Harry, Shirley, and Jo lay pressed to the slope, faces on their folded arms, but Lew pulled down his face mask, and lay watching, fascinated by the searching swath of hard-edged light. Engine barely audible, the car rolled by, then the others lifted their heads to stare after it.

Her voice awed, pleased, Shirley said, "Just think, he's looking for *us* . . ."

The car merged with the darkness ahead, only its headlight beams visible, then these were cut off by the little motel half a mile down at the foot of Ricardo Road.

They resumed their climbing, the men occasionally reaching up to give the women a boost, and once Shirley said, "Harry, god damn it!"

"Only helping."

"At least I trust it was you."

"But hoping what?"

They reached the top, Harry moving past the women to turn and give them a hand up onto the path that wound along the ridge, then he took Lew's sack, and Lew scrambled up. His mask still down, Lew turned to face the direction of the vanished car and, slowly thumping his chest with a fist, called in a pseudo-shout, "Hey, Floyd! Come and get us!"

Harry said, "Che, I've got a machine gun buried up here. And a cache of rice; we can hold out for days. Shirl, Jo: now's the time to leave, if you want to rat out. It's no surrender once the action starts."

Shirley said, "Did Bonnie leave Clyde? I'm staying right here. With my foot on the bumper and a cigar in my mouth."

Lew said, "Remember, Short Pants Pearley is mine."

"What if a cop comes up here?" Jo said. "When they don't find us along the roads."

"No," Lew said. "The sheriff isn't going to come climbing around up here in the dark; it's not a big enough thing. And you know Short Pants won't."

"Anyway," Harry said, "they'll think we had a car somewhere —who walks? The sheriff will cruise around for a while, then let it go; probably get another call. And Short Pants will have to pick up on checking doors again. We'll just keep off the roads for a while; work our way back along the ridges as far as we can." He picked up the canvas sack. "Probably break our ass in the dark."

"I don't allow anyone to say 'ass' in front of Jo," Lew said, and they laughed quietly, and began following Harry along the ridge.

A mile and twenty minutes later, when finally they had to descend to the roads, it again became possible that headlights might suddenly pick them up; or that, rounding a bend, they could come upon a police car parked in the dark waiting for them. But in fact they encountered no one. And when presently they turned into their own driveway to stand indecisively between the two buildings, Lew understood that to simply say good night now would be anticlimactic. The adrenaline still flowed, and when Harry lifted the canvas sack to rattle the glass, saying, "Well, come on, there's some champagne left," turning toward his building, the others followed. "We're not letting the fucking cops spoil Jo's party."

In the Levys' living room, a newly opened bottle on the table beside Harry on the chesterfield, they sat in semi-darkness, each holding a filled glass. Harry had circled the room, pouring, then turned out the lights, drawn back the drapes, and slid open the glass doors to the balcony. Now, sipping, they sat watching the motionless green-lighted street just outside, curious to see whether or not a slowly cruising police car would prowl by. Voices low but still tinged with the exhilaration of their encounter and flight, they talked about what had happened, laughing at the cop and at themselves, quietly hilarious.

Then—it was very late now, the street outside utterly still—they fell silent. On the chesterfield beside Harry, Shirley sat watching her glass, slowly revolving it to and fro by the stem. "Damn cop," she murmured. "I was having the most marvelous, nutty kind of time."

"I know," Jo said. "And then he spoiled it. He's spoiled them all."

"What do you mean 'all'?" said Harry.

"Well, we can't go out again after tonight." She smiled. "Bc a long time before they forget four people dancing and drinking champagne at the shopping center. At three in the morning."

"Of course," said Shirley. "From now on any cop cruising Strawberry at night will have an eye out for that foursome. And would see us sooner or later."

"So?" Harry demanded.

"Well, it spoils it, Harry, that's all."

"*Why?*" he insisted, wriggling forward to sit at the very edge of the chesterfield, glaring at the others. "If the cop is Short Pants we deny it was us; must have been four other people. He'll know better, but let him try to prove it weeks later. And if it's some other cop, we're just out taking a walk; so what?"

"At like 3 A.M.?" said Shirley.

"Why the hell *not* if we feel like it! It's what we've *been* doing, isn't it? No law against it! Jesus Christ, we've gotten to believe the police are all-powerful!" He snatched the bottle from the table beside him, jumping up to refill their glasses. Then he strode over to the balcony doors, and closed them: "The cops aren't coming, screw the cops." He turned on the nearest lamp, yanked the drapes closed, then turned to grin at them, lifting the nearly emptied bottle to his mouth, and draining it. "*Pah!*" —he popped his lips in a long, satisfied exhalation, rubbing his stomach. "Stuff's beginning to work its familiar magic once more. Right, Jo?"

She nodded, smiling. "Most ridiculous night I ever spent," she said, and surprised herself by giggling.

"Lew?" said Harry, and Lew said, "This may be the answer to everything. Unlimited champagne, day and night. Piped into every house."

"Shirley?" Harry said. "Report, please."

"Oh, sure," she said, shrugging, "I'm feeling fine again: Why not? Pour enough of this into me, and I'll go back to the shopping center, and dance with the cop."

"Right." Harry returned to the chesterfield, and began peeling the foil from another bottle. "You know," he said conversationally, "coming back tonight I was almost a little sorry that ducking the cops was quite that easy. Lew, the first few times, when you were out alone, you kind of liked a little excitement, didn't you; that little feeling of risk?"

"Well, yeah, except there really wasn't any risk, Harry. I kind of instinctively ducked one night when a patrol car went by. It was sort of fun—memories of Halloween—sitting in the shadows watching him." He grinned. "And I did sit on a guy's porch swing one night. Deliberately. Creaking it a little. Courting a little trouble, I guess. The guy came out, and I had to duck behind a hedge."

"You never told me that." Jo looked at him, startled.

"I forgot." He sipped at his drink.

"Why'd you do that? What *for?*" She was frowning.

"For the hell of it. Playing the fool, acting the kid, just out of boredom. For whatever risk, as Harry says, that it amounted to. Which wasn't much." He laughed, shaking his head. "I don't know what I could have said or done if he'd come busting down to where I was, wanting to know what I thought I was doing. Plead insanity, I guess."

"Yeah." Harry sat smiling, twisting the stem of the little wire basket enclosing the cork. "So here's what I'd like to say, as self-appointed chairman of this little gathering here in the deep of the night under the great majestic wheel of the eternal stars. The young ladies say things are spoiled. But I'm not so sure. What *I* think would have spoiled things, actually, is if we'd kept *on* at the shopping center. No interruptions, I mean, no cops. Till we were ready to go home. Would have been a great outing. Best we've ever had; all hail to Jo!" He popped the green plastic cork, letting it fly, to bounce off the ceiling. "But it would probably have been the end of the Walks." He stood, and began refilling glasses. "Because damned if I know what we could ever have done to top it. Or even compare. There isn't anything much *left* to do, actually. In the old way," he added. He sat down again, setting the half emptied bottle on the table, glancing down into the sack. "Only one more. Too bad; party's going good again: right?"

"Right," said Jo; she sat well down in her chair, holding her glass in her lap, smiling lazily—and just a little drunkenly, it occurred to Lew, amused.

"Beats sleeping," said Shirley.

They were companionably silent then, Lew conscious of how very comfortable he felt, slouched in the big upholstered chair. Was he drunk, too? No: they'd only had . . . how much? Over a quart of champagne apiece. But was that a lot, was champagne strong? He had never had enough to know but doubted that he was drunk. He felt only very content, smiling at Harry and Shirley across the room on the chesterfield, and at Jo opposite in her low, deep chair. Content, and conscious of an enormous good will toward these three people, so loving and complete that he knew it was exaggerated. But he was happy to be here, drinking champagne in the deep middle of the night and grinning at his friends, and he understood that he *was* drunk, a little, anyway. But in a completely clear-headed way, it seemed, strangely.

He hadn't seen him get up, but Harry was crossing the room toward him, palm extended. He stopped, and Lew saw two cigarettes, home-rolled, fat and puffy. "No, thanks, Harry."

"Come on!"

"Harry, it's work tomorrow. Work, work, work! I don't want to get completely messed up."

Harry shrugged, and turned away. "Jo?" She shook her head, and Harry sat down on the chesterfield again. He and Shirley lit up. They inhaled, held it, then Harry let his breath whoosh out, and grinned at Lew. "Hey, man," he said in a parody voice, "join the scene." He hopped up, crossed to Lew, offered the cigarette, and Lew took it. He inhaled, and tried to return the cigarette to Harry, but Harry turned away. "Keep it. You and Jo. Shirley and I'll have the other." Lew nodded, and still holding the lungful of smoke, he reached forward, and handed the cigarette to Jo.

They smoked, sipping champagne, talking and laughing steadily now; presently Harry brought out two more cigarettes. Things got funnier. When Shirley merely shook her head at a remark of Harry's, everyone else laughed in delight at the funny way she did it. Lew felt too warm and unzipped his jacket, but that didn't help, and he sat forward to pull it off. He had trouble doing it, and when he got it off both sleeves were inside out. He wadded up the jacket, tossed it toward the bookshelves, but the lightweight nylon fluttered to the floor, falling short; he made a kicking motion at it, and the others laughed happily. They, too, peeled off jackets and sweaters, and Harry wadded his up, and threw it at Lew. Both were still wearing caps, and when Lew snatched his off to throw at Harry, Harry yanked off his, they threw at the same time, the caps struck each other in midair, dropping to the rug, and the men roared.

Harry pulled off his sneakers without untying them, pretended to throw one at Lew, then tossed it, twirling, high into the air. It thumped the ceiling, leaving a smudge, and they all laughed. Shirley was pulling her sneakers off, and Harry stood up, yanked open his belt, unsnapped the top of his pants, and pulled them open, forcing the zipper down. He let them drop, and began kicking them loose from his ankles.

Grinning, watching Harry, Lew's eyes were caught by a movement: he turned his head and his heart jumped: Shirley was standing, body turned at the waist, fingers flickering at her side. Was she . . . ? *Yes*: she shot the zipper, and swiftly, one knee rising, then the other, stepped out of her denims.

Lew sat hypnotized, staring at the long length of her bare legs. *Lovely, lovely,* he kept saying to himself, and didn't know till it hit him in the face that she'd pulled off her blouse and thrown it at him. It dropped to his lap, and he looked up to see her grinning at him from across the room, in snug white pants and brassiere, and he grinned back lazily. "Take it all off," he said.

"Yeah. You, too, Jo," said Harry, voice muffled, and Lew turned. Face hidden, Harry stood pulling off his underwear T-shirt, exposing the mattress of black hair that covered his stomach, chest, and shoulders.

Lew knew Jo would not take off her clothes, and looked at her, curious to hear how she'd refuse. But without losing a flicker of her contented smile, she stood and began unbuttoning her blouse. Harry dropped his T-shirt to the floor, stooped, and picked up his baseball cap, slapped it across his thigh, put it on, then yanked his elastic-banded shorts down, and kicked them off. "Ahhh, that's better," he said, smiling around at the others. Naked except for his cap, he sat down on the chesterfield, and picked up his glass.

Jo's blouse was off, hung across the back of the rocking chair, and she sat bent forward to the floor unlacing her shoes. Shirley stood, chin ducked to chest, elbows winged out, hands busy behind her back, and—*Jesus!* Lew cried out to himself—the brassiere sagged loosely forward. Then she did it: plucked off the brassiere, and Lew saw her breasts, so beautiful, so *actual*, that he heard his teeth grind.

Then, realizing, he shouted silently, *No, I'm too skinny, I won't do it!* He picked up his glass from the floor, and held it at his chest as though it were a defense. Then he drained it angrily, thinking, *What's the sense of this, what's the point!* But he knew he was angry because he had to do it, and he set his empty glass on the rug, forcing his face to smile, and sat slowly unbuttoning his shirt. *Damn Jo:* if she'd refused, as she should have, he'd have been able to say no too. He got up, and stood watching his fingers slowly unbuttoning his cuffs, afraid of what his face would show if he looked up at Shirley. But he couldn't help it: he lifted his head, their eyes met, and she grinned mischievously, standing there in her snug white pants, her breasts full, solid, round as bowls, incredibly exposed to his eyes. With both hands she pushed her pants down off her hips, lifted one leg and ankle to step out of them, let them fall to the floor around the other ankle, and stepped gracefully sideways out of them, and Lew stood stunned.

Harry shouted, a single bark of laughter, his arm rising to point across the room at the front of Lew's pants, and Lew blushed, and quickly sat down again, glancing at Jo. She stood watching him, still smiling as though in a dream, unfastening the side buttons of her plaid slacks: he didn't know what she was thinking or what she understood. She stepped forward out of her unlaced shoes, daintily drew down her slacks, and Lew looked away, his mind a roar of confusion. For a moment he sat staring at his knees, then looked up: Shirley smiled at him, shrugged a shoulder, and then it was all right. *To hell with it, hell with it all*: he could stand now, and did, and quickly took off his clothes.

It was okay. It felt strange, the air cool on his skin, all his skin everywhere, but he assured himself that it felt good and—glancing down at his naked body—that while he was skinny, you couldn't say scrawny.

Lew sat down, able to look casually around the room, careful to look at Shirley no longer than at the others. She sat on the chesterfield now, leaning across Harry to take her glass from the table, her back momentarily turned. Facing front again, raising her glass, she drank, chin and breasts lifting, and Lew looked away to watch Harry who had stood and was walking out of the room into the short hall. *Too heavy*, Lew thought smugly—the roll of fat at Harry's waist extended around to his back—*I'd rather be skinny*.

He turned to Jo beside him, but she wasn't watching. Frowning in concentration, eyes intent on what she was doing, she stooped to the red-plaid wad of her slacks on the floor; picked up and shook them, then laid them across the chair seat. Then she hung her brassiere across the back of the chair on top of her blouse. This was the way, he suddenly realized, and felt a rush of tenderness, that she got undressed at home in her own bedroom. As he continued to watch, Jo's face and thoughts focused on her own actions, she stepped carefully out of her pants, white with a flowered pattern, laid them on her slacks, turned, and stood there in the room naked with the rest of them.

As though only in this moment realizing what she had done, she quickly sat down on the floor, drawing her legs to her chest, hugging her knees, trying to smile. She flicked a glance up at Lew, he saw her eyes, and saw that she was hiding herself from *him*. She glanced away, then immediately back, and the look in her eyes had become an appeal. Lew smiled uncertainly, thinking that maybe he'd sensed something of what she was feeling, he wasn't sure. Then he made his smile confident and reassuring, nodding at her, and she smiled back at him, eyes relieved.

What they had communicated he didn't know, possibly nothing, but his smile and nod seemed to have made what was happening all right for Jo.

What the hell are we doing! he thought in sudden irritation. *We're not a bunch of suburban wife-swappers!* Then Harry came walking out of the little hall back into the room so ludicrously naked in his baseball cap that Lew had to smile. Harry had a tan leather and chrome camera in his hands and, still walking toward them, he aimed it at Shirley, it flashed, he stopped to open the back of the camera, and Lew understood that it was a Polaroid.

Harry peeled off the picture, looked at it, nodded approvingly, then walked on to hand it to Jo. "Free souvenirs for the ladies." Jo reached up for it, and Harry gripped her wrist and drew her to her feet. "Okay! Everyone up for the class photograph!" He gestured toward the hearth, and Lew watched himself and the others obey, wondering why. He didn't know how to object, that was why: On what grounds? Their clothes actually off, the possibility of refusing anything lesser didn't seem to exist. He knew—the champagne, the marijuana—that he wasn't thinking well, that his thoughts and reactions were sluggish, trailing events by too long to affect them. On the brick hearth they stood accepting Harry's positioning; he pushed the women apart, indicating that Lew was to stand between them, and Lew obeyed, feeling the fixed quality of his smile. "Okay . . ." Camera at his eye, Harry retreated, bringing them all into frame, then he lowered it. "Let's see a little life, for crysake! You look like a stand-up morgue. Put your arms around them, Lew! Like you were actually pleased you're standing between a couple naked ladies. Just keep your hands off my wife's tits, is all." Lew carefully put an arm across their shoulders, smiling rigidly. He made his mind blank, simply refusing to think about Shirley's naked shoulder unfamiliarly in his cupped hand; he drew Jo close, for comfort and to get through the moment. "Okay"— Harry demonstrated a little sideways step-and-kick—"dance step!" Obediently the women began it, a step and kick to each side alternately; Lew had to join or be shoved off balance. *Flash!*

The flare struck his eyeballs and, still trying to dance, bumping into Jo, Lew watched the great blind circles float up and to one side. He was interested: they dimmed, turned maroon, strengthened again, then Harry was pushing the camera into his hands, showing him where to press to take a picture. Lew walked to where Harry had stood, raised the camera, and for a moment watched the three of them, small in the viewfinder like a tiny television, the smiling women graceful, Harry heavy-legged and leering out from under the peak of his cap. Lew pressed the stud, the unreal little scene whitened, then he handed the camera to Harry and in that instant felt the focus of his attention move out of the room, and knew the party was over.

Harry insisted on one more of the four of them, and using the camera's built-in timer, took it: the four dancing, and this time thumbing their noses at the camera. Now he could get dressed, Lew thought, and turned to cross the room toward his clothes. But at the join of the heavy drapes across the front windows he stopped, and drew them apart an inch. The street and the sky had turned gray, and a light showed in an apartment up at a bend of the road. The others looked, too, murmuring in surprise. Then Lew and Jo dressed, Shirley bringing out robes for Harry and herself. For a few further moments they talked quietly, looking at Harry's photographs to smile again, but the strange, glossily colored little scenes seemed already to have receded into the past.

Outside as Lew and Jo walked through the parking area, two more lights had come on, in the next building, and a Toyota sedan passed the end of the driveway, the driver young, wearing suit and tie. "A stockbroker, I'll bet," Lew said. "I think the New York Exchange opens in half an hour."

Jo nodded without interest, turning in at their place. "How do you feel?" she said.

"All right. Kind of fuzzy. Muzzy. Buzzy. But not as bad as I thought."

"Me too." They stopped at her door, and as she found her key in her sweater pocket, Jo said, not looking at him, "I didn't really like that, Lew."

"No. I didn't either, especially. No real point to it."

She opened the door, they stepped in, and now she looked at him. "Then why didn't you stop me?"

His mouth opened for the quick, angry retort, but before he could phrase it, he changed his mind: she was right. "I should have, god damn it. Why didn't I?"

Instantly she put her hand on his arm. "I could have said something myself; I wasn't gagged." Then: "I'm glad I didn't. I'm too prim, it's incredible. I'm actually prudish."

"No, you aren't. Not when it counts."

She smiled. "Shirley's lovely, isn't she?"

He studied her face for an instant, but her expression was serene. "I guess so. So are you."

"You, too."

"Of course. But not Harry."

"No."

Lew walked on to the balcony doors, and as he rolled one open, they heard from far off, across the distance between them and the invisible freeway, the faint diesel whine of a truck. Jo walked forward, and both stepped out onto the balcony, their eyes moving across the graying landscape. She said, "When you think about it, it *was* an adventure tonight. The cops. Sneaking home over the hills. Even just now at the Levys'."

"Yeah." Lew nodded, wondering which would make him feel worse, to stay up now or sleep for only an hour and a half.

"It'll be fun thinking about it tomorrow—today. After I've had some sleep. Till like noon. Lew, I hope the Walks don't stop!"

"Well, we'll see." He yawned suddenly, blinking. "Maybe Harry'll come up with something."

CHAPTER 7

They didn't see the Levys for several days. Harry began a trial on Tuesday, going directly to court each morning, so the men drove separately. Shirley and Jo spoke on the phone during Shirley's lunch hour: the Levys would be gone next weekend, visiting Shirley's parents down the Peninsula. In the early evening, Lew and Jo drove in to the Mill Valley library for a new supply of books; and each in his own apartment were reading in bed by eight-thirty, asleep before nine-thirty. At Lew's office on Wednesday a typist unaccountably lost the last two pages of the memorandum she was typing for him; it had to be finished next morning, and Lew worked Wednesday evening at the office reconstructing them from his notes.

On Thursday afternoon the two couples played tennis, in the way they sometimes arranged. Mostly young people occupied these apartments, no children allowed, and in good weather there was often a late-afternoon scramble for courts as people came home from work. Lew and Harry left the office early enough to beat the worst of the commute traffic, quickly changed clothes, then trotted across the street, rackets in hand, to join the women, who were already occupying a court.

Lew and Jo against Harry and Shirley, the most evenly matched foursome, they'd learned, they played one long set, the Levys finally winning. Then, still in tennis outfits—the women in white singlets, the men in T-shirts and shorts—they sat on Lew's and Jo's balcony sipping cold white wine: behind them Jo had her big recorder playing, the volume way down. She'd prepared a casserole that morning, and put it into the oven just before leaving for the courts. Presently they'd have dinner out here, staying out as long as the fog didn't come in.

Though the sun had set, daylight still held strong. Harry sat tilted back against the wall in a webbed aluminum chair, legs extended to the railing, ankles crossed, his heavy legs very dark against the white socks. His glass comfortably balanced on the roll of his stomach, he said, "Well, if no one else is going to say it, I'll have to: this is the life."

"You stole that from Jo's father," Lew said, and the others smiled. Lew sat on the railings at the corner.

Beside him in an aluminum chair Jo said, "It *is* nice. I feel very contented."

"Me too," Shirley murmured. Legs crossed, glass in hand, she sat beside Harry.

After a moment Harry turned to look at Lew quizzically. "Well? You want to make it unanimous?"

He smiled. "Sure, why not. Be ungrateful not to. I was just thinking—sitting here all relaxed, glass of wine in hand, music, feeling good—we're probably all of us part of the one-tenth of one percent of the world's population both present and past, who may just have the easiest, most comfortable lives anyone ever lived. In spite of all the problems, with new ones coming up, that everyone talks about. So who am I not to love it?"

"You don't, though," Jo murmured.

"Oh . . ." He grinned at her. "I probably belong in the Middle Ages. In a Walt Disney hovel with a half-door opening onto the street: look in as you walk by, and there I sit in my Robin Hood suit and Chico Marx hat, cobbling shoes. Because that's what my father did, and his father before him. Never entered their heads or mine that I'd do anything else, so it suits me fine.

Couple days a week I work on the cathedral, like everyone else in town. The way we've all been doing for four or five hundred years. No hurry; just string enough lives together, and it'll get done. I'm just one of an endless series of drops dripping on the grinding wheel of life or something. And I never question it because that's my lot, what God ordained. So I'm happy."

"But now?" Jo said.

"Well, the cards are punched differently now: nobody's willing to be ordinary any more: it's how we're programmed. The guys still in their jeans and leather hats, getting on to forty, the long hair thinning, but still cranking out the talentless paintings, crappy jewelry, blobby candles and piss-poor leatherwork instead of driving a truck, pumping gas, or cobbling shoes as nature clearly intended. Because we're all *unique* now, everybody talented, all 'creative.' They even have *classes* in creativity, for godsake. For the backward geniuses who haven't quite got the hang of it, I guess." Lew sipped at his wine, then shrugged. "And I'm not one damn bit different than the leather-belt makers in the Munchkin hats. At best I'm an okay lawyer; about what anyone could be who's able to hang on through law school and get through the bar exams. Not special, it turns out. Not talented or creative. But with the feeling I *ought* to be—you know? Punched in. And that keeps you a little restless and dissatisfied, is all."

He looked over at Harry. "What about you? Are you unique? Like everyone else?"

Harry sat looking at him, blinking slowly, consideringly. "Well, god damn you," he said then, "I wasn't quite ready to say this. In the back of my mind I still thought—maybe justice of an appellate court. Not quite nobody. A little *bit* special. But shit, I guess not even that. I haven't really believed it for quite a while now. But I wasn't quite ready to say it out loud. So okay, you've brought me down. Now what?"

"Drink." Lew leaned down to pick up the jug from the floor. "What else?"

Jo sat steadily shaking her head. "I don't believe that. We're not all programmed to think we're so special."

116

"Oh no?" Lew said. "Look: none of us owns much, we're pared down long since, we travel light. We own very little of our own pasts; there's no room. But one thing you've got and hang onto—is the album; the photo album and scrapbook your folks kept. Pictures and souvenirs of everybody, but especially you. Starting out black and white, from literally the day you were born, then on through the birthdays, changing to color, dozens and dozens of pictures. Plus old report cards, clippings. You *were* special; programmed from the start to believe it. And we've all got something like it, I'll bet."

Shirley said, "Could I see your album, Jo? I'd love to."

"Sure. I'll check the casserole, and bring it out."

Harry said, "You know, you're right. Jeez, the stuff my parents kept: they sent me a cartonful of crap when they moved to Florida. Too bad I'll never make President; history will lose the best-documented life of all time. There must be ten pounds of photographs, newspaper clippings, a high school year book, stuff I made in first *grade*. All my Boy Scout merit badges!"

Lew smiled. "I've got a box full of scout stuff my mother saved; it was with some things of hers. It even included my hat badge. I made Star Scout, incidentally."

Jo walked out with a large tan-leather gilt-ornamented book. She handed it to Shirley, who nodded and said, "My folks have one something like this. Of me and my sister; I'll bring it up." She opened the cover, said, "Oh, these are darling!" and bent close to a page of black-and-white baby pictures.

"*Star?*" Harry was saying contemptuously. "That's nothin'! I made . . . my god, I forget. What is it? I got the badge at home; it's heart-shaped. *Life*, I think! I made Life Scout. My father was going to kill himself because I didn't make Eagle."

Lew said, "Can you still tie a sheepshank?"

They drank more wine, and—no fog rolling in over the hills—had supper on the balcony. As they ate, it grew dark, the street gradually taking on its night-time look, and when the street lights came on, Harry stared out over the railing, nodding, chewing. He'd been working on something, he said, for Monday's Night People. But, smiling and shaking his head no, he wouldn't say what. It was a good evening, and after eleven when the Levys left.

In the kitchen, Lew washing dishes, Jo drying, Jo said, "Shirley doesn't really look forward to going down the Peninsula."

"Oh? Why?"

"Her parents always have questions. Very casual and subtle. But what they all mean is: when is Harry going to be a partner?"

"Well, he could be. If he wants."

Jo nodded absently, putting dishes away in the small cupboard as she dried them. "You know, you may be right. I had to finish college; my parents insisted. And now I make models for a living, something I could do in high school. That's fine, they say, as long as I like it. But it isn't what they expected."

"I know. You really screwed up; they even have to smile about me." He lifted the plug, then moved the swing faucet in an arc, trying to rinse away the artificial suds. He turned from the sink, wiping his hands on the front of his shirt, "Well. Speaking of your father, it's another day, another dollar. And time to hit the hay. Right?"

"Right."

So the week passed. On Friday, Harry's trial recessed, he and Lew had lunch, and as they sometimes did in good weather, had a quick sandwich, then walked idly around in the sun. Today they looked at display windows; stopping at Brentano's, at a stamp and coin shop, at Brooks Cameras. Here Harry inspected everything in both windows, and Lew said, "Harry, the deal is you can have one thing here, anything in the windows. What is it?"

Harry shook his head. "No: I want it all. One of everything they got in the entire store, doesn't matter if I can use it or not. I want that enlarger, both the sixteen-millimeter movie cameras, and all the telescopic lenses. I even want the used theater projector; it's a bargain."

"Two hundred and fifty bucks?" Lew looked at the foot-high crackle-finish metal box, from which a lens projected.

"Sure, the thing's got a twelve-hundred-watt light, and that's a tremendous lens; it'll project stills for a mile. I want the stereo camera too; you ever see what they do?" Lew shook his head. "Incredible 3-D pictures; color transparencies in three dimensions; they look alive. Terrific effect."

"Harry, why don't you *be* a photographer? It's the one thing you get excited about."

"I might. I just might some day." He looked at his watch, and they turned back toward the office.

On Saturday morning, accepting a standing offer from a couple in a neighboring building to lend their bikes, Lew and Jo cycled to Tiburon along the shoreline bike path, watching the sparkling Bay beside them speckled with weekend sails. At Sabella's, sitting out on the deck with the weekend crowd, they had a gin fizz, then biked home.

After dinner Lew got out a yellow legal pad and, Jo reading on the chesterfield, worked at his desk on a talk he'd been invited to give next month, along with the other council candidates, by the League of Women Voters. After half an hour he put down his pencil to stretch, and Jo looked up. "How's it go?"

He shrugged. "I'd sell my soul for a new idea." Lew raised a hand to his mouth, and leaned toward the floor. "How about it?" he called. "One slightly used soul for a really new, fresh political talk! That a deal?" He waited, hand at ear, then shook his head. "No dice, I guess. For where is the fearful pink smoke, the dread odor of brimstone?" He sniffed the air. "You smell anything?"

"Lew, cut it out," Jo murmured quietly, and he looked over at her, amused and surprised.

"That bother you?" She didn't reply, and he said, "Hey, it *does*, doesn't it! You're actually a bit worried: a little primitive fear that there just *might* be a sudden puff of smoke, an awful stench." He leaned toward the floor again. "Price not right? Well, how about just one new phony political promise, then? For this used-up, retreaded old soul!"

"Lew."

"Okay," he shouted to the floor, "I'll throw in Jo's!" He waited, hand at ear, then sat up, shaking his head. "Doesn't look like you've got a thing to worry about. But it worries me: look at guys who sell their souls to be President, and I can't even make city council. What a miserable, shriveled-up little soul I must have."

He worked for another ten minutes, then folded the dozen long yellow sheets and tucked them away on the bookshelves.

On Sunday evening, a few minutes past ten, Shirley phoned Jo. They'd just got home, she'd just walked in the door: Harry had asked her to phone while he emptied the car. On the way home he'd decided he ought to give them an advance briefing on tomorrow's Night People: could they come over to Jo's after supper tomorrow?

They arrived a little past nine, Monday, the doorbell ringing several times exuberantly. Jo, in a yellow jumpsuit, stood closing cupboard doors in the kitchen, giving various surfaces a final wipe with a wrung-out cloth. Lew, who had rinsed and dried the dishes, then wandered out onto the balcony, came trotting in to answer the bell, knowing who it was, glad to see them, shadow-boxing on the way: he wore after-work tan wash pants and a long-sleeved lemon-yellow shirt, knowing his tanned skin, black hair, and mustache showed off well in this outfit.

Harry stood filling the doorway, grinning so broadly it pulled his mouth slightly open. He wore ragged denim shorts, sandals, a gray sweat shirt; all Lew could see of Shirley in the corridor behind him was a strip of one leg of red velvet pants and the sleeve of a blue denim coat. "Hi, come on in"—he stepped aside —"welcome home." Harry walked past him, grinning euphorically, and Lew lifted his eyebrows questioningly at Shirley, who shrugged. "He's out of his mind with whatever he's planned for tonight: chuckling, shaking, twitching all through dinner. Hi, Jo." She walked into the kitchen area, and Lew led Harry out to the balcony.

"Sit down." He nodded at a chair. "And quit grinning, for godsake; makes my face hurt just looking at you." Under his arm Harry held a large gray manila envelope, their firm's name printed in a corner, and he sat down, leaning over the chair arm to prop the envelope against the railing beside him. "Jo's still got coffee hot from dinner, or you want a beer?"

"Beer," Harry said, still grinning, and Lew walked to the refrigerator, and opened two cans; Jo stood folding a kitchen towel, Shirley at the little white table filling two coffee cups.

For a few minutes the four sat on the balcony idly talking about the Levys' weekend. Then Harry set his beer on the rail, and picked up the manila envelope. Glancing around at the others, pleased with the drama he was creating, he bent up the metal clasps and opened the flap. Lifting the envelope to peer into it, he reached in, simultaneously turning the envelope over, so that as he slid out whatever it was, it emerged blank side up: it appeared to be a sheet of thin, flexible white cardboard.

Lew sat facing Harry, both directly beside the railing of the narrow balcony. Jo sat near Lew, her back to an end wall; Shirley in the open doorway just inside the living room, on Jo's wheeled work chair. Leaning toward Lew, Harry extended the letter-size sheet, blank side uppermost, but as Lew reached for it he could see that the bottom side was a glossy color photograph, and he understood what this was: Harry owned an enlarger Shirley had given him for a birthday present.

Taking the sheet, Lew turned it over, and yes: it was the nude shot, rephotographed and enlarged, that Harry had taken of Lew, Jo, and Shirley. Before rephotographing the original print, Harry had apparently pasted narrow black strips over the girls' faces, because the strips appeared in the enlargement as part of the print. They made Jo and Shirley only a pair of anonymous bodies, but Lew's vapidly grinning face showed clear and sharp.

He sat staring at the enlarged photograph in his hands: Jo and Shirley had gotten up to lean over the back of his chair, looking over his shoulders; he could feel the faint warm breath of one of them on the right side of his neck. Lew shook his head slowly, reluctant to look up: he felt embarrassed, not so much at his photographed nakedness as at this irrefutable evidence that he had once really been this foolish, even semi-drunk.

Squatting down beside him at his right, Shirley said, "That's a brave, brave smile, Lew," and nodded at the photograph.

"I know. And your hair was lovely." Leaning forward, he offered the photograph to Harry, who gestured it away.

"Keep it. I printed up three or four of them."

"Oh, thanks," Lew said sarcastically. "We can all sign it. 'Fifi Levy, Cuddles Dunne, and Lew, the Stud: in memory of a great gang and a great evening!' I'll frame it. How come you blacked out the faces? I'd know them anywhere."

Harry smiled mysteriously. "Well, it makes the picture even more salacious, don't you think?"

Lew looked. It was true: the black strips across the women's eyes reminded him of photographs he'd seen outside topless night spots on San Francisco's Broadway, before they'd stopped troubling to use black strips. "I guess so." He passed the photo over his shoulder to Jo. "But so what? Why bother?" Lew smiled to conceal his annoyance.

"I just thought it would be more effective." Harry sat back, hands clasping behind his big head. "For the poster," he added, watching Lew's face.

"Harry, for crysake! You sound like Abbott and Costello! *What* poster?"

"Your campaign poster, Lew. It's not a bit too early to get started." Harry picked up the gray envelope from his lap, and began poking through it, saying, "Get the jump on your competition." Again he slid something out of the envelope face down, and again Lew could more or less see what it was; another copy of the same 8x10 print, this one pasted onto a larger sheet of white paper. The top and bottom of the larger sheet were folded over onto the photo, partly covering it.

Lew took it impatiently, flipped open the two paper flaps, and, the women leaning over the back of his chair again, they all looked at it. It was the same print but on the paper to which it was pasted, in careful felt-pen lettering just over the photograph, was printed, GET YOUR JOLLIES WITH "JOLLY LEW" JOLIFFE! Then came the photograph, Lew stupidly cavorting between two naked girls with blacked-out faces. And below the photo in smaller lettering: *A vote for "Jolly Lew" is a vote for*

Sexual Freedom! Your future Mill Valley Councilman, Lew Joliffe, between four of his consTITuents!

The crude poster in his hands was so absurd that when Lew looked up at Harry he was smiling genuinely. Shirley said, "Harry, for godsake, that's just plain *dumb*. It's not worthy of you! That's high school humor!"

"Right!" Harry nodded vigorously. "You've got the idea: that's exactly who it's for."

"*Who?*" Lew shouted. "Who's on second! No, who's on first, *what's* on second!"

Voice patient, Harry said, "I was in the Mill Valley library one night last week." The women sat down again. "And the reference section was crammed with teen-agers, a fairly startling sight. When I checked out my books I asked the woman at the desk how come this burning thirst for knowledge? She said it was term-paper time. At Tamalpais high school. Happens twice a year. Term papers are due this week, so every night last week the reference section was packed with kids, because you can't take reference books out. Well, the climax is today and tomorrow; all day long from the time the library opens in the morning till it closes at night. Because most of the papers are due Wednesday and Thursday; all of them by Friday.

He paused, and Lew nodded. "Well, thanks, Harry, that clears up everything. Who's not on first, he's at the library."

"I was at the library again tonight," Harry said. "And just before it closed at nine o'clock, I waited till the last of the kids got out of the reference section. Then I left one of these splendid posters behind. A duplicate of the one you've got there, but even more carefully lettered. I tucked it into one of the reference books left on the table." Harry sat back, thumbs hooking into the band of his shorts, grinning around at the others. "I'd say that the odds that it won't be found tomorrow are minuscule. It's just about impossible, in fact, that one of the crowd of kids in that reference section tomorrow won't open up that particular book. And discover an absolute sensation: Jolly Lew Joliffe, Mill Valley's very own centerfold! Naturally he or she will show it around to absolutely every other kid in the library.

And then—well, god knows where in Mill Valley they'll stick it up, but you can bet your ass they will. Somewhere. Prominently. Maybe Xerox a batch of them on the library machine, and plaster them all over town."

Bewildered, Lew sat staring at Harry with a weak, one-sided smile. He didn't understand, didn't know how to react or what to say. The women sat unbelieving, looking from Harry to Lew. Finally Lew said, "You're kidding, of course."

"No," Harry said judiciously, hands dangling from his hooked thumbs. "No, I'm not, Lew. I really did it."

Her voice stunned, Shirley said, "Lew, he *did*. We stopped at the library just before we came here; he said he had to reserve a book. I waited in the car. He had that envelope in his hand when he went in."

"Right." Harry nodded. "They were just starting to turn off the main lights when I tucked a magnificent specimen of your poster into one of the books in the reference section. So it's there right now. Just waiting for the kids who'll descend on that section like knowledge-devouring locusts when the doors swing open in the morning."

"*Why? Why*, for crysake!" Lew lunged forward in his chair toward Harry, eyes fierce and demanding.

"To give you a chance to get it out, Lew. *Tonight.* Before those doors open tomorrow!" Harry sat forward suddenly, leaning eagerly toward Lew, their faces hardly a foot apart. "It's tonight's *project*, Lew! You and Jo go in after it! Shirley and I out front in the getaway car!"

Shirley said, "You've finally done it, Harry. You're out of your mind."

Her voice tight, Jo said, "Harry, you can't *do* this. You've got to go back there! To the library! First thing tomorrow! And get that thing back the very minute it opens."

Harry didn't answer or even glance at the women; just sat leaning toward Lew, grinning, waiting, watching Lew's face.

The things he ought to be saying were rising up in Lew's mind: that Harry's insane poster shown around town could kill any chance he might have in local politics, or later on in state;

any chance at a partnership in the firm, perhaps any real career in law at all, he wasn't sure; at the very least it would cripple his prospects at work, might even lose him his job. Yet he found himself unable to hold back a smile, and what he said was, voice thoughtful, "You mean sneak back in there tonight. And get that thing back."

"Lew, *no!*" Jo said sharply.

"Harry, cut it out," said Shirley. "This isn't what the Night People is about at all."

"You're wrong"—he swung toward the women. "It's the essence of it! Did you think it was sitting on the shore on Silva gazing over at the city? Or dancing under the stars at the shopping center? That was nice, and I liked it, but when did the real fun begin?" He leaned closer to them over the arm of his chair. "It was when the *risk* began. The little touch of trouble. The chance of actually getting arrested. Lew sensed it from the start; when he stepped up on the curb, and watched the cop cruise by. When he sat on the guy's porch swing deliberately making it creak. Hell"—he threw himself back, glancing around at them all—"what do you think got us all so god-damned *high* last time that we didn't come down till dawn! Stripped off our clothes. Damn near had a gang bang! It wasn't a little booze or marijuana. What sent us up was the run-in with the cops! Which we won!" For a moment or two Harry sat glancing from one face to another, then he resumed quietly. "I don't know what life was like in times past. Back in Lew's Middle Ages. But these days it's mostly a lot of shit. Well, we stumbled onto something that puts a little boost into things: The Night People. And tonight I'm leader and that's tonight's project. Your turn next week, Lew, and you can tell *me* what to do." He grinned, "If you aren't in jail."

After a moment Lew said, "What book is it in?" but Harry shook his head, still grinning. "Harry, make sense!" Lew said. "There must be two thousand books in that section! Or more!"

"That's why you can't just wait till the library opens in the morning, and then walk in and get it. While you were hunting through thousands of books, one of the kids would stumble onto it first."

Jo leaned forward, but Lew heard the squeak of her chair, and turned to waggle a hand, and she sat back, lips compressing. Lew said, "Harry, what if I insist you go back there first thing tomorrow, and get that thing."

"Now, listen to me; all of you. Reference books were scattered all over three or four tables tonight. Dozens and dozens of them. Left lying there for the library staff to put back on the shelves tonight. I just folded the poster in half, and stuck it into the back pages of an open book lying on one of the tables. I didn't close the book or even look at the cover—deliberately. Because to make any sense, this has to be *real*, Lew; you know that. The danger has to be real, not something we can decide to call off, or something I can retrieve in the morning if you can't find it tonight. You're right: there's two, three thousand books there. And I haven't any idea—*I really haven't*—which one it's in. You have to go in and get it, Lew; you've got to. You *have* to find it. Tonight."

Lew sat blinking slowly, thinking about it, the women waiting, Jo's eyes narrowed and hard. "In the dark?"

Harry laughed, his belly trembling under the gray sweat shirt. "I don't know: have to leave something to your ingenuity, won't we, Lew?" And at that, the appeal, the absolute necessity of having to work out how to *do* this crazy thing flared up in Lew tangibly, he could feel it in his chest. Looking at Harry's big, tough grinning face, he had to grin in response: his heartbeat was up; he wanted to do it. Harry saw it in his face, reached down for his beer can, stood up, and stretched. Pleased with himself, he winked at the two women, and walked into the living room toward the kitchen area, can tipped over his mouth, finishing the beer.

Jo got up, came over to squat beside Lew's chair, and put a hand on his knee. "Lew," she said gently, reasonably, "you could get arrested. You *could*."

He had covered her hand with his, turning to smile down at her. "You're talking to Le Chat, famed cat burglar of the Riv-

126

iera." But she wouldn't smile, and he closed his fingers to squeeze her hand. "Jo, I won't get caught: it's the *library*, not the Federal Reserve Bank. And it shouldn't be too hard to work out some way of doing this. To just sneak in, find that stupid poster"—Harry came strolling out onto the balcony carrying a new can of beer—"and show our juvenile friend here how easy it is."

"Right on." Harry lifted his can in salute, and sat down again.

"But there's no point in your going, Jo; it doesn't need two of us. I can—"

"Oh, I'd love to go!" Shirley cried. "I'd *love* it! Jo, if you don't want—"

"Oh, I'll *go*," Jo said quickly. "If you're really going to do it, Lew, then I want to help." She made herself smile, and stood up. "It might be fun."

Lew got up to go to the kitchen; it seemed to him that what was happening called for more than beer. In the doorway he turned. "One thing, Harry; I won't break in. No matter what. I like the library."

"Oh hell," Harry said easily, "you'll find some way to get in. They're understaffed; I don't think they check every last door and window each night."

"I'm not so sure."

Harry shrugged, lifting his beer. "You'll get in."

For a while then, it was fun; everyone chattering, even Jo, presently. Lew mixed drinks, handed them around, said, "To crime!" and they drank to that. Shirley made them synchronize their watches, then Lew got a yellow legal pad from his desk, laid it on the balcony railing, and drew a large rectangle with a felt pen: just the empty rectangle, nothing else. Inside it he printed FLOOR PLAN, and held it up. "I want everyone to memorize this!"

Harry said, "Jeez, boss, *all* of it?"

"Yeh: till you know it in your sleep."

They began talking movie-gangster talk, but in drawing even his joke plan Lew had begun thinking about the library, picturing it: a low, handsome concrete building less than ten years old, and built on the edge of a large park of huge redwoods inside the town. One side of the park and of the library fronted on a quiet residential street.

Lew sat down and, sipping his drink, visualized the building as though standing across the street from it: a low tiled roof with huge skylights; three enormous multiple-paned windows on the street side, eight or ten feet tall, rising from floor to ceiling; the entrance of double glass doors. In the daytime, light flooded the interior from these windows, doors, and skylights, and from banks of fluorescent tubes, but at night . . . Lew said, "Listen: there's not much of a moon tonight. And there are redwoods all around the place. Damn big ones on all three park sides, and in that little strip of dirt along the front. So the street lamp out there won't help much. It'll be dark as hell inside! And we *can't* show a light with all those windows. Even a match would show up like a bonfire."

Harry stood leaning back against the balcony railing facing the others. "It'll be late at night: how many people go by there then?"

"I don't know, I'm not around there late at night. It's a quiet street but that doesn't matter: one phone call to the cops about a light in the library is all it would take."

Shirley said, "This is great: real problems!" In Chico Marx accent she said, "So whatta we gonna do, boss?"

Jo said, "I don't remember any windows in the women's washroom. We could carry books in there and turn on the light."

"Take forever," Lew said. "It's a long way from the reference section to the washrooms. And we'd be carrying them back and forth in the dark."

"Why take them back?" said Harry.

"No." Lew shook his head. "I'm not leaving the place messed up."

"What about a little pen flashlight?" Shirley said. "We've got one, if the batteries are still—"

"Any light at all would show; those windows are *big*."

They discussed and discarded ideas, enjoying it, quietly excited. Presently Lew made more drinks. Then Jo found the answer. They worked her idea over, criticizing it, but it seemed to hold up, and Lew said, "That's it, then; that's how we'll do it."

"Okay, what time?" said Harry. "Two-thirty?"

"Make it two; we may need every minute."

"Let's get some sleep, then." Harry glanced at his watch. "We'll go in my car; the getaway car, souped up to do a hundred and twenty-five in second. See you at two, Les Chats."

At a quarter after two, Harry driving slowly past the library from the north, they stared out at it as though they'd never before seen it—as they had not; not like this. In the front seat the Levys were dressed as they'd been earlier, except that Harry now wore his baseball cap; Lew wore his usual, the mask front of his cap rolled up; Jo a chocolate brown pants suit. In the darkness only the widely separated street lamps and the yellow parking lights of the slowly rolling Alfa showed. Beside the car just across the sidewalk, a ragged line of redwoods rose from a narrow strip of earth: behind the trees the long street façade of the library slid past. One by one the great floor-to-ceiling windows moved by, their panes shiny black, each reflecting light from the one dim street lamp ahead, and Lew thought he could sense the silent darkness on the other side of the wall. The busy, friendly, early-evening place this had always been for him had turned sinister now, drained of warmth and welcome; beside him Jo sat nibbling her lip.

No one spoke. A hundred yards beyond the dark building, and well past the street lamp, Harry stopped in a pool of darkness beside the redwoods of the rustic park. Across the street on the other side, the low white buildings of a grade school stretched for a short block, dark and still. Harry switched off lights and engine, and Shirley and Jo rolled down their windows a little. For a moment they heard only the small pings of the cooling engine, then became aware of the faint sough of moving air high in the redwoods. Except for the tree trunks and lower branches directly beside them across the walk, most of the park was a solid black wall; through the trees a single light bulb indicated the public toilets and a phone. Quietly Harry said, "All right," turning sideways to look back at Lew, his arm stretching along the seat back. "I'll keep watch every second. And if you two come a-running, I'll start the engine, ready to haul-ass out of here. Shirley will stand on the walk with the door open. You two pile in the back, and she'll—"

"Yeah, we know, we know," Lew said, suddenly irritable. He sat turned to look through the slanted rear window, studying the front and end walls of the building behind them. It looked tightly closed, locked up, and he wondered how and where they could possibly get in; he didn't feel quite sure, in this final moment, that he wanted to leave the safety of the car.

"You got the ground cloths?" Harry said, and Lew wished he'd shut up.

In a small, tight voice Jo said, "Yes. Ours and yours."

"Right." Harry turned front to search the motionless street as far ahead as he could see, to a sharp bend. Then he turned with difficulty, his body too big for the cramped space behind the wheel, to study the street to the rear. "All clear," he said, and grinned at Lew; Harry was happy, Lew realized, hugely enjoying this, and he smiled, too, suddenly excited again.

"Harry, let's go along!" Shirley said. "Instead of just *sitting* here!"

"We can't. We just can't; I've got a hunch they may need a getaway car; we have to stay here." He grinned at Lew and Jo. "Good luck. And good hunting."

Lew nodded. Shirley got out, and they slid past the front seat to the sidewalk, each carrying a folded ground cloth. On the walk, Shirley in the car again, Lew eased the door shut, and stood with Jo looking around them. Nothing stirred. Except for the school and the library this was a street of small, old Mill Valley houses, some built in the early years of the century. No light showed in any of them as far as he could see in both directions. Behind the library Mount Tamalpais filled the lower half of the sky, black on deep blue.

Lew touched Jo's arm, and they turned to walk back along the sidewalk toward the library. They had no plan for entering except to try doors and windows, hoping to find one unlocked. A few steps short of the library, Lew touched Jo's arm again, and they stopped on the walk, looking up at the dark bulk of the night-time building. "You really want to go in there?" he said gently. "You don't have to. There's no need at all."

"I don't know what I want." Still staring at the looming building, so close now, she said, "It gives me the creeps to think of feeling my way around in there. But to just go back and sit in the car waiting would be too drab to bear. What I really want, I suppose, is to have it over with. Do you want to? Really?"

He nodded. "Yeah. Now that we've started. Now that we're out here and really going in if we can. But I want to bring it off, not mess up, so let me think."

The front doors of the library, twenty yards ahead near the center of the long street façade, were a pair of heavy glass sheets opening out onto a wide, brick-paved veranda a few steps above sidewalk level. These doors especially were sure to be locked, Lew felt certain. In any case, he did not want to walk onto that open veranda and try them in full view of every darkened window across the street.

The library was built on a slope: only one story high on the street side, it was two at the rear. Along much of the rear face ran a wide wooden balcony overlooking the woods and the small stream that curled through the park, a fine, secluded place to sit and read on a sunny day. This balcony hung a story above the ground; underneath it ran a row of windows and doors opening into the basement which was divided into rooms for storage, exhibitions, board meetings. They could hope one of these doors or windows had been forgotten.

They stood directly beside the dirt path leading down the slope along the building's end wall, and Lew took Jo's hand, and turned onto it. Feeling their way with their feet through the almost complete darkness, they moved down the slope beside the end wall, and turned under the balcony. Here the darkness was absolute, and Lew reached to the back of his belt where he'd shoved a powerful four-cell flashlight he'd bought for a camping trip. They had to see; the building stood between them and the street, and he pulled the flash out, cupped his hand around the head to confine the beam, and pushed the stud. Aiming the hard white light, he found the first window, and in the light reflected from it gestured to Jo; she reached to the metal frame and pushed. It was locked, and they moved on to the first door. Jo gripped the knob, turning, but it barely moved.

The next window, next door, and the following window were locked. Lew found the knob after that, a dull weather-mottled bronze in the blob of light, tried it, and it turned, the door opening toward him, and Lew said, "I'll be damned."

"Lucky," Jo murmured, but her voice didn't sound as though she felt lucky.

They stepped inside, Lew pulled the door shut, pressing the stud that locked it, and they stood warily listening. Then he swept his beam across the room: it was the boardroom, a long, narrow table surrounded by a dozen neatly pushed-in chairs; at the room's other end stood the door to the inside corridor. He said, "This wasn't luck. Harry unlocked the god-damn door."

"How do you know?" She was whispering now.

"I know, that's all. They didn't forget to lock it: tonight at the library Harry just came down the stairs, into this room, and turned the knob, that's all you have to do to unlock the stud. When they closed, no one checked down here: why should they? They keep these doors locked all the time, you know they do." For a moment longer they stood hesitating, then Lew said, "Come on," and walked across to the inner door. He switched off the flash, slowly and soundlessly opened the door, and they stood, leaning forward in the opening, breaths held, listening. Nothing; no sound. Lew touched Jo's arm, and she stepped past him, out into the dead-black corridor. Behind her he eased the door closed, pulled down his face mask, and pressed the head of the flashlight to the underside of his chin. "Jo," he whispered, and as she turned he pushed the stud. The light flared up onto the Africanlike mask, weirdly illuminating it, and she punched at him, hitting his shoulder hard.

"Cut it *out!*" She began to snicker, through her nose, trying to repress it. "Damn it, if I wet my pants, I'm taking yours!"

The light still on, Lew shoved up his mask, grinning at her. "Well, we're in. Good old Harry; he wasn't taking any chances."

Their light on the carpeted stairs, they climbed quickly, feet making only faint muffled sounds. On the top landing Lew switched off the flash: they stood facing a pair of doors paneled with opaque glass, the shape of the panes barely visible against the dark of the other side. These doors opened into the great main room, and Lew slowly eased one open. Staring across the width of the room, they saw the dim silhouette of the big main desk against the lighter shape of the glass door which led onto the outside balcony. No sound, from inside or the street, and they stepped through, Lew noiselessly closing the door behind them. He led the way, half a dozen steps to the desk, a long waist-high counter at which books were checked in and out. Here they turned to face left, looking ahead into the main room of the library. Jo stood close, a shoulder lightly touching Lew's arm.

The great hushed room lay in deep shadow along the windowed side, and in almost complete darkness along its center and opposite side. But they knew the room, knew what lay where they could not see. The room occupied the entire width of the library and two thirds of its length; behind them lay the children's section. Far ahead, the distant back half of the huge room was stacks, shelf after shelf of books rising from floor to as high as could easily be reached. The stacks stood in a row across the width of the library like a dozen parallel walls. All they could see was the ends of the stacks, their lengths dissolving on into not-quite darkness—a huge window of the distant end wall admitted a tinge of light from a street lamp.

Lew stood studying the front half of the room, lighter than the stacks because the dim illumination from the enormous side windows was uninterrupted. This front area was divided into sections by waist-high standing shelves; the section ahead and to their left was reference. Directly to their left stood the wide glass doors of the main entranceway, clearly defined against the street outside. With Jo close behind, Lew walked over to them.

His memory was correct: a hinged bar ran across each door at

133

waist level, probably required by fire ordinance. Though the doors must surely be locked on the outside, he knew that if they had to, they could plunge through these doors at a run, the hinged bars unlocking them.

Taking Jo's hand, he turned back, leading her into the main room toward the left. Here vaguely defined parallelograms of yellowed light from the street lay distortedly across table tops, chairs, low divider shelves, and along the carpeting. Reaching the reference section, eyes now accustomed to the faint light from the windows, they moved quickly. The section was bounded by waist-high shelves, enclosing a small area of several tables and chairs. These shelves were packed with encyclopedias of various kinds, specialized dictionaries, Who's Whos of many varieties—references of all sorts, the largest local collection outside the university at Berkeley, larger even than the county's library. Standing at one of the tables, they set chairs aside, then unfolded and snapped together their two ground cloths to form one sheet. This they draped around the table on the three sides nearest the windows, making sure it touched the carpet all around. The cloth was heavy, rubberized, completely opaque; it came up onto the table top by only six inches, would slide off unless held. Jo stood, arms wide holding the cloth in place as Lew weighted it all around with a stack of books from the new-fiction shelf. He tested, tugging gently, and it held. Handing the flashlight to Jo, he whispered, "Crawl in, and wait till you hear me whistle. Then flick the light on for a second."

He walked to the street wall to stand beside a window, facing the draped table. Watching intently, he whistled softly, saw nothing. "Did you hear?" Her voice muffled by the heavy cloth, Jo called yes, and Lew walked to the first reference shelf.

From the top row, he took the first dozen books, and carried them balanced on his left forearm, right palm pressed to the top of the stack. At the open front of the little hut, he knelt carefully. "Turn on the flash." Jo pressed the stud, and the inside of the little enclosure lit up, the shadow of Jo's head and shoulders immense behind her. Lew set his books down, and crawled in. Sitting cross-legged beside Jo, he looked around him appreciatively, sniffing: the rubberized walls had the look and smell of a tent.

He positioned the light, balancing it on its end between them. The strong beam, striking the underside of the light-wood table, reflected downward, illuminating the floor before them, and when Lew took the first book from his stack, and riffled through it, it was well-enough lighted for their purpose.

Within minutes they had searched through two thirds of the stack, riffling through each book, then shaking it. As one of them finished with a book, Lew set it beside him on a new pile, carefully restacking them in the order he'd brought them in. Jo leaned toward him. "This is fun," she whispered. "Ridiculous but fun. It's so *cozy!*"

"Makes me think of camping out in Wisconsin when I was a kid. Listen: find the stupid poster quick, and there'll still be time for me to have carnal knowledge of you right here on the main floor of the library. A first, no doubt."

"First, nothing: you just haven't noticed some of the kids in here."

Leaving Jo to search the remaining few books, Lew crept out, carried those they had searched back to the shelf where he'd found them, and returned with a new load. For twenty minutes then, Lew returning searched books and bringing back others, they riffled through and shook out book after book; finding a canceled envelope addressed to V. Banheim at a Mill Valley address, and a claim check for The Clock Shop.

"How many have we done?" Jo said. They were no longer quite whispering.

"Oh . . . a hundred or so."

She thought for a moment, then her eyes widened. "Lew: they've got over three thousand reference books; I've heard them say it! We'll never finish!"

He frowned, then shrugged. "Probably won't have to; it could be in that one." He nodded at the book Jo had just taken from the pile.

But it wasn't, and presently Jo changed position, getting to her knees to lean forward over the book on the carpet before

135

her. Again and again Lew crawled out with a load of searched books, and returned with a new load. Then, returning once more, careless now in the repeated action, he bumped hard against a corner of the table with his hip, and a side of the tarpaulin and a few inches along the back dropped loose, the light inside beaming across to and reflecting on the window behind them. Instantly Lew set down his books, plucked up the tarp, pulling it snugly around the table again, and blocked off the spill of light. Weighting it down again, he glanced over into the open front of the enclosure, and looked down onto Jo's bowed neck, her hair hanging forward over her face as she knelt riffling through the pages of the last book before her.

She hadn't even known that the tarp had slipped; but Lew knew that for two seconds a light clearly visible outside had shown from inside the library where no light should be. He set the new stack down before Jo, and took the others. These he replaced on their shelf, then walked on to the great window, and —invisible in the darkness—stood searching all he could see of the street through the intervening trees. Nothing moved that he could see. No light had come on in the windows he could glimpse across the street. He walked on to the next window for a view from a new angle, but saw no sign that their light had been seen.

A small rectangle hung in space before him at waist level an inch or two in from the window panes; he touched it, felt cold metal, and remembered what this was. In daylight he had read the block letters, invisible now, enameled across the face of this panel: PUSH TO OPEN AND SOUND ALARM. The panel was attached to a short rod which would unlock the lower hinged half of the big window, allowing it to swing outward as an escape from fire. Fingering it now, Lew smiled at the thought of pushing it: in his mind he could see Harry in the car somewhere ahead whirl in his seat as the gong ripped through the quiet of the street, could see Harry's face as he and Jo ran laughing down the walk toward him.

"Lew, what're you *doing?*" He turned to see the blur of Jo's face at the corner of the draped table.

"Just checking." He walked back, and saw that she had nearly finished with the new stack.

She knelt looking up at him. "Lew, we have to face it: we'll never finish at this rate."

"I know, I know." He frowned, squatting down to face her. "Each load I keep hoping we'll find it."

"I've been thinking: would Harry *really* put it in just any old book? That doesn't sound like him. He'd look at titles to find one he liked."

"You could be right"—Lew nodded. "I can see him; it would appeal to him. But what book?"

"Encyclopaedia Britannica?"

"Maybe; if there's a *Joliffe* listed."

"Where are they?"

"I don't know, but I think now we've got to take some chances. Turn off the flash, bring it along." He gathered up the books in the enclosure, and, Jo following, returned them to their shelf. "Turn sideways," he said. "With your back to the windows. Facing me. Press tight up against the shelves to shield the light." Jo did this, and the light snapped on, her hand cupped around the lens, narrowing the beam. She held it to the book spines on the top shelf where Lew had just replaced the last books, her body keeping all or most of the light from the windows behind her. As she walked slowly backward, Lew followed, scanning titles. They found the lineup of Britannica volumes, then the moving blot of light touched Jerez-Liberty, Vol. 13, and Lew pulled it down. Jo holding the light, Lew flipped pages, then looked up. "Nothing here. No Joliffe ever made it; typical." He replaced the book.

"Try Who's Who."

He thought he remembered where these were; on the other side of the section. They found them, and searched: first through the current Who's Who; then the volume for the past decade; finally through Who Was Who, which sounded promising to Lew, but found nothing; no Joliffes. "Is there one called Who Ain't Nobody?" he said, replacing the last book, then saw

137

the title of the book beside it, and yanked it out. "This is it: I *know* it!"

"What?"

"Who's . . . Turn off the flash!" Her light vanishing instantly, they froze. He'd been waiting for this sound ever since they'd come in, knowing it could happen. Yet now he could hardly believe he had actually heard the small preliminary snick of key against lock plate at the front doors. But he had, and now distantly but distinctively they heard the small *whoosh* of air pushed inward by the opening front doors. Lew tugged Jo's arm, silently laid his book on top of the shelves, and they sank soundlessly to the floor in a squat, heads ducked below the level of the waist-high shelves surrounding the reference section.

Silence; not a sound; it was as it had been. But this was illusion now: someone had come in . . . was up there now at the main desk where they had stood, staring ahead into the gloom hoping to catch them unaware. They didn't move. Squatting low, Lew's hand gripping Jo's wrist, both aware of their heartbeats, they breathed shallowly through their mouths, listening for the listeners.

Two brilliant beams of solid white light shot the length of the library, crisscrossing it fast, searching for a body moving through the dark. "*All right, we see you!*"—it was a cop-voice, astonishingly loud in here. "Step out with your hands up, or we'll shoot!"

"They don't see us," Lew whispered, lips at Jo's ear. "Down on your knees now. Keep low. Crawl over toward the windows, then back into the stacks."

"Where the fuck is a light switch?" a voice up front said.

"I don't know," said a second voice. "The office maybe. How should I know?" Again the pair of lights swiftly swept the library wall to wall, crisscrossing over their heads. Moving fast and silently on hands and knees, Jo, with Lew following, crept along the side wall toward the blackness of the stacks. "Last chance! Stand up now, and you're okay; if you don't, we shoot on sight!"

Would they? Were their guns actually out? Maybe he should

call to them: warn them he wasn't armed, and that he would stand up slowly. He could say he was alone, and let Jo hide. But she had reached the stacks, Lew right behind her, and now one of the cops betrayed his mind by using the past tense. "Hey, somebody *was* here! Look at this."

In the almost pitch-dark of the stacks, they crawled on, down a narrow aisle toward the far end.

"What the hell is it for? Some hippie sleepin' under that?"

"Nah, for crysake. Why would he sleep under something indoors?"

Silence. They reached the far back end of the stacks. The stacks paralleled the length of the big room, and very likely the cops would look down the length of each of them now, searching the aisles with their flashlights. But a back aisle ran across the width of the building here, along the ends of the stacks, and Lew rose to stand hidden behind the end of one stack; at the end of the next Jo stood facing him. Now a beam searching the lengths of the aisles wouldn't find them, and the cops might not —they just might not—come back here.

Standing very straight, Lew watched down the aisle along a ragged line of protruding book spines: at the ground-cloth-covered table the cops stood dimly visible behind the brilliance of their two beams held on the little hut. "Beats me," one of them said finally. "Kids maybe," and the pair of lights lifted to search the room again; but perfunctorily now, randomly. Lew watched a chair back become momentarily visible, then slide into darkness again as the hooded microfilm viewer appeared and vanished, then the arm of a chesterfield at the fireplace on the other wall. For an instant a flashlight beam slid across a blue-shirted chest, a silver star winking into visibility, and in that instant Lew saw the face above the star, under a peaked cap: it was the dull and hostile wedge-shaped face of Pearley, the cop they'd encountered at the Strawberry shopping center. Lew glanced at Jo, but her face only a white smudge in the semi-darkness, he couldn't tell what she'd seen.

Suddenly he was scared. The possibility that even if they were caught nothing much would happen—that they might explain, and be let off with a warning since they'd caused no actual harm —that possibility was gone: the man out there was an enemy. He was mean, was probably scared, almost surely vindictive, and would certainly remember them—with pleasure. And he was a cop, and a cop willing to use it had enormous power to hurt with impunity.

Lew felt certain now they'd be arrested if caught, and driven to the county jail a dozen miles north up 101; very possibly to be locked up for the night, if Floyd Pearley had anything to say about that. *What if he drove them up alone!* Lew stood suddenly remembering what had happened in Marin County, not to an unknown like Jo and himself but to an important, powerful man, a member of the State Public Utility Commission, and well known throughout the state. He'd come out of a Sausalito restaurant to the parking lot with friends, at night, had an argument with a cop there, been arrested, handcuffed, and driven to the county jail—alone in the car with the cop. On the way, he charged, the cop had alternately driven at high speed, then hit the brakes, over and again, causing him to fly helplessly off the rear seat smashing his face against the steel screen between him and the cop. He arrived battered and bleeding—caused by a fall in entering the car, the cop asserted. That kind of explanation, Lew knew, was always accepted; and remembering the anger last week of the man out there in the library now, Lew knew they mustn't be found. Yet they stood trapped in a cul-de-sac, no way out except past the cops who stood between them and the only exits.

The searching flashlights had steadied, oval splotches of light momentarily motionless on the carpet before the covered table. "Well? You think he's still here?" Pearley's voice said.

"Don't look like it. *Hey, you!* You still here?" A silence. "Don't answer; must be gone." The other voice laughed, the beams lingering indecisively on the carpet. "Well, what do you think?"

"Could be in them bookshelves."

A considering pause. "Okay, let's search them."

Sweeping up off the rug, the beams sliced ahead through the

dark, bobbing gently as the cops walked toward the stacks: Lew stood holding his breath, then had to force himself to exhale and resume breathing. "Okay," said the other cop, and his beam swung to point off toward the park side of the room, "go walk up the first aisle with your flash. Walk around the far end, and come back down the second aisle. Keep on like that. Search every aisle, up and down. I'll stand out here, and see he don't try to come sneaking out."

Lew reached over, took Jo's wrist, and—there was nothing else left to do—led her around the end of the stack, and into the aisle along the street side of the library. Here they stood between building wall and the final stack. For the moment now, the entire row of stacks stood between them and the searching cop. The shelves were backless, and not solidly filled. Between books of one category and the next there was often empty shelf space, sometimes as much as several feet without books. Through these gaps, and across the tops of shelved books, they caught glimpses, looking through the dozen intervening stacks, of the searching cop's flashlight bobbing rhythmically up the first aisle across the room from where they stood watching.

The beam reached the end of the distant first aisle, then swung to shoot across the back aisle, searching it, touching and brightening the wall not a yard from where they stood. It swung away then, the cop started down the second aisle, and just as Lew thought of the possibility so did the cop on guard out front. "Hey, Floyd! Walk backwards coming out! So he can't sneak along the back aisle, and get past you!" Through the shelves Lew and Jo saw the light swing around to shine back along the aisle, lighting up the end wall. Then, the beam holding the end wall, it steadily lengthened as the man moved backward down the second aisle.

Steadily holding on the back wall, the flashlight reached the end of aisle two, and Lew stood staring through the stacks, fascinated. The cop out front was intelligent: he stood holding his flash down the same aisle, keeping the back wall lighted during the moment it took Pearley to side-step to aisle three—and now Lew knew there was no way at all to get past either cop.

The searching cop walked up the third aisle, his light bright on the back wall. The cop out front still stood at aisle two, his light on the back wall also. And now Lew made himself turn away, staring at the rug, trying to think. Within—what? Two minutes? Less?—Pearley would turn into this final aisle to find them standing here; there was no escape. If he'd been alone, Lew thought, he might have run for it; sneaked to the front end of this aisle, then run out into the library past the cop standing guard; ducking, dodging, trying to make it to the doors, out, and then down the street as fast as he could sprint to Harry's car. But the thought was time-wasting: Jo couldn't do that, and even if she could, he wouldn't risk the possibility of a shot. "Lew, I'm scared," she whispered, and Lew lifted his head: through the stacks he saw the cop begin to back down an aisle, the bobbing circle of his light remorselessly fixed on the end wall. "What if they have their *guns* out?" she whispered. "What if he turns into this aisle, and shoots when he sees us. It happens! You read about it."

"Take it easy," he whispered. But *would* Pearley have his gun out? Yes, he would: he couldn't know what he might walk into each time he turned into a new aisle; Lew knew the gun was in his hand right now. Would he shoot when he saw them? He damn well might; he'd be scared! Lew understood that he had to call out. Right now. Call to them, say where they were, and . . . what? That they were lying face down on the carpet, hands clasped at the backs of their heads, and *don't shoot, please don't shoot!* At the front end of an aisle, he saw across the book tops through the backless shelves, Pearley side-stepped and began to walk up the next, his light on the end wall, the other cop's light shining down the previous aisle. Hating it, hating to abjectly surrender to this man, Lew opened his mouth to call out.

Instead he continued to stand for a moment, motionless, mouth still open. Suddenly he squatted, sliced both hands into the books of the bottom shelf, and lifted out a length of them pressed between the flats of his hands. Very swiftly he rose, set them onto the vacant space of a shelf at eye level, and as fast as he could move squatted down again to seize a second length of books, and set them onto still another vacant space above.

Again squatted at the bottom shelf, making the least possible sound, he slid a third length of books as far as he could, to a vertical divider; and now he had cleared a space perhaps five feet long. He looked up at Jo but she had already understood, and she quickly lay down on the carpet before it. The cop reached another aisle—only two away now—and began backing down it; they could hear his rapid, muffled tread.

Lew turned to run silently half a dozen feet farther along the aisle, squatted, and began clearing another space along the bottom shelf. Watching Jo in side vision as he worked, he saw her lying on the carpet, her back to the emptied section of shelving just above the floor. Then she wriggled up onto it, facing out, and lay motionless. Her knees protruded slightly but so did books on either side of and above her, and now Lew no longer had time to look at Jo.

Hardly more than a yard of bottom shelving stood cleared, and he could find no other large gaps on the shelves above. Lew stood desperately hunting, the searching cop side-stepped to a new aisle—the next aisle but one, he saw—and there was not going to be enough time. He squatted, and seized between his flattened palms the greatest length of books he had yet tried to lift, more than two feet of them. Now he had cleared enough space, just barely, if somewhere he could find space for this stack. But as he straightened his knees and stood up, his arms began trembling; the books were big, their weight impossible to hold for more than another second or two, and there was simply no space for them anywhere.

The cop was well up the aisle, would turn next into the one just beside them—and the long stack of books Lew held at his chest like an accordion began to sag. His arms shaking with the impossible strain, there was no more holding them, and he thrust them straight out before him into the nearly solid wall of shelved books. They gave way—were shoved violently back on their enameled metal shelf onto the filled shelf in the next aisle behind them, tumbling the books there onto the floor, pages fluttering, spilling onto the carpet in a thudding cascade of noise Lew knew must be audible even out on the street. Feet instantly pounded, and Lew dropped to the floor careless of sound, and pushed himself back, up onto the five-foot length of empty space he had created, yanking down his face mask, knees drawing to chest.

Lights bobbing, feet thudding, the cops reached both ends of the aisle at his back. An instant's silence, lights frantically searching—"Keep your light outta my *face*, for crysake!" Then: "Not here! Next aisle!" Feet pounded again and lights glared from each end of the aisle in which Jo and Lew lay motionless on the shelves. "God damn, he made it out front!" One light vanished, the other hurtled down the aisle toward and past them, feet thumping as the cop from the back end raced down their aisle hard as he could go—watching through the eye-slits of his mask, Lew felt a terrible urge to reach out and grab a flying, white-socked skinny ankle.

Silence: peering past his knees Lew saw the two beams sweeping the main room, crisscrossing, touching ceiling, then floor, trying to search every inch of the great room in an instant. Then: "He's *gone*, god damn it! You shoulda stayed *out* here! What the hell you come inta the shelves for!"

"'Cause he was *in* there, that's why! Who the fuck you think dropped the books! He was in there with you, and you *missed* him, you asshole!"

"I didn't miss a god-damn—"

"All right, all *right!*" A pause. "Shit."

Again the two beams searched but slowly now, without hope. "Lousy hippies," Pearley's voice said then. "Stealin' books. They sell 'em to buy drugs, you know."

"I know, I know, for crysake."

"Wonder how he got in; the front door was locked."

"Came in downstairs," the other said shortly. "It's how he got out too."

Lew inched forward onto the carpet, and stood; Jo, too, getting to her feet in the dim light from the street lamps through the big windows beside them. Lew walked down to her, and she gripped his forearm hard, laughing silently. "We made marvelous bookends!" she whispered: her shoulders shook with suppressed laughter, and Lew put his arm around them, squeezing her to him, calming her as he led her to the front of the stacks. He felt exhilarated, wanting to *do* something, felt like yelling in sheer wild exuberance.

A flashlight emerged from the library office behind the big checkout desk up front, the other approaching from the children's section. The lights met, and with weary irritability one voice said, "All right, let's check downstairs." The lights bobbed across to the double doors of the interior staircase up which Lew and Jo had come, the doors swung open, closed, and again the library stood silent and dark.

Lew stepped forward, a hand clasping Jo's wrist, and they walked quickly along the street-side wall toward the outer doors, moving past the tall windows through the light patches from outside. Abruptly, Lew stopped, Jo bumping into him. Lying on top of one of the low standing shelves enclosing the reference section was the book Lew had put down when he'd heard the police arrive: he could make out the gold-leaf title: Who's Who in the Law. Without picking it up, he began riffling through it, certain that he would find and feeling no surprise when he immediately did, the crude photo-and-poster Harry had put there that evening. Lew held it up triumphantly, and Jo nodded rapidly, frowning, pushing at him to move on. Their tarps were still there, enclosing the table, and he stepped over, tugged them loose from the book weights, and walked on with Jo, bundling the tarps up under his arm, and looking down at the absurdly titled photograph of his naked grinning self between two anonymous women.

For this they had actually risked arrest and jail, maybe worse, and looking at it now, it didn't seem enough to Lew merely to have recovered it. Now what? Just toss it into a drawer at home? Lew murmured, "Wait here," and on pure neural impulse, without rational thought, he turned left, walking rapidly across the library along the main desk, away from the front doors. On the other side of the big room he stopped at the large bulletin board facing the main desk, felt for and found a thumbtack in its surface, and stuck the poster to the center of the board, overlaying the notices already there.

Just behind him, Jo fiercely whispered, *"No!"* and, reaching past his shoulder, yanked it from the board.

He didn't care. Walking back toward the front doors with Jo, an arm across her shoulders as she folded the paper, and gave it back to him, Lew was grinning: he felt wonderfully alive. Again it occurred to him that he'd like to yell, as loud and long as he could hold it, a Tarzan yell, and give the cops downstairs something to make their visit worthwhile. But he didn't. At the double glass doors he pushed one open for Jo; a white-doored car labeled MILL VALLEY POLICE stood at the curb, its lights out. As Jo stepped past him onto the brick veranda, Lew murmured, "Meet you at the car, and don't waste time. Now do what I say: *run down the walk! Fast!*" He pulled the door closed, leaving her outside staring in at him through the glass, astonished. He gestured hard, waving her on, and after a moment she turned away.

Swiftly now, Lew walked back along the street-side wall to the second window: leaning to one side, he looked out toward Harry's car. It lay out of sight somewhere ahead, but he saw Jo pass his window, not quite running along the walk, walking rapidly toward the car. Then, behind him, he heard the beginning murmur of voices coming up the inside stairs. He waited, letting Jo move on, then shoved hard against the waist-high, rectangular metal plate at the center of the window. As the lower half of the big window swung outward, a frantic electric trill sounded abruptly, directly beside him, and astonishingly clamorous, an enormous *bung-bung-bung-bung-bung-bung* that split the air of the motionless street.

Lew stepped outside, edged between the trees of the narrow dirt strip between library wall and sidewalk, then ran. Ahead, the door of Harry's car stood open, Shirley standing on the walk beside it, waiting. He reached it—laughing hard, the others staring in wonder—sidled into the back seat beside Jo, and Shirley jumped in, and slammed the door.

In the moment of silence that followed, Lew realized that the engine wasn't running. Behind them he heard the crash of the library doors bursting open, and he swung around to the rear window: the two cops came hurtling down the shallow brick steps to the sidewalk, actually skidding on the soles of their shoes as they stopped, heads whirling, searching. "Let's go!" Lew said, swinging to face front, still laughing. But Harry sat motionless, head and shoulders thrust far out his window, looking back. Still watching the cops, Harry's hand moved to the dash—to start the engine, Lew thought. Instead, Harry pulled a knob, and their lights came on.

"*There they are!*" a cop's voice shrieked over the clamor of the alarm, and again Lew's head swung around: a cop was running hard around the front of the police car, the other yanking open the door beside the walk. They piled in, doors slamming . . . and still Harry sat staring back at them, making no move to start.

"Harry, *start, start!*" Jo cried, but he didn't move, and now the cop's headlights flashed on. Harry turned from his window to smile back at Lew. "Here you are, Lew"—he brought up his hand, something dangling from a finger—"a souvenir." Lew reached forward, and took it, a ring of keys. "The cops' ignition keys," Harry said. "They ain't goin' nowhere." He turned to shove head and shoulders out his wondow. "Hey!" he yelled back. "You're too late! We got away with it: Tom Swift in the City of Gold, and you'll *never* get it back!"

Lew got out, pushing Shirley's seat, squeezing out to the sidewalk. The cops' doors opened, too, and they got out staring at Lew; the alarm clanging unendingly, lights coming on now in houses across from the library. Laughing, Lew yelled, "Hey, Slats! Your pants are too short!" He drew back his arm, and threw hard toward them. Their keys landed on the street, and before they'd stopped sliding along the pavement, Pearley was running for them.

Lew ducked head and shoulders to slip back into the car, then froze in astonishment: feet sliding to a stop, Pearley had yanked

147

out his gun. Bringing it down to a point, he was yelling in rage: "You mother-fuckin' bastard, I'll shoot your fuckin' head—"

The other cop cut him off, voice loud but matter-of-fact. "You fire in town, the chief'll have your stupid ass." Pearley stood motionless, hesitating, and Lew shoved himself into the Alfa. The other cop yelled it now: "Get those *keys*, god damn it!" and Pearley holstered his gun, and ran for them.

Dropping to the seat beside Jo, Lew realized that it had simply never occurred to him—this had been a *joke!*—that the cop might shoot, and he felt his face flush, deeply, cheeks hot, because he knew that it should have. Harshly, angry with himself and Harry both, he said, "Okay, sonny: you better drive like hell now: you got maybe sixty seconds' start." Harry's starter was whirring before he had finished, the engine caught, and Lew looked back. The cop was snatching the keys from the pavement, then Lew was flung back in his seat as Harry shot forward, scorching rubber, the cop behind them racing for his car.

The two-block-long Mill Valley business district lay just around the curve ahead, and Harry swung into it at forty-five, accelerating. Street lamps on, curbs oddly empty of parked cars, the green twin of the Alfa Romeo flashed across dark store windows beside them as they reached fifty-five, touched sixty for an instant, then Harry braked, the squeal prolonged. They rounded the right angle onto Blithedale, fishtailing, then Harry's hand swept through the gears to fifth. A two-mile dogleg length of narrow city street lay ahead now, and Harry hung at sixty-five. Halfway, Lew watching behind, headlights swung into view at the second turn, and the glaring red eye flipped on. Shirley said quietly, "Harry, they could still decide to shoot."

Harry hesitated, and Lew said, "No, we haven't murdered the mayor." Yet he wasn't quite sure. Watching at the slanted rear window, he first thought and then knew that the headlights behind them had enlarged, but he let Harry do the driving.

Ahead the traffic light flashed yellow, no other cars at the intersection. Reaching it, Harry downshifted to third—to cross with caution, Lew supposed—then Harry startled them by swinging left instead, and Lew understood. Even if Harry had wanted to drive all-out, and he probably did not, the police car would be faster still; they'd have been caught before they reached Strawberry. Instead he'd entered the old, two-lane county road to Corte Madera, an endless succession of short curves, left and right, left and right, over and over again for half a dozen winding miles. On this kind of road they could drive as fast as the other car would dare—and, in fact, Harry's shorter squatter car could swing through the short curves just a bit faster than the bigger one behind them.

This happened, Harry's fist sweeping unceasingly through the gears, accelerating hard up to each curve, then swaying around it, engine braking, and instantly accelerating again; hanging in their own lane, never crossing the line to risk a head-on. The trees grew thick along the shoulders here, the houses set well back mostly—high up the slope at the left, well down the slope to the right. Lew sat watching across the curves through the trees, and for three minutes or more caught occasional glimpses of headlights and red eye across several bends. Then no more: they were gaining; a few feet; a yard, on each short swing. Lew said, "Harry, they've radioed. They'll have Corte Madera blocking the other end."

"I know." Harry said no more, head and shoulders ducked toward the windshield, a big hand gripping the wheel at eleven o'clock, other fist on the shift knob. He probably didn't know it, Lew thought, looking at Harry's profile, but Harry was smiling. Another long minute, possibly two, swinging left, then right, left, then right, the four of them leaning out on each curve, possibly helping to cut down the fishtailing. Then Harry moved closer to the windshield, ducking his head to watch for something on the left, never slowing. "Okay! Just ahead!" he said. "Hang on!"

Around the curve to the right, then Harry flicked off the lights and swung the wheel hard left. They shot across the road and up into a steep driveway, curving back toward the direction they'd come from. Harry's hand cut the ignition as he shoved in the clutch, and he toed the brakes. The driveway he'd remembered was a half-moon touching the road at each end. Its center, marked by a flight of wooden stairs leading still higher up the embankment to a house, stood perhaps eight feet above the surface of the road below and beside them. They waited, still rolling slowly forward, and almost immediately twin sharp white beams touched and swept along the dirt embankment beneath them, swinging back onto the road as the car and its red light appeared behind it. The car passed, and now, still slowly rolling, the Alfa dipped onto the downgrade, rolled faster, and re-entered the road in the opposite direction, Harry's fingers holding the ignition key, clutch shoved in. They rolled silently around the curve, then Harry's wrist turned, his leg rose from the clutch, and the motor quietly caught.

He drove fast as ever, pressing hard as he dared on each curve —the cops might have sensed what they'd done. But watching across the curves behind them, Lew saw nothing, and when they came to the Blithedale intersection again, Harry dropped to a moderate speed. On across the freeway overpass into Strawberry, down the service road past the great dark shopping center, then up and around the end of the ridge to home.

In his stall behind the buildings, Harry turned off the ignition, and Lew said, "That was damned fine driving, Harry; you've redeemed yourself, you stupid bastard."

Harry turned to grin at them. "Oh man," he said softly. "I've wanted to do that all my life; race them, and beat them. I tried it once in college, and got caught."

Shirley said, "I feel I ought to scream at you for twenty-five minutes. But it would be a lie, I feel so *good*."

"Well, I'd like to send him over Niagara in a barrel," Jo said. "With spikes in it. We could have been *shot*, we really could!" Then she smiled. "But it was more exciting than anything I've done for days. Weeks. Months. Ever."

Voice lazy and content, Harry said, "Yeah, you got to admit the old adrenaline sure flowed tonight."

"By the bucket," Lew said. "I could be a donor." He sat slouched in a corner of the back seat, hands clasped behind his head, grinning. He leaned forward, feeling in his pants pocket, then reached over the seat-back to drop the folded poster they'd rescued into Harry's lap. "Who's Who in the Law," he said contemptuously.

"You guessed, did you?" Harry turned to grin. "If you'd missed it, I'da gone in and got it first thing in the morning."

"That's not going to help you, Harry. I doubt if you'll survive whatever I work up for you next week. Better take out a big policy for Shirley."

"Yeah," said Shirley, "and I'll help Lew plan." Then her voice altered. "But no more cops! Okay? We keep *away* from them!"

Neither of the men replied, but they both nodded, getting out of the car. As Harry locked it, Jo said politely, "You want to come in? For tea, coffee, a nightcap?" She yawned unexpectedly.

"No," Harry said, then glanced at the sky. "Be strange," he murmured, "driving to work and respectability in just a few hours." He grinned at them. "G'night, Group: your fuehrer is proud of you."

CHAPTER 8

Harry's trial over, the men resumed driving to and from work together. Jo finished a model Tuesday afternoon, the interior of a movie theater modified to show it divided in two; delivered it in the van; and brought home sketches for a new job, the "face-lifting" of a small apartment house. Shirley worked at the clinic. And the weather held, a typical Bay Area October, cool or even cold at night but the days more summery than the actual summer had been.

On Wednesday evening Lew and Jo had dinner on the balcony, Lew in jeans and long-sleeved plaid shirt, Jo in denim skirt and an old white blouse, the left sleeve streaked with black where she had wiped a drawing pen. Working together, they broiled hamburgers, then carried them out.

"You thought of anything for the Levys next week?" Jo said as she sat down.

His feet pressing the balcony railing, Lew tilted back in his chair; chewing, he held a finger up, meaning wait till he swallowed. "A couple possibilities," he said then, "I'm not sure. What do you think of some sort of treasure hunt? A few choice items they'd have to come back with."

"Like what?" Jo raised her feet to the railing, too, tipping back in her chair. Her skirt slid up, Lew eyed her, and she rolled her eyes.

"I don't know. Sneak that dumb cop's pants off when he wasn't looking—I don't really know. Can you think of anything?" He bit into his hamburger again.

She shook her head, and they sat silent for a time, eating. Then Jo said wistfully, "Lew, why can't we go back to the four of us doing something again. Just for fun the way we did."

"Well." He considered it. "Actually I don't know what more there *is* to do, just wandering around. We've about done all that. Anyway, I owe Harry something for that library stunt."

"What's your other possibility?"

"Well, I'm not too sure about this one; and it wouldn't include Shirley. Of course it doesn't have to this one time; Harry's the boy I'm after. It would be something he'd have to get. Like we did. Just one thing, it wouldn't really matter what. Because it's where he'd have to *go* that makes it interesting."

"Where's that?" A sparrow appeared on the railing, and Jo leaned forward to set a fragment of hamburger roll down, but the bird flashed off toward the eucalyptus trees across the street.

"Well." Lew hesitated. "To the top of a bridge tower."

"Bridge? What bridge?"

"Golden Gate."

She turned to stare at him. "Are you serious?"

"Well. Maybe. Why not? It could be done."

"*How*, for heaven sakes!"

"Walk up the cable."

She brought her feet and the chair legs down. "Lew, you're *crazy!* You're kidding, aren't you?"

"No." He shook his head. "Take a good look at the bridge cables next time you drive across. I've been looking them over, driving to work the last couple days, and those cables are thick. Immense. Maybe four feet across. And they come right down to bridge level at the center; walk along the sidewalk, and you can reach across the rail and lay your hand on the cable. On the ocean side, there's even some little metal stairs to make it easy; an old lady could get up onto the cable there."

No longer eating, her hamburger on its paper plate in her lap, Jo sat slowly shaking her head in rejection, and he said, "Jo, they're *made* to walk on. There are a couple wires strung all along each one for handholds. Bridge workers do it."

"*Bridge* workers, yes! But Harry's not a br—"

"Harry's done climbing; plenty of it. And rappelled *down*, which is more dangerous. We both have. Higher climbing, and more dangerous than walking up the cable."

"If it's so easy, what's the point!"

"It would be at night." Lew grinned. "The fog coming in, the wind sort of whistling through the wires. Walk up that damn cable with the ocean a million miles straight down under your feet. Have to walk up, and bring something back; that'll learn him!"

"Bring *what* back? How would it get there?" Her eyes widened. "Oh no!"

He began to laugh. "Yeah! That's the trouble! I'd have to put it there!"

"Lew, *no*. I mean it! *No!* It's ridiculous! Like boys playing chicken! I won't have you—"

"I didn't say we were going to: it's only an idea, is all. But it just wouldn't be that hard, Jo. It's been done. More than once. I don't mean bridge workers, I mean that every once in a while somebody has just hopped onto a cable, and walked on up to the top. Some go part way, and change their minds. In the daytime they're seen and arrested. But no telling how many have done it at night. It's no problem then; I've been thinking about it. Do it very late. Wait for a time when there isn't a car in sight. Then hop up onto the cable, grab the handrails, and walk up fast, don't stop to think. Any car comes along, freeze till it's g—"

"Lew, stop. Just listening to that gives me the chills. It's nightmarish! Even the bridge workers don't do that!"

"Yeah, well, I'll admit it's a sobering thought. Stand on the walk looking over the rail in daytime, and that water's a long

way down. Be twice as far time you climbed to the top. But still
. . . to finally stand up there, Jo. On the very top of the tower.
At night, and look around. Across the Bay, and out over Marin.
Walk around up there, and look out at the ocean—Jesus. It's
why people climb, you know."

"Lew. Please think of something else. The treasure hunt.
That sounds like fun, it really does, and I'll help you figure out
things for them to get. But I don't even want to *talk* about you
walking up that cable at night."

"Well, it was just a thought. Any dessert?"

"No; I could open some canned peaches."

"That's not dessert. Ice cream is dessert. Chocolate cake is
dessert. Canned peaches are nothing. We doing anything tonight?"

"No, unless—*California Split* is on. In Tiburon. We've been
waiting for it to come back."

"What time? The Levys want to go?"

"Eight twenty-five is the earliest we could make. No, they've
seen it; I talked to Shirley at noon."

"Well, all right, let's see it. I like Elliot Gould, don't you?"

"So-so."

"You think I look like him? A little?"

"No."

"Okay, I thought you looked like Faye Dunaway, but now I
don't."

On Thursday Jo finished a job, the façade of the face-lifted
apartment house, and when Lew got home they went food shopping, driving down to the shopping center in Lew's VW. Daylight saving had ended, but it was still light, the sun near the horizon. Tonight the fog and chill were rolling in over the hills,
and Jo wore her white knit sweater and cap, Lew a tan pullover
sweater. Jo needed india ink, and they parked at the stationery
store around at the side of the big center. Leaving the car there
when she'd finished, they walked on, crossing one of the interior
streets, to the big main building facing the freeway, and the
Safeway store there. At the Safeway entrance they saw Harry

and Shirley just leaving their car, up ahead by the bakery. They waved, and Shirley waved back, continuing on into the bakery; under a blue cardigan sweater she still wore her white work dress. Harry came walking toward them in tennis shorts and blue sweat shirt.

"Hi, where to?" he said, stopping. "Safeway?" Jo said yes, and to Lew Harry said, "Walk me to the camera shop." Jo went on into the big whitely lighted store, and the two men began walking along the store's long glass-fronted length.

As Harry began describing an incident of his recent courtroom experience, Lew casually noted a man standing up ahead at the other end of the store front: then he saw his face. Today he wore a short-sleeved sport shirt patterned in acid green, actually a blouse, hanging well down over the top of his pants, but only partially hiding the bulges of holster and folded handcuffs in the back. The pants were dark blue uniform trousers, too short, the ankles exposed; and above the blouse, the long, too thin and too bony face of the cop they'd encountered some ten nights before, almost at this very spot. Even in repose the face looked hostile.

It was too late to touch Harry's arm and turn back. The man would see it and recognize them, understanding that their turning back was an admission that they were who they were. Keeping his face calm, walking along listening to Harry, Lew turned his eyes from the man ahead. He might not recognize them; with luck they'd simply walk on by.

The man's head turned casually toward them, eyes uninterested. Then they narrowed. Lew glanced at him momentarily without apparent recognition, looking back at Harry again; listening, nodding. But it didn't work: abruptly the man stepped forward, directly into their path, blocking their way, brown eyes bright and belligerent. "Hold it; hold it right there!" They stopped, Harry looking at him in blank surprise, and Lew spoke first, hoping to somehow end this quickly.

"Yes?" he said in polite question, face unrecognizing, ready to bluff it out.

But Harry's voice overrode Lew's. "What do you mean, 'Hold it'? Who the hell are you!?"

The man hardly heard him; he stood staring at Lew. "Yeah," he said softly then, and nodded. "You was the guy at the li-berry." Suddenly excited, he said, "I seen you!" poking a forefinger at Lew, jabbing the air at his chest. "You flang the keys!"

But there was a tinge of uncertainty in his voice. It had been dark, the street poorly lighted, the distance between them great, and Lew knew he should deny it—making his voice sincere, brows rising in innocence, persuading the man he was mistaken. But he couldn't: everything about this man had the quality of almost instantly antagonizing him; the nasal accent, the per-manent look of know-nothing hostility, the aggressively short hair and blatant sideburns, even the skinny ankles. "Li-*brary?*" he said, stressing the pronunciation, brows lifting in a parody of pleasant exchange, helpless to stop himself. "Why, yes, I often visit the li-brary. To read Byron, Keats, Shelley. And others of my favorite poets."

"Your favorites, too, no doubt?" Harry added with leering po-liteness.

The man stood slowly nodding. "A wise-ass. A real wise-ass. The both of you. You was the other sumbitch at the liberry, wasn't you," he said to Harry. "They was two of you in there!" Again his eyes narrowed, studying them intently. "And you was the guys fuckin' around *here* that night!" His voice tried for the triumphant note, but again it had the sound of a question: they'd been wearing caps then, been dressed very differently. "*Wasn't* you!" he demanded. "With the wimmen!" He began looking rapidly around him, hunting for the women that would confirm his impression.

"You don't know what the fuck you're talking about," Harry said pleasantly.

"Don't talk to *me* like that, god damn you! I'm a cop!"

"So what?"

"Why, god damn you"—the man's voice had lowered in sud-den rage—"you're *askin'* for it!" A woman passing by glanced at

157

them, then looked quickly away, hurrying on. "And by God and by Jesus, I can give it to you! You hear? I'll make you wish you was *dead!*"

Almost conversationally Harry said, "Tell me something. If you will, *Officer*. If you please. *Sir*. You don't come from around here, do you." He waited. "Well? You ashamed to answer?"

"Hell, no, I'm not ashamed. I'm from Oklahoma, and proud of it."

"That figures. Been here what? Couple years, maybe?"

"Eighteen months: so what?"

"Well, I'll tell you so what. I've lived here in the Bay Area a hell of a lot longer than that. Since before you even heard of it. I *belong* here. Now I don't seem to have broken any law you know of or can prove. So how come, *tell me how come* some unemployed jerk from nowhere comes drifting up here and lands himself a job on the cops, how come he thinks he's been handed the power to make me wish I was dead? Because he doesn't like what I *said!* Where'd you *get* that kind of power! Who *gave* it to you!" A middle-aged man stopped on the walk to stand staring; Harry glanced at him, and he moved on.

"You'll find out, shitheel."

"Yeah, well, you'll find out something, too." Harry stooped, leaning forward to bring his face closer to the other's. "That's *not the reason you're on the cops*: that's not the job!" He stood erect again, and spoke quietly. "You catch me breaking the law, arrest me. But until then, cop or no cop, it's just man to man. You aren't God because they pinned a badge on you. You start tough-talking me, I'll tough-talk *you*." Harry turned to Lew. "*Look* at him!" he said incredulously. "A god-damn *king* couldn't be madder than this guy! It's like some dirty commoner spit on his robe!" Again Harry shoved his face forward. "You think a cop is some kind of king!? Nobody dares talk back to him? 'Yes, *sir*, Officer,' no matter what *you* say? Well, buddy, I won't *let* you shove me around. Try it, and you won't wish you were dead. You'll *be* dead, you stupid asshole."

The man stood speechless, eyes rapidly moving from one face to the other, then he nodded as at some finality. "Couple of mother-fuckers," he said in a low voice, still nodding. "Couple of real mother-fuckers, aren't you!"

"Yeah." Lew nodded, leaning forward to bring his face close. "*Your* mother," he said. The man's eyes widened, he stood stunned, and Harry stepped forward, brushing him aside.

They walked on, Harry without looking back, but Lew looked: the man behind them stood hunched, neck pulled to his shoulders, watching them from under his brows; his face had gone paper-white. His eyes met Lew's and he swung away.

Turning into a passageway that cut through the face of the long building, they walked through to the other side. There they entered the camera shop, and Harry stood waiting, his face serene, merely glancing once at Lew to smile. A clerk arrived, and Harry leaned forward on the counter on his big forearms, hands clasping, and began questioning him about several types of film. Presently he bought two rolls of different kinds. Standing erect, pulling out his wallet, he saw in the rack a new kind of film labeled "professional." He discussed it with the clerk, nodded, and bought a roll. He asked for mailer envelopes; the clerk hunted and found they were out of them. While he was waiting, Lew wandered the store, reading display signs, looking at photo blowups, trying to distract himself from what had happened outside. He didn't like the encounter now; neither the cop's part in it nor his own; his mind kept rerunning every word and move of it like a looped film, and he wanted to stop.

He strolled to the store windows, and stood looking out at the walkway, and the parking area, much smaller here on this side of the building. Faintly, he heard a woman's voice outside calling someone: "*Lew,*" he almost thought she had said, then he heard it more loudly: "*Lew! Harry!*" It was Jo's voice, and he turned, and shoved through the door.

She was running along the walkway toward him, people turning to stare. "Lew! Lew! *Harry!*" Behind Lew the store door knocked open violently. "*It's Shirley!*" Jo cried, eyes wild, and Lew felt his stomach knot: *She'd been hit by a car!* "She's been *arrested!*" Jo whirled to point toward the distant end of the long walkway ahead. "He's *handcuffing* her!"

159

Harry plunged past them full tilt, arms rising to pump hard; people yanked themselves out of his path. Then Lew and Jo were after him, sprinting on their toes, and Lew's mind began to work. "Listen. I don't know what's going to happen; Harry may go wild." Digging for his keys as they ran, he said, "Go move the car. Out in back. In the street by the cleaners so we'll know where to look. With the motor running." He shoved the keys at her, Jo snatched them, and angled off across the street.

Harry, and then Lew, hurtled out onto the parking lot at the end of the long building, heads twisting, searching: along the covered walkway across the end of the building a dozen people stood staring in open-mouthed uneasiness at something in a vacant parking slot. Between Lew and Harry and the empty slot stood a sun-faded old blue sedan, its rear fender an unmatching gray: they couldn't see but could hear on its other side feet shuffling on the asphalt, harsh, gasping breathing. Harry ran on, around the back of the old car, and Lew whirled to run around its front, pushing through the crowd on the walk.

The rear door of the old car stood open on torn, dirty upholstery. Directly beside it, arms handcuffed behind her, Shirley frantically fought with the man in the acid-green shirt. His arms clasping her bearlike, he stood struggling to shove her in through the open door of the old car, actually lifting her off her feet now, Shirley writhing wildly, kicking back at his shins, straining her head down to bite at his forearms, blocking the narrow entrance with her legs, tears of rage sliding down her face. "*Help* me, god damn you!" the man cried to the crowd, "She's under arrest! You're deputized!" But no one moved, and a man turned his head to one side and spat.

Harry's fist hit the side of the man's head with a loud popping sound like striking a melon, and the man's arms flew out to the side seeking balance or support as he staggered sideways toward the curb in a bent-kneed shuffle. He kept his feet, swinging to face Harry, a hand curving around to the rear hem of his shirt and Lew understood that Harry was about to be shot and stepped off the curb, knocking the man's groping arm up, and plucked pistol from holster as Harry rushed him. Harry hit him on the chin, sending him scuttling backward to the curb, the crowd parting as he struck curb with heels and went over, landing hard on his back with an audible thump.

Lew shot a glance toward the street: Jo was slowing at the curb, looking anxiously toward them. "*Harry!*" he cried, and as Harry looked toward him, he jabbed his finger in a moving point. Harry whirled, saw Jo and the car, grabbed Shirley. A hand gripping her under the armpit to support her, he ran her across the asphalt toward the wide driveway and street. Sprawled on his back, eyes closed, the man on the walk groaned, rolled to his knees, groaned again, and lay forward on his forearms, head between them in prayerlike attitude. His green shirt lay rucked up over his back, exposing paper-white skin above the top of his pants. Attached to a belt loop, a thick bunch of keys on a ring lay on the blue cloth of his pants, and Lew reached down, gripped them and yanked, tearing the belt loop open. Gun in hand, he turned, spectators stepping quickly aside, and ran for the car.

Harry and Shirley were in, and their door slammed. Jo drove the car slowly forward to the middle of the driveway, shortening Lew's run, and he ran straight on, down the driveway and past the end of the car; Jo's knit cap hung tautly stretched over the rear license plate. The front door stood open, and as Lew threw himself onto the seat beside Jo, she started instantly forward, his door slamming of itself.

A hundred yards ahead the road angled right: watching behind them as they approached the turn, they saw no one following. Then, in the moment of turning, a red Mustang bounced down onto the street from the shopping-center lot, and swung in behind them. Fifty yards, and Jo curved onto the Tiburon road, merging with the traffic, not speeding. Lew turned to pass the key ring to Harry, smiling at Shirley, hand dropping to squeeze her knee, and she smiled wanly, her breathing hiccuplike, just short of a sob. "You're okay now," Lew murmured.

"I know." She nodded rapidly, swallowing. "Oh, *God*, it was so good to see you guys! I'd have *gone*—I'd have got *in* if it had been a police car! And if he'd been in uniform! But that awful man in a *sport* shirt! That terrible *car!* It was like being *kid-naped!*" She began to laugh, silently, shoulders shaking, tears welling. Harry had found the small key, and he turned Shirley away from him, fitted the key, and unlocked the cuffs. They had reached the next intersection, and, turn signal flashing, Jo swung off the highway back into Strawberry again. They watched, and a moment later the red Mustang flashed past the intersection behind them, the driver not even glancing their way. Jo drove on then, over and around the hills to their building, and parked in Lew's space behind the apartments. Quickly, they got out, doors slamming, hurrying to be gone from here before someone else drove in. Walking around the back of the car, Lew snatched Jo's cap off the back plate.

Inside his apartment, Lew bolted the door, and turned to Harry, intensely conscious of his hyperexcitement; but controlled, it seemed to him, his thinking lucid. "Well?" he said. "What do you think? The cops on their way here?"

Crossing the room toward the balcony doors, Harry said, "If someone down there knew us and identified us, then sure: they could be here in the next minute. If not, we may just be all right." Standing at the glass doors he searched the street: Jo sat with Shirley on the chesterfield, steadily patting her forearm. Turning from the doors, Harry said, "We're not surrounded at the moment anyway," then clapped his hands together in sudden exuberance, rubbing his palms. "Let's get in a fast drink while we're waiting to find out!"

Lew turned to the kitchen area, and began setting out glasses. He said, "They come here, we'll identify ourselves right away as lawyers: lawyers worry cops. You got a business card?" He was still interested in his own reaction: was he really thinking clearly or only sounding like it?

"In my wallet." Harry dropped into the upholstered chair across from the women on the chesterfield.

"And what do you think we claim illegal arrest?" Lew said; he stood pouring. "Because in that case you have every right to rescue your wife; he'd have no special standing. And I have a right to hel—oh, Jesus!" He clapped a hand to his back pocket, then brought out the pistol. "My god, Harry, what's the penalty for this—*life?*"

Harry rocked in his chair with sudden laughter, then drew the handcuffs from his back pocket. "If it is, so is this. We'll be cell-mates!" He laughed again, Shirley and Jo smiling sadly, and Lew began passing drinks around. "Well, hell," Harry said then, still smiling, "if the arrest was illegal, everything's all right. If not, then nothing is. Shirley, that bastard read you your rights?"

She nodded. "While he was handcuffing me."

"He tell you the charge?" Lew said, handing her a drink.

"Yes: resisting arrest. The night we were all down there."

"Well, screw all that," Harry said. "It was an illegal arrest any-way, days after the fact." He took a swallow of his drink.

"That's our defense, at least." Lew sat down on an arm of the chesterfield. "But I'm afraid the arrest was legal; the son of a bitch *is* a cop, incredible as that sounds." He looked down at Shirley. "He identify himself?"

"Well, he stuck his wallet in my face; I didn't know what he was showing me or what was happening. Then he said he was a police officer, and that I was under—*oh!*"

"*What!?*" Harry sat forward abruptly, spilling a little of his drink.

"My cake! He took my cake, and set it on the hood of a car! It could still be down there!"

At this they roared, all of them now, longer and louder than her words justified, in sudden release from tension. Grinning, Shirley said, "Don't laugh, Harry: it was your favorite, a choco-late log! I ordered it special."

"Hell with them then: let's go down there and eat it!"

"I'll bring champagne!" Jo said. "We'll have another party!"

"And invite the cop!" said Lew.

They finished their drinks, and Lew gathered up their glasses. "Let's get in another while we can." Jo and Shirley began quietly talking, and Harry stood to follow Lew into the little kitchen area.

As Lew poured new drinks Harry said, "You know what gets me, Lew? We sit around worrying about legalities: was the arrest *legal*, for crysake. It had nothing to *do* with legality! That wasn't an arrest, it was an act of revenge! It had nothing to do with what happened ten days ago: it was to get even with *me*. The only crime committed is that I talked back. Didn't say, Yes, sir, Officer! And the punishment—handed out right on the spot! No trial!—is public humiliation for my wife."

Lew handed him a drink. "Yeah, well, *we* know that's true, but it won't be in a courtroom." He picked up the other drinks, and walked out with them. Standing before the women as they took theirs, he said, "Shirley, how you doing?"

"Very much better. You know, ever since I was about eleven I've wanted to be rescued from something by a good-looking stud. And now *two* of them! My cup runneth over. I want to give you about a fifteen-minute kiss."

"My fee is thirty." He sat down in the upholstered chair.

"I'll pay! Harry, I want to marry you all over again."

"Beg me. Again." He stood with his drink at the balcony doors, staring out at the street.

"Jo, you were spectacular," Shirley said. "That whole thing with the car was marvelous."

"Damn right," said Harry.

"Any time," Jo said. "That was something *I* always wanted to do."

Silence for a few moments: they sipped at their drinks. Then Lew said, "You know something? They're not coming."

"Could be." Harry leaned toward the glass doors to look both ways along the street. "Maybe nobody down there knew us. I didn't see anyone I knew."

"You never do down there," Jo said. "You hardly ever see the same face twice."

Grinning, Shirley said, "So we got away with it? Huck, is we free!?"

"Oh-oh," said Harry, and their heads swung toward him.

They stood watching at the glass doors: the sun down, dusk near, it was still gray daylight, and down on the street a black-and-white Mill Valley police car moved slowly along the curb toward them, the uniformed driver leaning out his window to look up at the buildings, searching the house numbers. "Oh, god *damn* it!" Harry said.

Shirley said, "Maybe this has nothing to do with us; it's not the same cop. Where's our cop?"

"Sitting in the chief's office," Harry said shortly, "explaining what happened to his gun." The car outside stopped, and Harry said, "Our building: it's us, all right. *Shit!* How did they know?"

Silently they watched as the cop set his brake, opened his door, got out: dark-haired, hatless but in uniform, about thirty. He slammed the door, turning to start across the street, and now in the hand nearest them as he turned, they saw something pink —a square cardboard box which he held by the white string wrapped around it. "Oh, *nooo!*" Shirley moaned.

"What!?" Harry swung around.

"It's my chocolate *log!* Oh, *Harry* . . . it was all ready, all wrapped. It's got our *name* on it . . ."

Lew and Harry turned simultaneously to walk quickly toward the bedroom. The women followed, and at the side window they stood watching the Levys' entrance.

The parking-area lights had come on, and the cop appeared, walking along the side of the building. "The only Levys in Strawberry," Harry muttered. "All they had to do was look in the phone book." The cop turned the back corner of the building, looked for and immediately found the Levys' door, labeled by Harry's business card inserted in the small brass frame under their bell. He pushed the bell, and stood waiting, pink cake box dangling from his hooked finger. Presently he pressed the bell again, and waited. Glancing at his watch, he turned away, with the cake.

Back at the balcony doors again, they watched him reappear, walking down the driveway, cross to his car, get in, and start it, glancing up at the Levys' dark windows. He drove on, and Shirley said, "Oh, *Harry*; I'm so sorry."

"Not your fault." They all turned back into the room, faces solemn. "It's mine: I eat too much. My god: done in by a chocolate log." Harry suddenly set down his glass, and walked swiftly toward the door. "Got to get our stuff out of there!"

"I'll help," Lew said.

"No, no sense both of us getting busted."

"Harry, if they grab one of us, we're all in the soup. Come on: everybody. Many hands make busy work."

"Is that how it goes?" Shirley said, walking to the door.

"No," said Jo. "Many hands make—is it quick work? That doesn't sound right."

"Many hands . . ." Shirley said, and walking across the parking area they discussed it to the Levys'.

In less than ten minutes they emptied the apartment of everything the Levys owned, carrying their armloads to Jo's apartment, heaping the chairs, chesterfield, and Jo's work tables with tumbled armloads of clothing, sleeves dangling; a jumble of Harry's photographic and sporting equipment; a ragged tower of paperbacks; and Shirley's few cooking utensils. Then, in the camper, Lew and Jo drove to the shopping center, Lew hidden in the back, Jo at the wheel; she would be least vulnerable to recognition, they thought; Harry and Shirley should not be seen at all. Jo parked beside the Alfa Romeo, most of the stores closed now, plenty of room. She looked around as she turned off the motor; no one seemed to be watching. She got out, and walked along the covered walkway to the drugstore; it was nearly dark now. She stopped, looked in the lighted drugstore window for a few moments, then turned to walk back, bringing out Harry's ignition key. She got into the Alfa, started it, backed out, and drove away.

Half a minute later Lew moved from the back of the camper to the driver's seat, turned the ignition key Jo had left there, and backed out. He drove to Belvedere Drive, a quiet residential street a mile from the apartments. The Alfa sat parked at the curb, lights out, and he drew up beside it. Jo got out, stepped up into the driver's seat of the camper, and drove Lew home. She drove on then, parked half a mile away on Reed Boulevard, and walked home in the dark.

Supper was ready: Shirley had prepared it in Jo's little kitchen from canned goods Jo kept in supply for her lunches. Each of them with a plate wherever he could find room—Jo and Shirley

166

on arms of the chesterfield, Lew sitting on the floor, Harry leaning back against the sink—they ate, talking about what had happened; joking, laughing, still excited. The Levys would take Lew's apartment tonight, they decided; Lew and Jo would use hers. Presently they grew quieter. Jo opened canned peaches for dessert. When Shirley walked to the kitchen to rinse out her dish, she said to Harry, standing beside her, "So okay: we're all right tonight. We hope. But what about tomorrow?"

"Tomorrow we move."

She smiled uncertainly. "We already have."

He shook his head, chewing, then swallowed. "First thing tomorrow we throw our stuff in the car, and head for the nearest state line."

"*What?*"

"Shirl, listen. This isn't some little hit-and-run fender-bender: *I took a prisoner away from a cop!* And for that every cop in the county—Mill Valley police, deputy sheriffs, even highway patrol —will be very happy to nab me. *And* Lew." He glanced at Lew, who nodded. "I beat up a cop, took his prisoner, we took his handcuffs, took his keys"—Harry grinned suddenly—"and Lew took his god-damned *gun!*" He tossed his hands into the air. "They'll hang us!" Both men laughed genuinely, the women staring at them.

"Everything but his pants," Lew said, and they laughed again.

Harry set his plate on the sink, and began wandering the living room. "I can't even go to the office again. Ever. My full business address right under our doorbell for the cop to read: address, phone number, extension, and zip code. Everything but my photograph, front view and profile. Oh boy." Passing Jo's big supply cabinet, he reached out to touch one of the lineup of models on its top.

"You think they'll go to your *office?*" Shirley said. She stood shaking liquid soap into the sink, preparing to wash dishes.

"Sure they will! Why not? They'll find out who Lew is at the office, too. We can't risk it anyway: I don't want to serve a god-damn jail term! Become a felon. Be disbarred. No kidding, that's what they're planning for us. Right now. They'll be back tonight." He stopped at the glass doors to nod at his apartment. "And the cop I hit will work twenty-four hours a day, he'll give up sleeping—oh, *man*, would he like to find us! They'll have warrants out: we won't dare risk being stopped for anything. They're going to break their collective *ass* to find us! We really could do six months in jail. Any of us. All of us. That's the handwriting on the wall, and what it says is—move. Fast and far. While we can."

After a moment Shirley said, "Well, we've talked about trying Seattle some day; now we can. Just throw everything in the camper—"

"Not that pile of scrap. It wouldn't make it over the next hill."

"Well, cram everything into the Alfa then, and leave the camper where it is." She began running water into the sink. "How about it, you guys? Anyone for Seattle?"

"Sometimes I've thought about Santa Fe," Lew said slowly. "I've heard that it's different there." They laughed, and so did he but insisted, "Really. I've heard it really is." He glanced uneasily at Jo. "If that suits you?"

She didn't reply to this but said, "Couldn't you guys beat the charges? You're lawyers."

"We might," Lew said. "Our defense would be the simple truth: bring out the cop's real motive, no true arrest, we were within our rights. But he'd lie about what really happened; you know it. And juries believe cops, God knows why, these days. And judges pretend to. Frankly, I wouldn't take my own case."

"What about notice at work?" Jo said.

"I'll phone Tom Thurber in the morning."

"And then we leave? Just like that?"

"Well, the rent's paid till the first, of course. On all three apartments. And the furniture. No lease, it's month to month, and they've got our cleaning deposits. All we have to do is leave a note for notice." The room was silent then, except for the little clinks and watery swishes of Shirley's dishwashing. Lew sat looking at the others, frowning, and when he spoke again his voice was startled. "You know, it's funny: it gets easier to move every time. I could leave in ten minutes from a standing start; pack most of what I own in my suitcase and backpack, and carry the rest under one arm. All our stuff will fit in the VW, with the skis on top. What about your tables though, Jo? And the supply cabinet?"

"Well," she said slowly, "I bought them used; I expect I could sell them back at the same place. Just take them over in the van."

"And sell the van when we sell the camper," Harry said: he stood at the glass doors to the balcony watching the street. "First used-car lot we come to in the city. Might get a buck and a half apiece."

"You'll want your models," Lew murmured uneasily. "The Town."

"Yes."

"Well, we can manage." He looked around at the others. "So? That's it? We leave in the morning?"

Harry nodded. "By way of the city, lost in the commute mob; our last battle with that, anyway."

Again, for some moments they were silent; Jo got up to begin drying the dishes. But it was an uneasy, dissatisfied silence, and presently Lew said, "Son-of-a-bitch," and they all looked at him, sitting on the living-room floor. "Less than three hours ago we were solid citizens. And now we're on the run. That little creep was right, wasn't he, Harry? We didn't say, Yes, sir, and snap to attention; now he's running us out of town." No one replied. Harry stood at the balcony doors, frowning. Lew stood up to take his plate to the kitchen, saying, "Well, all right, okay. We have to run; Harry's right. Pile our stuff in the cars, and *drive*." He turned back into the living room. "But not in the morning, not tomorrow; not me, anyway. Before I leave, god damn it, I want to say good-by."

"How do you mean?" Harry said, swinging around to look at Lew, voice sharp with interest, and Lew grinned.

"I want to fix that red-neck son-of-a-bitch first."

"Why, yes," Harry said softly, and grinned, too. "How!?" he demanded. At the sink the women stood motionless, listening.

Lew shook his head. "I don't know exactly." He shoved his hands into his back pockets, and walked to the balcony doors to stand beside Harry, staring out at the street; dark now, the street lamps on. "But, you know?—I've been sitting here feeling like some kind of invisible man. We'll all be *gone*, vanished. Wiped out without trace. Someone else in our apartments in a day or so; there's a waiting list. Our furniture scattered all over the Bay Area." He swung around, speaking to them all. "Yet we lived here, damn it! We *belonged* here, didn't we? As much as anyone else. I had a job, maybe even a career." He smiled. "Lew Joliffe, city councilman; state senator; governor; head of the firm, finally; known, loved, and respected by all." He shrugged, baffled. "Instead I'm being wiped away like chalk off a blackboard. Well, I don't give a shit about the city council, you all know that. I just don't like being erased. And before I am, I not only want to fix the guy who did it; I want the whole damn county and Bay Area to know Lew Joliffe was *here*."

"Right. *Right!*" Harry began walking the room, gesturing, hands flinging out angrily. "A creepy little shit of a nobody starts mouthing off at us. And we don't just stand there and take it. That's all that happened! That was our crime! And for that— he's a nobody, you wouldn't spit on him!—but he's got a job on the cops so he's free to punish *me* by humiliating my *wife*. Publicly! Handcuff her! Before a crowd! Manhandle her around a parking lot!" He was addressing Shirley directly now. "So what am I supposed to do? Stand there saying, 'So long, Shirl'? I take you away from him; I *have* to. And now I'm supposed to run like a fucking rabbit. Well, god damn it, Lew's right: first, we fix that guy, then we say good-by." He swung around to face Lew. "But *how*, Lew? You must have something in mind!"

"Well, yeah. Sort of. We'd have to work it out." He stood looking at Harry appraisingly, then smiled suddenly. "You feel like some climbing? Some really weird climbing?"

"No!" Jo actually stamped her foot on the kitchen floor. "No, Lew: I know what you're talking about, and I won't have it! I won't! Oh, why can't we just *go*," she cried out. "Just leave in the morning, and forget the whole—"

"Because we wouldn't forget."

"*What, what?*" Harry demanded. "What's she talking about?"

"Well," Lew said, and he pushed aside a mound of clothing on the chesterfield, sat down, leaned back, and began to talk.

When he had finished, Harry, sitting on the floor at the balcony windows, began to laugh, silently, his big shoulders shaking. He said, "That's the worst thing I ever heard of. It's terrible, you know that: we'd be crazy." He shook his head, still laughing. "But it's too good to pass up."

They argued then, the women with the men: Lew sitting back on the chesterfield, hands clasped behind his neck, the others sitting on the floor. Then presently Shirley said, "Jo, look at them: look at their faces. They're going to *do* it. With or without us," and Jo nodded shortly, her lips compressed. Looking curiously from one to the other of the men, Shirley said, "Do you really have the nerve? Do you really?"

Lew smiled. "No. I haven't got the nerve at all. Except for one thing—the result. Oh, man, the *result* if we can bring this off! That's what will get me through it, I think. Like the carrot in front of the donkey."

Harry sat nodding, smiling, and Jo stood up abruptly. "All right, what the hell," she said. "It's late, the police haven't come back, and we're not going to Seattle or Santa Fe; not for a while, anyway. Let's get to bed."

CHAPTER 9

At five-forty in the morning Shirley's eyes opened. She lay listening, hearing only Harry's slow breathing beside her. Yet something had awakened her, and she got up quietly, walked to the side windows, and in the gray dawn saw Floyd Pearley walking soundlessly up the driveway on the balls of his feet.

He wore uniform, including his cap. Behind him—hands busy under her chin knotting a green scarf over her gray hair—Mrs. Gunther, manager of the buildings, followed in slacks, red slippers over bare feet, a raincoat buttoned to the chin. Harry said, "What's going on?" and his blanket flew aside before Shirley could answer.

They stood watching, Shirley shivering a little in the morning chill. Pearley had pressed their bell, Mrs. Gunther turning casually to look carefully around her. Now he pressed again. A token wait of a second or two, then he nodded abruptly, and Mrs. Gunther brought out a key from her raincoat pocket, unlocked the door, and followed Pearley in. "Can they *do* that?" Shirley whispered. "Without a warrant?" and Harry shrugged.

In less than two minutes they reappeared, Pearley walking swiftly down the driveway as Mrs. Gunther pulled the apartment door shut; and Harry turned away. "Back to bed. If Stupid knew this was Lew's place he'd be pounding the door down."

Promptly at nine every morning Tom Thurber arrived at the office, the only partner to do so; and at nine-five Lew phoned him, tilting the earpiece so the others, standing close, could hear. "Lew! What the hell is going on!"

"Why, what's happened, Tom?"

"A cop was just here! Waiting at the doors when Freddie arrived to open up." The cop had asked about Harry, and then, Thurber was afraid, in reply to further questions Freddie, the office manager, had given him Lew's name and address as a friend of Harry's.

Lew covered the mouthpiece. "Start emptying my apartment!" As the others ran to the balcony doors, he said, "What'd the cop look like, Tom?"

Thurber described Pearley, then: "Now, what's this all about?"

Lew told him. For himself and Harry he apologized for their having to leave without notice, and Thurber said he understood. They were all packed, Lew went on, were leaving within minutes to drive out of the state today, and Thurber said quickly, "Don't tell me where!" He added that he was sorry, and that he wished them luck: Could he help? Lew said no, and as he replaced the phone Jo and Shirley hurried in from the balcony carrying armloads of clothing, Harry following with Lew's skis, his wet suit, his tennis equipment. From the clothes Jo dumped onto a bed, Lew took his tweed coat and, buttoning it as he ran, clattered down the outside stairs, and ran to the VW.

Standing at Mrs. Gunther's desk, the VW at the curb, engine running, Lew laid his apartment keys before her, smiling pleasantly. He had to give up his apartment immediately, he said; he'd been "transferred to Atlanta," to report on Monday. Since he had a long drive and wanted to get started right now, would she mind notifying furniture rental? She asked for a forwarding address, and Lew gave her one, slowly and carefully as she wrote it down on a printed form: 808 . . . South Crescent Drive . . . apartment 2B, the home of a friend in Atlanta with whom he'd

173

be staying till he found a place of his own: no, he didn't know the zip. The Levys? Yes, he knew them slightly; had sometimes played tennis with them. No, he didn't know they'd moved, let alone where; was surprised to hear it. And the young lady next door? Miss Dunne? Was she staying? Lew shrugged, his face going coldly indifferent. "Far as I know." Then he smiled charmingly, offering his hand. "Good-by, Mrs. Gunther; I've enjoyed knowing you." She flushed slightly, and her eyes dropped.

Entering his car, Lew didn't glance back: what she had believed or thought, he didn't know. He drove on in the direction of the freeway. Making a three-mile loop, he returned to the apartment from the other direction, and parked behind the first of the buildings, four down from his own. With the pliers from his glove compartment he removed both his license plates, shoved them under a seat, and walked through the parking areas behind the buildings to Jo's van. He took off the front plate, returned, and attached it in the VW's rear plate-holder.

As Lew entered the apartment Jo, standing at the balcony doors, cried, "The cop's back!" and with the others Lew hurried over in time to see the Mill Valley black-and-white, Pearley at the wheel, swing into the driveway beside the building and disappear, accelerating.

They heard the brake squeal, the door-slam, then—all standing silent, the women's eyes widening—they listened to the faint peal of Lew's bell on the other side of the living-room wall. A moment's pause, then it rang four or five times in rapid, angry succession. Back at the balcony doors they watched the car bounce down into the street, shoot ahead to the manager's office and, brakes screeching, tires patching, park on the wrong side. The door flew open, and Pearley ran up the short walk to the manager's office.

On common impulse Lew and Harry stepped into movie pose, backs to the wall at each end of the double doors, hands on the butts of imaginary shoulder-holstered guns. "Shirl, *look* at them," Jo said. "They love this, they really do." Half a minute later Pearley reappeared, got into his car, and drove on.

In Jo's van all but Harry drove into Mill Valley—a chance

174

they had to take—and emptied their bank and checking accounts. When they returned, Harry was kneeling before Jo's white table, set in the light beside the balcony doors. As they stood watching he sighted through his 35-mm camera mounted on its tripod; propped before the lens, against a stack of paperbacks, stood a small photograph. Harry unscrewed one of two closeup lenses he'd attached to the camera, refocused, made a short time exposure. He began arranging his next setup, a long yellow card, its blank spaces handwritten in ink, and the others began carrying Jo's long paste-up table out to the van.

In the van Lew and Jo drove to the city, Lew in back out of sight. As she entered the bridge, the empty Pacific sliding past her side vision far below beyond the red-painted railing, Jo sat conscious of the knot of dread which had appeared under her breastbone as soon as she'd awakened. It would stay there for the next three days, she knew, but she'd become aware that along with it during the morning there had come a sense of anticipation: now, she decided, she felt simultaneously frightened and intensely alive. She drove on beside the long loops of the great support cables, passing under the two great bridge towers, thinking how placid and almost entirely without risk her life had been; and at the toll plaza, dropping her coins into the collector's cupped hand, she smiled at him genuinely, thinking, "What would you say if you knew what I knew?"

It took five hours to draw a line through everything on their list. On Kearney Street, Jo dropped Lew off at Brooks Cameras, and drove on to Market where she sold her worktables and supply cabinet at the office-supply shop at which she'd bought them. She delivered her finished model at a California Street office building, enjoying the luxury of parking directly at the building entrance in the clearly marked NO PARKING zone. There she asked for and got her check immediately, and—no ticket on her windshield yet—walked a block to the bank it was drawn on, and cashed it. When she returned, a folded white ticket lay under her wiper; she slipped it out, tried to crumple and throw it into the gutter, and couldn't. She put it into the glove compartment and drove on to pick up Lew.

He stood waiting on the curb, straddling a cardboard carton, as she pulled into the yellow zone. He opened the back doors, and when he heaved the package up onto the floor, it shook the van.

At a Mission Street electronics store, Lew bought a good-quality transformer; at a hardware store, a hundred-foot coil of light cable, two one-hundred-yard rolls of nylon fishline, and a bolt cutter. At Sears, out on Geary Street, he bought four of their cheapest twenty-four-volt automobile batteries.

Just outside Sausalito on the way home, Jo stopped at Big-G market to buy food. This was the waterfront industrial area, and Lew walked across the road to the nearest sail loft and bought the cheapest and widest nylon sailcloth they sold. This turned out to come in 44-inch bolts at $2.42 a yard, and he took all they had, five hundred feet. At another loft nearby he bought two hundred feet more; at the building-supply store eight fourteen-foot lengths of threaded two-inch plastic pipe, and a sackful of couplings and caps. From their garden shop he bought a sack of gravel. They drove to San Anselmo, and at The Alpine Shop bought four hundred feet of eleven-millimeter perlon rope.

Shirley stood at the stove in Jo's purple terrycloth apron when they returned, potatoes boiling, frozen vegetables in their plastic sacks ready to heat; she took the wrapped package of steak from Jo. Harry sat on the chesterfield with a drink, his camera in its case on the mantel beside the folded tripod. "Get it all?"

"Yeah." Lew dropped two bundles of sailcloth, ninety pounds of it, onto the floor before the newly exposed fireplace. "But it's good you're sitting down; wait'll you hear what it cost."

"Who cares? It's a bargain."

Saturday morning Jo walked to the camper and brought it back, and Lew and Harry drove to San Rafael, Harry in the back. In the nearly empty living room, crawling on hands and knees, Jo and Shirley cut the sailcloth into fourteen fifty-foot lengths. Each took two of these strips and, sitting cross-legged on the floor, tailor fashion, began sewing them together in big, looping stitches along the sides. Beginning at ten-thirty they

176

watched on the Levys' portable television set the morning cartoons, as they worked, and then whatever else came on, discussing it. They finished just before five, all the strips sewn together to form a fifty-foot square, a great white billow of cloth heaped along the side of the room.

In San Rafael Lew stopped first at a lumberyard, and bought several lengths of two-by-fours, some carriage bolts and washers. In the electrical-supply department he bought a short length of heavy insulated copper wire and some cutters. He drove to a tool-rental shop in the industrial area along the canal and rented a handsaw and drill. In an empty parking lot beside a closed-up cabinetmaker's—most of the small factories, supply, and service shops closed today—he and Harry cut and fitted inside the camper a solidly braced and bolted two-by-four frame, level with a side window. Harry connected the batteries and transformer, and lashed them together on the floor under the new framework.

On Sunday, breakfast over, they had very little to do. While Jo and Shirley washed dishes and made beds, Lew and Harry folded the giant square of sailcloth with great care and difficulty. One end of the wadded-up mass they dragged onto the balcony. From there they laid it, a huge puffed-up worm of white cloth, the length of the living room and on into the short hall. Even so, they had to curve the last dozen feet or so back on itself. Shifting it frequently as they worked, they folded this in accordion folds a yard wide. Then Lew knelt on the yard-wide fifty-foot length and, working his way backward, flattened and compressed the many-layered bulk with forearms and palms. Harry followed on his knees, rolling the long length into a coil, as tight as he could squeeze it. They wrapped it with a length of nylon cord, cinching it into a squat, fat roll which Harry lifted easily, though his arms wouldn't meet around it, and carried down to the van.

In the bedroom, Shirley and Jo packed Jo's Town, loosely wrapping each little building in tissue and fitting them into a small cardboard carton. Then, for most of the rest of the day they played a lazy, cheating game of Monopoly; each eating when he felt like it, searching the little kitchen area for whatever was to be found. In the afternoon they sipped white wine, not too much; Harry turned on the Raiders-Dallas game, and they watched it, continuing the Monopoly desultorily.

By four the Monopoly had dwindled into inaction; and when the Raider game ended at four-thirty, the men turned restless, glancing at their watches, walking to the balcony to glance out at the sky. At five Harry said, "I don't think a drink or two at this point could do anything but help," and Lew made them for everyone.

In the van after dark Jo drove north on the freeway in the slow lane at the steady fifty that was about all it could do; the men in back. Past San Rafael, she began, as always along this stretch, to watch for the break in the hills on the right that would suddenly reveal the great county Civic Center "in all its glory," she said to herself, meaning it.

It came: the van rolled on past a high bluff and then, no more than a quarter mile from the freeway, there it stood—exterior spotlighted, interior lighting on—the strange, beautiful building unlike any other she had ever seen; the last, she believed, ever designed by Frank Lloyd Wright. Slowing, glancing off at it as often as she could, Jo studied it again, thinking as always each time she saw it that some day she would make a model of it for herself. Long and narrow to give most of its rooms outside exposure, the building projected straight out from the side of a hill so steep that the end of the roof there nearly touched the ground. Jo had once stood beside it with Lew and, reaching up, had been astonished that her hand easily reached the eaves. Yet the other distant end of the long roof, extending out from the hillside far beyond its foot, stood several stories high. Now the roof lay in darkness, but Jo remembered it with pleasure, shooting ruler-straight out from the hillside, looking like a high-crowned road paved with tile of a rich, startling blue. The gold-ornamented eaves shone in the spotlighting from below, the beige walls exotically broken by enormous, scallop-topped windows. The black night-time hills began cutting the strange, lovely structure from view. Then it was gone, Jo smiling in the darkness of the cab, feeling that what she had seen was nothing so drab as a building of offices, courtrooms, a jail; it was more like Glinda's palace.

A mile past the Civic Center at a partly constructed building in a green-lawned industrial park beside the service road, Lew and Harry took two twenty-foot roof beams from a stack of them—heavy timbers half a foot thick, nearly a foot wide—and loaded them into the back of the van. Then Jo drove, fast, back along the narrow road—the obviously stolen beams projecting behind were a risk they had to take—and into the parking lot behind the Civic Center. Lights out, motor off, they waited. Nothing moved, the lot dark and silent, empty except for a lineup of orange-painted county road-maintenance trucks, and a single car. High on the hillside from which it projected, the great Civic Center loomed like a castle. Jo drove on, lights off, partly seeing and partly feeling her way up the dirt road at the back of the hill. Halfway up, she stopped at the padlocked gate in the high mesh fence. The men jumped down in back, dragged out the beams one at a time, and manhandled them over the fence. They climbed the fence, carried the beams on up to the Center, and dropped them in the weeds beside the road which ended here at a leveled area. Lew walked forward to the glass doors which, from up here on the hill, led directly into the top floor. He peered in: under the ceiling lighting the waxed floors shone; nothing moved. Turning away, he reached up as Jo had once done, and touched the roof edge, smiling. Back at the van, Lew tossed the bolt-cutter he had bought into the underbrush. Then they drove home.

From eleven o'clock on they tried to sleep, and presently did, lying partly dressed, women in the bedroom, the men lying on sleeping bags in the living room. Just before Lew drifted off, Harry said, "Lew?"

"Yeah."

"This gonna work?"

"Yeah."

"I hope so. I'd give a year of my life for a written guarantee from God."

At two o'clock when the alarm on the floor beside him rang, it took Lew some seconds to find it and shut it off; he could not understand what the persistent sound was, and didn't want to move and wake up. Then, heavily awake, thumb still on the stud he'd pressed, desperate to let his eyes close, he understood that he'd known what the ringing had meant, and that he was frightened.

It did not seem possible that they were actually going to do what it was time to do now. Propped on an elbow, blinking rapidly to hang onto wakefulness, he tried to find a way, a mental set, of accepting the truth; that there was almost nothing more between them and what they had said they would do. He felt unwell: was it possible he'd become sick while he slept? His stomach was an emptiness, and he was cold.

"Lew? How much you take to call off this whole fucking—"

"Don't say it! Or we will. We'll find reasons, and won't do it."

"Right: don't think, just get up." Lew heard Harry's movements, and he sat up, too. From the bedroom came the murmur of Jo's voice, and Shirley's muffled reply. Their light snapped on, slanting through the open door onto the nap of the beige hallway rug, and Lew was grateful that it didn't reach his eyes.

The drapes drawn, only a kitchen light on, they had coffee standing in the kitchen and living room. Lew wore his denims, blue zippered jacket, red mask-cap, and, tonight, a forest-green daypack. Harry was similarly dressed, his jacket dark green, his watch cap blue, his daypack red; and both men wore sneakers. Jo and Shirley wore pants suits, Jo's chocolate brown, Shirley's dark gray, and both wore berets. The coffee was too hot, Lew kept burning his lips, and he turned to the sink to cool it with water. Instead he took down the bottle of whiskey from the kitchen cupboard, and walked to the others, pouring a good slug of it into their cups and his own. It cooled his coffee and tasted good; burning his nose clear, warming him from throat to stomach in a palpable, glowing line, and what they were about to do once more became possible, just barely.

Lowering his cup, Harry said, "Bless you. Courage out of a bottle is a lot better than none at all." He swallowed down the rest, set his cup aside, and turned toward the outer door. "Well, c'mon, Sergeant; you want to live forever?"

CHAPTER 10

At the wheel of the van, Shirley beside her, the men hidden in the back, Jo curved onto the freeway, greenly lighted, empty and quiet in the night; far ahead across the blackness of the Bay the lighted city shimmered remotely.

Presently, near stalling, the van crested Waldo, then picked up speed, rolling down toward the lighted tunnel. Inside the tunnel, framed in the dome-shaped opening of its other end, the great towers of Golden Gate Bridge appeared, rising black against the night sky, the beacons at their tops winking red, the orange-yellow lights of the great span arcing across the black water.

On the bridge she slowed; headlights had appeared in her big side rear-view. They grew, the mirror glaring, the car drew abreast and passed, its driver glancing over at her. Then once more there was nothing behind, and only the single pair of rapidly shrinking tail lights ahead.

Jo leaned toward the windshield to stare out; first, at the long, empty, lighted roadway; then, lifting her eyes reluctantly, up at the enormity of its soaring north tower straddling the roadway like a giant ladder—a leg on each side, four huge transverses like rungs between them. In the orange light of the bridge lamps the first thirty feet of the great twin tower legs showed rust-red; beyond reach of the lights they turned abruptly black, endlessly rising into the night sky. The tower was so *high*, she thought, terrifyingly so, higher than in daylight, the winking red beacons at its top remote as the lights of a plane.

The rivet-studded red base of the ocean-side tower leg grew in her windshield to the size of a small building; then they were beside it, Jo braking, checking her rear-view, still blank and empty. She stopped, and the van's rear doors flung open, banging the sides hard; then the body jounced as Lew and Harry jumped down onto the roadway.

Instantly Harry seized the rolled-up sailcloth, heaving it up onto his shoulder. Beside him Lew stood dragging out the taped-together bundle of long plastic pipes. Harry swung away, trotting to the low, dirt-splashed steel divider between roadway and sidewalk. He jumped up onto it, down onto the walk, and ran across it. Lew followed, the long pipes balanced on one shoulder, a swaying plastic sack dangling from each end. They ran around the great tower base onto the little railed and concrete-paved bay facing the ocean behind it. Here, completely hidden from the roadway by the tremendous steel wall of the tower base, they dropped their burdens to the walk.

Back they ran, hurdling the short barrier to the roadway, and hopped up into the van, pulling the doors closed; it had taken less than fifteen seconds. At the slam of the doors Jo started up, the roadway still empty as far ahead and behind as she could see. On each side of the bridge ahead lay blackness, but between the railings the long empty roadway seemed warm and enclosed under the orange lights, artificial in its motionlessness. Shirley, sitting beside Jo, murmured, "It's fake, a stage set. Wouldn't surprise me if the chorus of *West Side Story* came climbing up over the rails."

Jo smiled tightly, nodding: she was watching at the right, following the long, slow curve of the immense support cable; black high above where it thinned into invisibility against the night; turning orange-red where it curved, thickening, down into the light. Just ahead at the halfway point of the long empty bridge, the barrel-thick cable seemed almost to touch the railing beside it. Jo slowed, then braked to a stop directly beside this center point, the rear doors of the van banging open again. They slammed shut immediately, she watched the two men run across her right-view mirror to the walk, and far ahead the lights of an approaching car appeared.

Before it could see she was stopped she drove on toward it, nothing else to do; a truck, she realized, from the height of its headlights. It moved slowly, and Jo continued on toward the city. If the lights of still another car should appear, she would have to drive on through the line of booths, paying toll, to wait somewhere on the other side, then return.

Van and truck, an aluminum-sided U-Haul, she could see now, crawled toward each other. They passed, a young black man wearing an enormous lopsided knit cap, glancing at her impassively. Nothing else had appeared, and Jo slowed, watching the pattern of red and yellow rear lights dwindle in her mirror. Then she stopped the van completely to wait, eyes moving between rear-view and windshield, until the bridge should be completely clear.

Two minutes . . . three; then the distant lights in her mirror vanished, cut off by the curve of the approach at the other end of the bridge. Jo checked—nothing coming now from behind or ahead—drove forward, then swung the wheel hard for the U-turn, and Shirley said, "Whee!"

"You like that?"

"Love it. I'll bet it's the first U-turn on the Golden Gate Bridge in twenty-five years."

Glad of the distraction, Jo said, "Well, we aim to please!" and swung the wheel hard again, holding it this time and the van made a complete tight circle, pressing Shirley against her door. "How's that?" Jo straightened, and they rolled on, back toward Marin.

"Marvelous. The fine for that must be ten thousand dollars."

Driving on back across the bridge they became silent, and each leaned toward the windshield, eyes searching. Approaching the point where the cable dipped lowest, Jo slowed, but the little ladder and platform beside it stood empty. She slowed still further, eyes moving along the great main cable, then Shirley cried, "There they are!" and Jo saw them, and shoved in the brake pedal.

After a moment she said, "Oh, my god." Then they sat motionless, staring up through the glass. Above and beyond the bridge lighting, the two small figures moved—flickered—along the dark cable in tandem. That was all, two blurs of movement no longer recognizable as men. Hardly darker than the sky against which they were just visible, they moved upward along the black line that, high, high above, faded away in the sky. Shirley turned suddenly and crawled over the seat. Stooped under the skylight, she slid it aside and stood erect in the opening, head and neck protruding above the roof. Jo set the parking brake and joined her. From this foreshortened angle the moving shadows seemed to advance very slowly; but within a minute, the women's heads gradually tilting upward, the two vague blots had moved perceptibly higher, then seemed to stop.

"I can't watch any more"—Jo reached for the seat back. "I hate this." She crawled forward, Shirley following. Glancing at each other as Jo released the brake, each saw that the other's face had gone white.

They drove on, and up on the great ocean-side cable high in the darkness above them Lew clung to the handholds saying, "Jesus. Oh, *Jesus*," and could not move.

"Lew, for crysake," Harry said, "we don't have to *do* this stupid thing. We can just turn around—"

"No. No. I'm all right. I looked down, that's all; dumb thing to do. You okay?"

"As okay as you can be when you're scared shitless. I'll tell you something else not to do: don't look *up*. I nearly puked. I saw the red beacon, and oh, man, it's *way* up. You say the word, and I'll race you down."

"No, it's okay." Focusing all his will power into his right foot, Lew made it lift off the cable, and plant itself six inches ahead. Then the left, and—the handhold wires sliding slowly and roughly through his curled palms, a film of sweat breaking out all over his body—he walked on. They'd climbed higher than this, and more dangerously: up nearly vertical cliffs. But in daylight. No one belonged up here in the dead of night.

One foot, then the other: he made himself a mechanical man, achieving a kind of rigid calm. Then he said to himself that that wasn't enough. It wasn't why he was *here*, walking up the main cable of Golden Gate Bridge. *God damn it*, he said silently, *this is something to remember forever!*

The ascent was steepening, they were having to lean into it now. But Lew forced his head to turn left, and stare off into the void. *That's the ocean*, he said. Another few steps, and he deliberately looked straight down to the right. The lighted bridge was an aerial photograph of itself, its narrowness emphasized by the limitless blackness beyond its sides. Toes pressing, calves tensing, he climbed on, the terror still waiting but forced outside him and held off. As nearly as possible he began to enjoy what they were doing again, appreciating its strangeness; and, the fear postponed, his exhilaration gradually returned.

Off the bridge approach, Jo parked just beyond it, out of sight of the freeway around the first bend of the dirt road leading to a small ocean-side state park. She and Shirley walked back onto the bridge and to the north tower, then around it onto the little railed bay on its ocean side. Looking up the riveted red wall of the tower, they could see only the darkness into which it rose; and they sat down to wait on the rolled-up coil of sailcloth Harry had dropped here.

Five hundred feet directly above them the men climbed the final dozen yards, the cable slanting up at nearly sixty degrees here, their bodies tilted sharply back; each step up now took the strength of an arm tugging on the handhold to bring the torso along. Now the huge, winking red beacon stood incredibly close above them, the great two-foot lens reddening Lew's sneakers, turning the air itself a blinding pink, then mercifully blackening, over and again.

Three steps to go, Lew's arm trembling. Two steps, one, then his hand lifted from the handhold to close down on the rung of the small steel ladder leading from cable down to the great topmost transverse. He swung off onto the ladder, Harry followed, then they stood safe, safe, *safe* between the waist-high guard rails of the gloriously flat steel surface.

They stood on the topmost rung, wide as a road, of the tremendous, ladderlike north tower of Golden Gate Bridge, faces reddening and darkening, and they grinned at each other. Harry stuck out his hand, and said, "Hey, pardner, we climbed the goddamn bridge." They shook, Lew saying, "Should have brought some wine, we could have drunk a toast," and Harry said, "Hey, yeah. How come you forgot?"

For perhaps two minutes they strolled the wide, high surface, feeling slightly stunned, tasting the joy of sanctuary attained. Gripping the railing then, they leaned forward to stare down at the strip, astonishingly narrow, that was the six-lane lighted roadway of the bridge. They watched a small dark rectangle push a pair of finger-length beams along it, till it passed directly under them and vanished. Harry said, "Yow." Then, loud as he could yell it, "*Yow, yow, yow, yow!*" HEY, down there! Look at *us!*"

Forearms on the railing, ankles crossed, they stared out across the Bay at the city lying darkly on its hills, its grid of streets picked out by dots of light. To the left stood the heaped shapes of its lighted downtown buildings shimmering distantly through the layers of night-time air; from them a dotted line across blackness, the lights of the Bay Bridge, led to the freckles of pale green light that meant Oakland.

They turned to the opposite rail to look out at the smoothly undulating Marin hill shapes against the sky, striped with the white winding of the freeway. Then they walked back toward the black nothingness of the ocean. Occasionally a remote dab of dingy white flickered on the blackness, an infinitely removed whitecap, and Lew said, "Harry, I was scared; I tell you I was *scared*. But this is worth it."

"Yeah, look at us. *Up* here."

And then, as they walked on, across the eighty-foot length of the huge topmost transverse of the tower, looking out over scveral counties spread across the night below, the prolonged moment of attaining it faded; and when they reached the ocean side of the tower again it was gone.

This was not their final goal but only a way-stop. It wasn't the topmost transverse but the middle one they had to reach, the second up from the roadway. They could not reach it from below—the great support cable led only up here. To reach the lower transverse they had first to climb to the top, then come down to the middle transverse; not down the cable—down the sheer wall of the tower leg, smooth and blank as the side of a windowless building fifty stories high. It was time to start, and Lew felt the tension re-forming: this was going to be worse.

The small ladder they had descended from cable to transverse led past a railed balcony. This balcony, made of thin steel rods and slats, was four-sided. It hung wrapped around the very top of the tower leg—higher than the transverse they stood on, lower than the great main cable. Lew climbed the ladder, Harry behind him, and halfway up it he stepped off onto the balcony. It was narrower than he could have wished, his right shoulder lightly brushing the side of the tower as he walked to the first corner. The steel rods on which he stepped were spaced more widely than he would have preferred; some were loose, rattling as his foot left them, the very soles of his feet conscious of the long black distance beneath them.

Harry following, Lew turned the right-angled corner, and as they walked on in the new direction toward the ocean, Lew saw themselves again as from a distance; two matchstick figures moving across the south face of the Marin tower at its very top; he wondered if Jo and Shirley stood far below at just this moment, heads tipped back to watch them. Passing under the great support cable, almost brushing his cap, Lew reached up to slap its cold solidity and, hearing the echoless smack, realized he'd become bored with being frightened. He knew what he was about to do, knew how to do it, felt sure of himself, and the elation of what they were doing tonight roared back.

Again they turned a corner, to move across the ocean-side face of the tower. At midpoint they stopped, and from his daypack each brought out a climbing harness of wide red webbing. They stepped into these and buckled them at the waist. Then Lew took out a small flashlight; Harry a rope coil, a fistful of webbing, and a rappelling ring: a two-inch metal circle, a slim doughnut of steel. Squatting at the base of one of the stanchions supporting the rails of the platform, Lew held the flashlight for Harry, a hand cupped under it to shield it from view below. Harry slipped an end of the webbing through the rappelling ring and knotted both ends around the base of the stanchion. He stood up, and tested this knot, gripping the rappelling ring in his hands and yanking till the stanchion shook. "Hold a horse," he said, squatted again, and began threading an end of the rope coil through the rappelling ring.

Lew stood clipping a carabiner to his harness; this is a metal loop with an opening in one side, called a "beaner" by climbers. The opening closed with a safety lock, and he closed it, tightening down the safety. Then he stood waiting for Harry to finish, emptying his mind of conscious thought, resisting a nagging urge to look over the side.

"All set," Harry said, and now Lew sat down on the balcony floor, legs hanging over the side: the rule was, least experienced man goes first. Beside him the loop of webbing hung from the base of the stanchion; from the rappelling ring at the bottom of the loop hung the doubled length of eleven-millimeter perlon climbing rope, dangling two hundred feet down the ocean side of the tower. Lew reached for the rope and brought it to his lap; to the rope Harry had attached a metal device, the "descender," and now Lew opened his beaner, clipped in the descender, refastened the beaner's safety lock. He was ready now, harness clipped to the sliding descender of the long rope. He gripped the doubled rope length in his left hand and glanced up at Harry to smile. "See you downstairs," he said, relieved to hear his voice come out calm.

"Right." Harry touched his shoulder. "Take it nice and easy, enjoy yourself."

Lew ducked head and shoulders under the middle railing, gripped the rope, squirmed forward, and slid off the edge of the balcony floor to hang suspended, legs dangling—swinging in a short, diminishing arc, twisting slowly toward the tower wall. He hadn't plunged, clawing at the air; everything had held. He had known it would, *known*, but still he felt the familiar, euphoric rush of relief.

Now he extended his legs to press both rubber soles against the riveted steel face of the tower wall, his back to the ocean, the sling and rope above him angling outward, the rest of the long doubled rope dangling below him into the darkness, a two-hundred-foot tail. His left hand gripped the rope, and now he slowly relaxed it, and the ropes began sliding through his fist, his body lowering. With the rope snubbed by the metal descender through which it was threaded and controlled by the pressure of his grip, Lew lowered himself at a steady speed, the steel balcony with Harry's face peering over it rising away like the underside of an ascending elevator.

In complete easy control of his descent, Lew watched the endless parallel rows of rivets just beyond his pumping knees rise into darkness: he could feel the small pressure of ocean air cool on his neck, and was conscious of the tendons steadily working inside the canvas of his sneakers. Walking backward down the ocean-side face of the great north tower of the bridge, he felt as happy, in the intensity of the moment, as he had ever been.

His heels bumping onto the steel-slatted floor, Lew backed down onto the next balcony below the top one; this balcony, identical with the one he had just descended from, hung wrapped around the tower leg just above the middle transverse. Unclipping his beaner from the descender, Lew turned to look down over the balcony railing. Three hundred feet below, the white blurs of two faces stared up from the walk at the base of the tower leg; and Lew thrust an arm over the railing to move his hand back and forth in a slow arc, hoping they'd see it.

Harry's swiftly walking legs appeared out of the darkness above. "Second floor," he called, "kitchenware, appliances, la-dies' underwear." His body straightening, he dropped the final few feet, shaking the floor—and now they had attained the level of the second transverse, where they wished to be. "Girls here?"

Harry turned to the railing, and Lew walked to the dangling, still swaying rope to pull it down from its loop high above them now, ducking as it came spilling onto their heads and shoulders. They would use the rope again, for their next descent, but before that happened they had work to do here; and Lew walked to the railing now, and began lowering an end of the rope over the balcony rail.

On the concrete walk of the little orange-lighted bay, Jo and Shirley stood waiting, faces upturned. When the rope end appeared, swaying down into the light, Jo jumped, missed, tried again, and brought it down. Shirley took it, knelt on the walk, and tied it to the rope enclosing the coil of sailcloth. She said, "Square knot, the one useful thing I learned in Girl Scouts. You in the Girl Scouts?"

"Oh sure."

"You like it?"

"I liked the camping."

"Me too." Shirley tugged the line, then they stood watching the fat white coil slide up the tower leg, bouncing outward occasionally. Shirley said softly, "Thank God they're down off the top," and Jo nodded, swallowing.

As he would roll a tire, Harry trundled the wheel-like coil along the balcony and around the corners to the ladder leading down to the transverse. He dropped it to the transverse, and climbed down after it. This transverse had no guard rails, and Harry unrolled the coil into a yard-wide, fifty-foot length of folded cloth, positioning it between the tower legs. As Harry worked, Lew stood on the ocean side of the balcony, hauling up the bundle of plastic pipes with its attached sacks of gravel and couplings.

On the transverse, the two men screwed pipe lengths together to form two fifty-six-foot-long pipes. One of them they filled with gravel, and capped the ends. The women had sewn sleeves across the top and bottom edges of the big sailcloth square; and Lew and Harry slid a pipe into each of these sleeves. They were nearly finished now.

The women stood waiting below, one on each side of the

roadway; when the lights of an occasional car appeared, they stepped around out of sight behind the tower legs. Leaning back against the railing on the Bay side of the bridge, the green light flecks of Oakland twinkling behind her, Jo stood wondering once more whether or not she would ever again see the Levys when this was over. She felt she would not; that that was the way such things generally worked out. She shrugged a shoulder slightly, a corner of her mouth quirking; it would be an important loss.

Shirley stood across the roadway, ankles crossed, a shoulder against the riveted wall, looking over at Jo. She, too, was thinking of the coming separation of the two couples, but what she wondered, smiling, was whether or not Jo and Lew would marry. Harry thought not, but Shirley told herself that he didn't know; and, nodding unconsciously to confirm it, she decided that they would.

Up on the second transverse the two men had unrolled a coil of thin light cable across its length. Now each twisted an end around the base of a ladder leg at opposite sides of the transverse, and the cable lay flat along the steel floor, tautly stretched clear across it. To this cable they tied the unweighted pole in its sleeve, using several forty-foot lengths of nylon rope. Finally, each tied the end of a hundred-yard roll of new orange-colored fishline to the ends of the other weighted pole. Checking both directions to make sure no cars were in sight, they dropped the spools off the San Francisco edge of the transverse to fall, unrolling as they dropped, to the roadway below.

As Lew and Harry walked back to the ocean-side balcony, and their next-to-final descent, Jo and Shirley stood taping the ends of the orange fishline high on the walls of the twin tower legs, using strips of orange-colored Mystic tape. They dropped the empty spools over the bridge rails.

The men back—first Lew, then Harry, walking down out of the darkness to drop to the walk of the little bay behind the tower leg—they were finished with the bridge for tonight, their preparations complete. Chattering, hilarious with excitement, they walked back for the van; when a car passed on the bridge approach, another behind it, they waved wildly—one driver slowly lifting an arm to respond, puzzled, the other only staring in bewildered suspicion.

In the van, rolling down Waldo Grade, the men kneeling behind the front seat, Shirley said, "What if a bridge worker goes up there tomorrow?"

"He'll see it right away," Harry said, "and that'll be that. Just hope no one does, is all; they don't go up there every day, or anything like it."

Out of the tunnel, they rounded a long curve, and Richardson Bay bridge and the dark shoreline of Strawberry Point appeared far ahead and below like a map. Lew said, "Harry, it's been quite a night: we could call it quits right now, if you wanted. Tomorrow night is the big one."

Shirley said, "Yes! I vote yes. So does Jo. Democracy at work."

But Harry was shaking his head. "No. I want it all. Not just tomorrow night—I want to fix the cop, too. Okay?"

"Sure. I do, too. Just checking is all."

"It's after three," Jo said. "How do you know he hasn't been and gone? Or that he'll even show up tonight?"

"Well, we don't," Lew said. "We're just guessing that it's an every-night routine. But if he doesn't show, all we lose is a little more sleep."

At Strawberry, Jo curved off the freeway onto the service road, and slowed, leaning forward to study the driveways of the Texaco and Standard stations, the car wash beyond them, and McDonald's after that. But no black-and-white, lights off, stood parked in any of them. Across the freeway the lights and sound of a car shot by toward the city, but here on the service road nothing moved ahead or behind. Jo swung into the Standard station, switching her lights off, and she and Shirley sat watching, motor running. "Okay," she said then.

"Got the dimes?" Harry said, and from her pants pocket Shirley brought a small handful of dimes, and passed two of them back. From under the seat she pulled out a slim blue-and-silver package, a roll of aluminum foil, tore off a ragged scrap from each corner, and passed them back.

The rear doors opened, the men slid out, eased the doors shut, and Jo immediately drove on, down the driveway back onto the service road. Watching her rear-view, she saw Lew and Harry walk quickly across its face toward the pair of phone booths at the edge of the lot.

Each in a booth, doors left open, no light coming on, the men wrapped their foil fragments loosely around the dimes Shirley had given them. Then they stuffed them into the coin slots, forcing them down, the foil crumpling and packing the slots. Leaving his booth, Lew saw the van stopped in the car-wash driveway next door, Shirley inside the phone booth there. He and Harry walked quickly along the side of the white-painted station and turned the corner at the rear. Safely out of sight, they stood watching the van leave the car wash, then swing into McDonald's to stop beside the phone booth there.

Standing in the star-lit darkness behind the station, it seemed to Lew that these were the first moments of relative calm in many hours, though he knew it had been less than two. He began to stretch slowly, enjoying it, arms out at his sides, fingers clenching and splaying. Then he walked in a slow circle, stomping softly, working the last of the climb and descent from his muscles, it seemed, preparing for what might come next. Harry sat down, his back against the rear wall of the station, then Lew joined him, and they sat silent and listening, waiting.

He arrived twenty minutes later: they heard the motor, a tappet ticking, then the small bumper scrape on concrete as the car jounced up the driveway; heard the faint brake squeal, then the parking brake ratchet. Silently they stood up . . . heard leather on concrete out front, fading as he walked to the other side of the building. On rubber toes they ran to the other back corner, stopped just short of it . . . heard the slight key jangle, then the quiet distinct snick of key sliding into lock. From out front the hollow click of a loudspeaker coming to life; behind a slight fuzz of static, a woman's distant monotone spoke a few unintelligible words. Harry nudged Lew, eyes pleased, to whisper, "Roof speaker's on; means the engine's running." From around the corner, the chain-rattle of garage door rolling up . . . the snap of a light switch . . . footsteps receding across concrete . . . a moment's pause. Then a coin rattled down a slot, and they whirled and ran hard along the back, full speed on tiptoes, around the corner, and along the side to the front.

There it stood, the black-and-white, facing south away from them, exhaust purring quietly, clouding gray in the night air. On the driver's door, standing slightly ajar, MILL VALLEY POLICE, dim but readable in the starlight. Moving very fast they walked silently toward it, Lew first to yank open the driver's door, slide under the wheel and—lifting a uniform cap out of the way— across the seat. Right behind him, Harry slipped in under the wheel, slowly pulled the door closed till the latch clicked, then pressed down the lock knob, and rolled up the window to within an inch of the top. He found the parking-brake handle, very slowly released it, set his foot on the brake pedal, and pushed the shift lever to DRIVE. Then he turned to grin at Lew who grinned back, their eyes elated. Watching the yellow patch of light spilling from the side of the garage, they waited.

Overhead the roof speaker suddenly squawked, and they jumped. Harry irritatedly jerked his head at Lew to find the cut-off switch. Lew pushed a toggle and they heard the speaker-hum snip off. In the same moment, as though Lew had caused this too, the light at the side of the building snapped out, and the garage door clattered down.

For just a moment in the dim starlight, they couldn't quite be certain it was he: only the top of his black-haired head visible, eyes on the filled Styrofoam cup suspended from his spidered fingers, he appeared walking slowly around the corner in uniform. For a moment longer they watched, then grinned as they recognized him—and Harry blasted the horn.

The cup dropped, split, a black gout of steaming coffee dashed over the man's skinny ankles as his head shot up, and Pearley's wedge-shaped face stared at them, eyes bright with fright, feet suddenly dancing as the scalding coffee bit through the white cloth of his socks. Harry howled a wild banshee-shriek of laughter, and shot the car forward, black-streaking the concrete. They bounced down onto the road, swung into the freeway-entrance almost directly ahead, and as Harry straightened in the lane they saw the man—motionless, long jaw hanging open—suddenly whirl and run toward the phone booths, both of them yelled with glee.

Harry held to the outside lane at a steady sixty-five, ten miles over the limit but easily acceptable, they felt certain, in a police car on a nearly empty road. After half a mile Lew handed the blue uniform cap to Harry, who put it on and grinned; it was half a size too small, but he left it.

Four trucks passed on the other side, nothing on this, and in just under eight minutes by Lew's timing they had passed San Rafael, and were approaching the Civic Center. Then the lights of a car approached on the other side of the freeway; and in passing they saw the red dome light and green-and-white car of a deputy sheriff. Could he be hunting them, could Pearley possibly have reached a working phone so soon? They hadn't planned what they'd do if this happened. The driver glanced over at them, lifted a hand in greeting, and Harry responded equally casually. Another mile, and he slowed for the turnoff, then onto the road they'd ridden early in the evening with Jo. Back along the road then, winding a little, up and down the occasional slight hill.

At the entrance to the back parking lot of the Civic Center Harry switched off the headlights, drove forward, and stopped, waiting for his eyes to adjust. Without lights then, he drove forward in low gear, foot on the brake, half seeing, half feeling his way. He found the dark bulk of the van, parked in the same place it had been earlier, and he pulled in beside it on the driver's side, and turned off the motor. Lew rolled down his window, and two feet away at the wheel of the van Jo said softly, anxiously, "Any trouble?"

"No, he's probably still hunting for a phone that works."

Shirley got out, closed her door silently, and walked past the front of the van carrying Harry's folded tripod, camera and flash attachment mounted. Lew put out his arm to take it, but Shirley brushed past to the rear door, and Jo got out of the van. "Hey, what're you doing?" Lew said.

"Coming along. We want to watch."

"No," Harry said, but Lew said, "Harry, if they get one of us, they've got us all. Let 'em come," and the women climbed into the back.

Listening, watching, they waited through a dozen seconds more. Then Harry drove on, lights out, creeping along in the ruts, the car slowly jouncing on its shocks up the hill to stop at the wire mesh fence. Lew got out, found the bolt cutters in the grass, and cut the lock chain. He threw the cutters down the hillside and opened the gate; Harry drove on through, Lew following on foot.

Harry stopped in the leveled area at the end of the long building which projected from the hillside here. Motor off, they got out, and the women watched as Lew and Harry carried the long beams they had left here to the narrow, slightly domed blue roof. One end of each foot-wide, six-inch-thick plank they set on the edge of the roof just above their heads, positioning them four feet apart, and stomped the other ends of the twenty-foot beams into the ground. Then, Lew squatting on the roof edge guiding him with the shielded flashlight, Harry slowly drove the police car up the ramp and onto the roof.

The roof ruler straight, wide as a road, and only slightly higher-crowned, he drove slowly on, keeping meticulously to the center: following on foot the others could hear the steady faint ripple of rubber on tile.

A dozen feet short of the end, Harry stopped, overlooking the asphalted entranceway five stories below. Parking brake pushed to its final rachet, gear lever in PARK, he got out, and they stood listening. Nothing moved, no shout sounded.

Harry set up his tripod at the front of the roof, facing the car and the open front door labeled MILL VALLEY POLICE. Twisting the lens to focus, he watched the others arrange themselves. Lew lounged at full length along the hood, his grinning head propped on an elbow before the windshield. The women stood each with a foot on the front bumper: Shirley with the shotgun from the front-seat rack held negligently in the crook of one arm, Jo with Pearley's pistol carelessly dangling from the trigger guard; both smiling sardonically at the camera in classic Bonnie and Clyde pose.

The camera set and buzzing, Harry ran toward them calling, "Ten seconds!" He dropped to a squat between the women, turning to grin at the camera. *Flash*—the car and their faces whitened, and Harry ran for the camera as Lew stood clicking Pearley's handcuffs through the two trigger guards and the ring of keys. The women already hurrying back along the roof, Harry trotted forward with his tripod, and Lew hung guns and keys from the base of the aerial, and the blue uniform cap from its top. Then they ran.

Four of them carrying the beams down the hill, stopping once for breath—listening, ready to drop them and run—they brought them back to the van: two minutes later they set them on the pile from which they had taken them.

Driving sedately home in the very first early widely scattered beginnings of what would swell to heavy commute traffic in the next hours, they twice watched police cars fly past at high speed, one in each direction, dome lights flashing; and they laughed softly and sleepily.

Five hours later at nine in the morning, Lew awakened, lying on Jo's chesterfield, closed his eyes again, then could not resist: he got up, turned on the portable television and, the volume low as he could tune it, he watched the news, including a black-and-white still photo apparently taken at first dawn showing the car and two uniformed men silhouetted on the Civic Center roof. It was a mystery, the announcer's almost inaudible voice murmured, the car first spotted at dawn from the freeway, and Lew smiled, turned it off, and returned to the chesterfield.

At noon they had lunch, watching the news, and saw a color film: the camera panning over a crowd down on the asphalt before the Civic Center, then up to others scattered over the hill beside the long beige building, finally lifting to the roof as a uniformed deputy sheriff, leaning out his open door, slowly backed the car along the blue road in the sky to the careful beckoning of a deputy behind him. The film continued till the car stopped at the back roof edge, then briefly returned to the faces of the watching crowd as it cheered mockingly. Latest word, said the announcer at his news desk, is that the car still stood at the roof edge awaiting a ramp workmen were preparing.

During the afternoon as the others desultorily played rummy, switching to casino later, Harry developed his films in the bathroom. Later, as he sat at the little white table mounting the pictures, the four of them watched the final descent of Pearley's car down an amply wide and well-braced ramp; this followed by a brief filmed interview with the Mill Valley police chief. With the good sense to know humor was his best refuge, he stood smiling on the walk before his police station, then responded affably to the interviewer's questions: Who put the car up there, and why? "That's easy," said the chief, "Officer Pearley was in hot pursuit. Of a stolen hang glider. Had him cornered up there on the roof. Unfortunately the thief managed to fly away in the darkness, and Officer Pearley didn't want to shoot for fear of hitting innocent planes. He has been commended, and will be transferred to our air force." The chief nodded pleasantly, and turned back toward the station, his smile fading quickly.

At three o'clock Jo walked to the camper, and brought it back to the building parking area. There she packed the VW and the Alfa, carefully cramming both trunks, filling the back seats and floors with their belongings, skis on the roof racks. She packed her own things into two suitcases.

At four-thirty, all dressed as they'd been the night before, the others stood waiting as Jo walked slowly through the apartment making sure it was empty of everything they were to take. For a moment or two then, she stood looking from Shirley to Harry, shaking her head. "I have the feeling that after tonight I'll never see you two again."

They protested. "We'll phone my folks the minute we find a place," Shirley said. "You phone them when you're settled, or we'll phone your folks—"

"Oh, sure, I know. And we will, of course. Then we'll all talk to each other. On the phone. And write. For a while. Send

Christmas cards a while longer. But . . . you're going to Seattle. You think. And we're going to Santa Fe. Maybe." She shrugged, and no one replied.

Harry left first, not certain the camper could make it over Waldo Grade, and Shirley followed in the Alfa. As Jo checked the balcony doors, making sure they were locked before leaving, Lew said, "I'll miss those doors," and she smiled.

Down at the van Jo stood beside it looking up at the building. "Well, so long, 2E," she said. "And 2D. So long, rented dishes, white table, and Scotch-guarded furniture: will you remember us? When someone else is using you? Think of us now and then? Lew and Jo?" She shrugged. "No answer: let's go." She climbed up into the van.

In the slow lane, Lew hanging a few lengths behind in the VW, Jo's worn-out van slowly climbed Waldo. Watching its big wooden bumper projecting a good foot to the rear, Lew urged it on with a slight rocking motion, then reached out nervously to snap on his radio. Louis Armstrong faded in hoarsely with "Mack, the Knife," and as the van crept over the summit, and began picking up speed rolling down toward the tunnel, Lew burst into voice, singing along in fragmented snatches ("'. . . scarlet billows! . . . gleaming white! . . .'"). Coming out of the tunnel onto the long curving downgrade toward the bridge, he saw that Harry and Shirley were nowhere in sight, no sign of a stall up ahead on the bridge, and he grinned in relief. Behind his rolled-up windows he began to shout out the words he knew of the song.

Rolling across Golden Gate Bridge a car length behind Jo, Lew studied the traffic. The forty-year-old bridge was only six lanes wide, the lanes narrow for today's cars. Now, during the evening commute, they were separated into four northbound lanes toward Marin, nearly solid with cars; and two southbound lanes toward San Francisco, more lightly used. Separating these opposing traffic streams stood a row of yard-high sausagelike posts of spongy plastic dyed bright yellow and red.

Lew heard the rackety clatter of helicopter blades, and saw the tiny KGO traffic helicopter a hundred yards overhead curving toward the bridge from the Bay like an insect. From his radio came the brief identifying musical theme, then the familiar voice over the beat of the blades in the background. "Northbound traffic on Golden Gate Bridge is heavy, moving slowly but normally for five o'clock on a weekday; no stalls, no congestion. Up ahead toward the Waldo tunnel, it's moving freely."

To his right, in snatched glimpses through the bridge railings, Lew saw the enormous dull-orange disc of the sun edging into the horizon far out across the miniature whitecaps below. It was full daylight still but would begin fading within minutes, and at the thought of what was to be done when the sun had set, Lew felt the sweat pop at the roots of his hair. Traffic report finished, the little bug-shape hovering over the bridge suddenly curved gracefully away toward Oakland, beaters chopping the air. A commercial began, and in sudden anxious irritability Lew switched the radio off.

He followed the van through the toll booths, then both edged to the right, out of the traffic stream onto a curving descending road. This led down into a narrow tunnel passing under the bridge approach. Van and VW came out on the other side into a large parking area facing the Bay, a view place for tourists, crowded in the summer. But now in the dusk of a late fall day, only Harry's camper stood at one end, the Alfa a little distance away, two strange cars at the opposite end. Jo parked at the low stone wall facing the Bay, and Lew nearby.

They walked to the camper: the Levys sat in the front seat, Harry rolling down his window. "Made it," he said. "It didn't want to, but I cursed it over the Grade." The area they were in stood at the side of the bridge, well below the level of its roadway. From here they had a spectacular view of the bridge, a foreshortened profile of the entire arched span. They stared at it now. Before them, close and enormous, the south tower filled half the sky. From its top the long, beautiful curve of the twin cables swooped down to almost touch the road, it seemed. Then it rose again to dwindle to a thread where it finally reached the height of the distant north tower. "Can you believe it, Lew?" Harry said. "We walked up that son-of-a-bitch!"

"Fair makes me stomach churn."

"I almost *was* sick," Shirley murmured, looking out at them past Harry, "when I saw those little *bumps* moving along the cable. Right, Jo?"

Jo nodded, then they all watched the sun visibly and rapidly sinking down into the water out beyond and under the bridge. First, half of it gone, then most of it, and finally the very edge of its upper rim flashed on the horizon line, and the great disc was gone. Its rays still filled the air, fanlike, at the horizon; and the daylight still seemed strong and clear, everything visible: the great rust-red bridge and its unending flow of cars high above them; the green-and-white Bay and its half dozen sails; the distant shorelines just beginning to speckle with light; the Bay islands.

Then suddenly, goldenly, the bridge lights came on all at once, and instantly the daylight diminished. The bridge's color vanished, and it stood stark and black against the luminous sky. Within seconds a few car lights flicked on, then very quickly all of them, the cars fading into darkness, and the commute traffic above became a stream of lights. "Jo, maybe you better start," Lew said, and she nodded. "You don't have to," he added quickly. "Really. Just say you've changed your mind, and we're all going to nod and agree, and feel damn relieved."

"That's right," said Harry.

"*You* say it," Jo answered. "Any of you. I've got the easiest job." She handed her keys to Lew, he gave her his, and she nodded at them all. "Well—good luck. See you." Abruptly she turned to walk swiftly to Lew's car, and he checked his watch.

The others watching, Jo drove up the narrow exit road to the bridge approach and stopped, the oncoming stream of traffic from the city flowing past her front bumper; it was nearly full dark now. At the first break, Jo wheeled swiftly into the lane, and they watched the VW's tail lights till they were lost in the Marin-bound traffic.

The two strange cars had left, and Lew walked to Jo's van, bringing out pliers, and removed her last license plate. Kneeling in the dark at the Alfa Romeo, he took off both its plates, and pushed them down into the Levys' heaped belongings on the rear floor.

Back at the camper he stood at Harry's door, and they waited: nervous now, wrapped in their thoughts, speaking very little. Harry sat frowning at the darkening Bay, his face set belligerently. Beside him, her face pale in the dark of the camper's cab, Shirley fidgeted: glancing out her window, at Harry's profile, and at Lew; yawning, checking her watch. Several times Lew turned away to pace slowly, returned, then walked away again. He looked up at the sky often, testing the quality of its deepening darkness.

Across the bridge on the Marin County side, Jo curved off into the view area there, which faced the similar area across the Gate in which the others waited. Only one other car stood parked here now, a man and a woman standing before it at the low guard rail, staring across the water at the lighted city. Getting out of the VW, Jo glanced at it, too, and stood for a moment, hand on the door. More lights appeared as she watched, the city taking on its shimmering night-time look, which always excited her. But she couldn't wait, slammed her door, and walked away toward the beginning of the sidewalk that led across the bridge.

Just short of the walk she turned onto a flight of concrete stairs, walked down its three shallow steps, and turned onto a narrow screened foot bridge which passed under the big bridge itself. She didn't like it here alone under the bridge, afraid of seeing someone turn onto it ahead and come walking toward her; and she hurried, half running. A few feet above her head the heavy bridge traffic rumbled steadily, and she didn't like this either.

No one else appeared, and Jo turned right on the other side to walk up a paved ramp to bridgeway level and turned right again onto the sidewalk leading across the ocean side of the bridge. Glancing brightly around, trying to appear as she imagined a tourist might look, she walked on, beside the double lane of traffic to the city. The sidewalk behind its low separating barrier stood several feet higher than the roadway beside it, and she could look over the roofs of passing cars. On the other side, the commute traffic toward Marin was a solid flow of headlights, the enameled bodies behind them winking yellowly under the bridge lights.

She reached the ocean-side leg of the south tower, and turned onto the little bay behind it where she had stood last night with Shirley. Hidden from the passing stream of cars on the other side of the enormous steel wall of the tower leg, she stood, hands on the railing, staring out at the night-time blackness of the ocean.

Across the bridge Lew looked at his watch. It had been fourteen minutes since Jo had left, time enough: she'd either be at her post or walking to it. But he waited the extra minute, then said, "Time."

"Okay"—Harry nodded from the open window of the camper. "What do you say, Lew?" he added quietly. "Still think this'll work?"

"Well, if somebody described it to me, I'd laugh. But it can work. Pretty easily. No reason it shouldn't, in fact. So logically, I say yeah, it'll work." He shrugged. "But emotionally, I won't even believe it when I see it."

"I wish we could stay and watch," Shirley said, climbing down to the pavement; she sounded eager, the waiting over. She walked to the Alfa, Lew walked to the van, and doors slammed. Lew started his engine, and waited, watching Shirley back out, brake lights brightening the pavement as she stopped to shift. Then, wheels turned hard, she drove forward, and up the short narrow roadway Jo had taken. Lew turned to watch Harry bring the camper up behind her, then he backed out the van, and joined the waiting line.

Shirley waited, her front bumper at the edge of the traffic stream moving sluggishly past it. Harry waited half a yard behind, Lew almost as close behind Harry. A break appeared only two car-lengths long but Shirley edged her bumper into it, the approaching car slowing to let her in. She swung into the lane, Harry riding her bumper, Lew following equally close, all crowding in together. Allowing no more than a few feet of space between them, the three passed between the empty toll booths, no toll being collected in this direction, and onto the bridge itself, staying in the slow lane directly beside the walk.

Careful never to allow another car between him and Harry, Lew watched the lane beside them in his outside rear-view. Here in the slow lane they moved at under forty, often having to brake, the line beside them moving a little faster.

He saw an empty space approaching in the rear-view, and flipped on his turn signal. A brown Mustang moved past him, the empty space behind it, and Lew slid smoothly over into it, his extended front bumper passing only inches from the slanted rear end of the Mustang. He touched his brakes, allowing the Mustang to move on, creating an empty space before him, and Harry slid over into it.

In the curbside lane where she would remain, Shirley moved along with the traffic. Harry, with Lew on his bumper, pulled abreast of Shirley, then held even. Maintaining his close distance directly behind Harry, Lew again began watching his rear-view, waiting now for an empty space in the third lane. Seconds passed as they rolled on, moving under the tower at the San Francisco end. Beside him, the slightly faster third-lane traffic flowed past, but no empty space appeared. Lew felt his heartbeat increase, and reminded himself that they had plenty of time, most of the length of the bridge yet.

Seconds passed as they rolled on under the orange lights, the commute traffic at its peak now. Then Lew saw an empty space coming up but before it reached him cars moved together, eliminating it, and again he felt the sweat start at the roots of his hair. He was worried now, and as they rolled on his eyes moved steadily between Harry's big wooden bumper and the miniaturized string of cars moving toward him in the rectangle of the van's mirror.

A break appeared in the mirrored lineup behind him, and Lew flipped on his turn signal. But as the empty space approached it began to contract. He could wait no longer, they were near the middle of the bridge, he had to move over *now*. Lew quickly rolled down his window, and shoved his arm straight out and pumping, pointing finger jabbing at the empty space as it came abreast. Now it was too short, obviously so, but Lew edged slowly toward it, his wheels crossing the lane-line, bumping along the warning nodules, the horn of the car behind blasting suddenly. Lew kept on, forcing, the rear of the van and the car's right front fender nearly touching; the man had to brake now or be hit. Lew pressed, edging fractionally closer, the horn stopped, the car slowing, and Lew slid into the line with no inch to spare. He waited for the renewed horn blast, but none came. A commuter, he thought, grinning, trained to resignation.

In the third lane now, Lew drew abreast with Harry and Shirley and they all held in a line. Then, passing the middle of the bridge where the cables dipped lowest, Harry began gradually slowing, dropping down through thirty-seven . . . thirty-four . . . thirty-two. Watching him intently, Shirley and Lew slowed with him, maintaining their lineup, and the cars in the three lanes ahead moved on, creating an empty space before them. The empty space grew to a car-length, then two, then three. At Lew's left the fourth lane moved steadily past him, drivers glancing curiously at the lineup of van, camper, and Alfa holding abreast and still slowing.

Again Lew watched his rear-view. Breaks in the fast fourth lane were more frequent, he saw one immediately, and as it came abreast he drifted left, wheels crossing the line, rumbling the markers. Simultaneously, Harry drifted over the line to edge into Lew's lane, and Shirley's left wheels slid over the line into Harry's. Each of them now straddling a lane-line, the three cars moving abreast blocked all four lanes behind them.

For eight or ten seconds no one protested: the bridge lanes were narrow, and cars did sometimes stray over the line. Then a horn tapped. Behind the three windshields, Lew smiled tensely; Harry grinned; Shirley frowned, glancing anxiously into her mirror. A long moment, then again a horn sounded, blasting this time, and immediately several more. An instant of silence again, as they rolled on down the orange-lighted roadway exactly abreast, straddling the lines, blocking all traffic behind them.

Then almost simultaneously dozens of horns blared and continued, some held down steadily, others honk-honking. It sounded almost festive; Lew thought of a wedding party.

Again he and Shirley watched Harry. Leaning forward, Harry stared up at the north tower, rapidly growing in his windshield. Harry lifted a hand, brought it slowly down in signal, and they carefully slowed together: to thirty . . . twenty-five . . . twenty . . . and on down to seven or eight miles an hour, speedometers now wobbling erratically.

Behind them horns raged. Far ahead, tail lights shrank in the distance, the strange emptiness before them lengthening. Across the road in the San Francisco-bound lanes, drivers slowed, rapidly cranking down windows, to stare over in wonder. Up ahead, her eyes wide, Jo stood at her post beside the north tower watching them approach.

Staring up at the north tower, Harry again raised a hand, waiting until they were approximately a hundred yards from it, the length of a football field. Then, in signal, his hand flashed down like an ax.

Instantly Shirley slammed the shift lever forward, flooring the gas pedal, and the Alfa shot ahead, burning rubber. In the same instant Harry swung his wheel to nose into the space she had just vacated, nearly brushing her rear bumper. And in the moment Harry moved so did Lew, yanking his wheel in a sudden right turn, his big wooden front bumper swinging in an arc toward Harry's rear one. Then they hit their brakes, and stood motionless, almost sideways on the roadway, across all lane markers, blocking all four lanes.

Brakes squealing behind them, the nearly solid four-lane commute mass came to a halt: from far behind as the stop moved peristaltically back toward the toll booths, they heard a bumper crash, then another. Ahead and still accelerating, the Alfa flashed along the empty roadway, body winking under the overhead lights. Behind van and camper slewed sideways on the road, the horns had gone momentarily silent in astonishment.

Lew set his parking brake, turned off the engine, and flung open his door. He jumped to the road, slamming his door, yanked at the handle to be sure it had locked. Then, grinning, he drew his arm far back, and exuberantly threw the ignition keys curving over the bridge rail to the water below.

Inside the camper, kneeling on the front seat to face the rear, Harry reached to the squat metal box bolted to the wooden framework there; the box stood directly beside the camper's side window facing north toward Marin. From it, heavy insulated black wire led to the transformer and batteries on the floor. Harry's hand smacked down on a toggle switch, and a brilliant, hard-edged beam of blue-white light shot from the lens of the squat metal box and through the camper window, whitening the air far ahead.

Like a searchlight, this beam touched the curving green trunk of the speeding Alfa a hundred yards ahead in just the moment that Shirley pressed the brake pedal hard. In the white light, black smoke sprayed from the rear wheels, and the Alfa slid to a stop directly beside the great north tower of the bridge. Its door flew open, and Shirley sprang out to race for the sidewalk beside the car—across the roadway at the other tower leg Jo stood watching her.

Waiting for Harry to jump down out of the camper, Lew simply stood beside the van; grinning and facing the massed headlights filling the four lanes for a mile behind them. Elation flowed wild in him. A driver in the front line of stopped cars sat watching him, and when Lew's eyes met his, Lew winked at the man. From the camper window, Harry's beam of light began to rise up through the night like a probing finger, reaching for something high above.

Up ahead, Jo and Shirley now stood with their backs to this rising searching light, one on each side of the roadway and facing the north bridge tower. Their hands rose high, reaching, then each found the patch of orange tape she had smoothed onto the steel side of the tower last night. Each peeled loose her tape, and then in unison both women yanked hard on the two long lengths of orange fishline stretching invisibly up into the night— and the weighted plastic pole the men had left high on the bridge transverse over the roadway, dropped over the edge.

It fell fast, the accordion folds of white sailcloth popping open, and now there in the darkness high above the orange lights of the bridge, a great white square of cloth hung swaying over the roadway, suspended between the enormous tower legs.

In the camper swiveling the metal box, Harry moved the long finger of light, found the swaying square of sailcloth, and centered the beam upon it. Then his fingers twisted the stubby lens, and the intense blue-white beam illuminating the great cloth sheet changed from fuzzy indefinition to a gigantic hard-edged square of light. Far below in one of the stopped cars facing the great illuminated sheet, a woman in the front seat leaned intently toward the windshield, murmuring, "My God, it's a screen." Suddenly delighted, she swung around to the other car-pool members—"We're going to have a *show!*"

Harry's palm smacked down on a push switch. A black drum on top of the powerful outdoor-theater projector revolved fractionally, and onto the giant screen hanging over Golden Gate Bridge flashed half a dozen carefully lettered words, enormously enlarged. In Harry's green, blue and red felt-pen lettering, they said, *Settle back, folks*. This . . . is our life! Harry jumped to the concrete, slamming and locking his door, and he and Lew began to run up the empty roadway toward the Alfa. Ahead and high above them, the huge screen went momentarily black, then lightened again, and Lew, running hard, began to laugh. A huge photograph now filled the screen—a face. Above it Harry's hand-lettered caption read, Lewis O. Joliffe, prominent S.F. attorney. Under the photo, in the careful, long ago white-ink script of Lew's mother: *Aged 3 months*. The photo itself, a sepia print, was a bonneted baby, the infant Lew Joliffe staring out as though astonished at the mile-long captive audience below—which stared back in equal astonishment at the huge round-eyed face in the night-time sky.

The Alfa was backing toward the two running men now, fast and erratically. Then it stopped, black-streaking the pavement, and Shirley flung open her door, then slid to the right. Lew piled in, squeezing into the back to sprawl across the piled-up belongings there; and Harry slid under the wheel. In the darkness off to the right of the bridge they heard the rackety clatter of a helicopter, and saw its running lights and dim dark bulk swinging down toward the bridge. Harry released the hand brake, slamming his door, and the screen high above them brightened once more.

They all leaned forward, staring up; an enormous black-and-white photograph filled the fifty-foot screen, a diapered baby on a lawn, an out-of-focus front porch in the background. JOSEPHINE DUNNE, said Harry's yard-high felt-tip lettering, WELL-KNOWN S.F. BEAUTY! Far behind the screen, down on the ocean-side walkway, the real Jo Dunne hurried toward the end of the bridge.

Blades clacking the air, the helicopter swung low over the car roof, and Shirley cried, "Harry, *move, move!* Let's *go!*"

"Wait! I *gotta* see this next one!" Again the screen darkened, the helicopter hanging directly over the bridge now, slowly lowering to hang over the car-jammed roadway. Under the clattering blades its insect body turned to face north as another giant photo filled the opening between the great legs of the north tower. A naked infant lay on his stomach on a wide white towel staring with interest at the tiny helicopter before it. Across the picture's top, hugely: HARRY D. LEVY. Underneath it: FAMOUS SAN FRANCISCO BAREASSTER. Harry yelled with laughter, shot the car forward, and punched a dashboard button.

From the car radio as they raced toward the bridge end, a man's voice over the running-water sound of his copter motor said, "—king all lanes is *not* a jackknifed truck as we thought at first sight. It looks like—whoops, *here's another!* Another child, this one in color! A girl of about two, looks like, leaning over the handlebars of her tricycle and smiling right at me. Written above it is, 'Shirley Rosen,' and underneath, 'Harry's bride-to-be.' Folks, in fourteen years of commute-traffic broadcasting, I've never seen anything like this! We're heading for the toll plaza now to see what's happening back there." Harry slowed, then swung off the freeway into the view parking lot. Almost directly below his wheels Jo raced along the dark length of the footbridge.

"Here's another!" said the voice from the Alfa's radio. "A boy of about twelve. On the front porch of a house. Holding a diploma. Underneath in a woman's handwriting it says, 'He made it! Lew's graduation, Proviso High School, 1958.' I can't *believe* it!"—the radio voice broke into astounded laughter. Harry pulled in beside Lew's VW, turned off lights and engine, and they sat staring back at the foreshortened length of the bridge, its distant half brilliant with motionless headlights, the back of the huge white screen in the north tower going dark. "I've reported accidents, breakdowns, tieups of every kind," the radio voice shouted delightedly, "but never anything like this! Down on the bridge below me people are standing between their cars, they're up on both walks, they're sitting on car hoods. A group of young people are sitting cross-legged on the roof of their van, and they're *applauding!* There's a highway patrol car down there, its dome light revolving, but it can't move, it's locked in, can't move! Here at the toll plaza and beyond everything is bl—. There's a *report card* up on the screen! I mean it! A tremendous yellow report card forty feet high!"

Jo appeared beside the Alfa. "Did it work, did it work!?"

"Take a look." Pointing, Lew got out, sliding past Harry, and Jo turned to stare back at the bridge. The rear of the great screen hung in the black sky, yellowly tinted, and Lew said, "That's your report card, and now the whole world knows: C in arithmetic."

"But A-plus in art." The back of the screen went dim, and Jo said, "Listen . . ." Motionless, heads cocked, the four of them waited, hearing nothing, and Jo said, "The horns have stopped."

"Yeah!" Lew grabbed her, grinning. "They love it!"

"They'll want it every night now," Shirley cried. From the north, very faintly, a siren sounded, and the radio voice said, "It's a dog! A black-and-white mongrel with his head cocked looking out at us! Says, 'Lew's old dog, Jake: he could sit up, roll over, and play dead.' Oh, my god!"

Lew bent forward to lean in at Harry's window. "Well, kids. We all better take off. We'll be in touch."

"Right." Harry put out his hand, they shook. "Good show,"

he said quietly, smiling fondly at Lew, "in more ways than one."

Leaning across Harry, Shirley cried out, "You've got my folks' phone number, Jo, and I've got your dad's. You phone now! You hear?"

"I will, I will!"

Lew said, "So long, Shirl. Remember me whenever you lie down on the freeway," and she nodded, blinking rapidly, unable to reply. The siren sounded, closer now, and Harry said good-by to Jo, kissed his fingers at her, then the Alfa's lights came on, and he backed out.

Behind the Alfa, letting the distance between them grow, Lew drove north on 101, beginning the Waldo Grade climb. A highway patrol car, dome light flashing, siren growling, flashed by on the other side toward the bridge, and Lew leaned forward to turn on his radio, punching the button for KGO. "—monitoring our radio," said the helicopter-voice over the watery sound of its motor, "and the truck at this end can't get through. But the truck that parks up at the tunnel during commute time is on its way down, and will be—here's another: a color photo of a boy in scout uniform, a yarmulke, and the beginnings of a mustache —it's our old buddy, Harry Levy, again! Written underneath—it *must* have been his mother—is: 'Harry's bar mitzvah. Life Scout the same day!' Screen's black now . . . I *wish* I had a TV camera to *show* you these things! Here's another color photo: bald, middle-aged man in suntans, woman in a dress, girl in shorts. The caption—oh boy—the caption says, 'Our summer in Yellowstone. Dad, Mom, and Shirley.' Oh, I tell you, there'll be a lot of late suppers tonight, but what an excuse!"

Driving through the night, the freeway strangely empty, Lew and Jo listened as the jubilant voice from the traffic helicopter described the scene on the bridge for late listeners, "There are a dozen or so men around the camper with the projector, but no one seems to be making any effort to break into it. They're just standing there, leaning against it, arms folded, enjoying the show. And so am I, so am I—forget traffic conditions on the Nimitz Freeway tonight! There's an enormous birthday cake filling the screen now high above San Francisco Bay: a woman's hands tilting the cake toward the camera. It has eleven lighted candles, and says, 'Happy Birthday, Jo!' "

They listened as the voice described Lew in Little League uniform . . . Harry's and Lew's law-school diplomas . . . Shirley in white uniform . . . Jo working on her Town . . . "And here's a great one—oh, this is great! Says, 'Harry and Shirley meet Lew and Jo.' A painted canvas; says 'Disneyland' in one corner. Shows four aerialists in costume: two men hanging from trapezes, arms out; one woman has just been caught by the wrists, the other is still flying through the air. And smiling out at us through cutout holes over the bodies are the four faces we've grown to know and love tonight! Oh man, I tell you! Screen's going black again . . ."

A huge tow truck, a Christmas tree of yellow, red, and white lights raced by across the freeway, and Lew glanced at Jo to smile. The radio voice described views of Lew, Jo, and the Levys skiing . . . playing tennis . . . lying by the apartment pool. "Here's the tow truck," the voice cried then, "racing along the bridge toward us! Up on the screen now there's a car. Looks like it's up on a—*it's the car on the roof of the Civic Center last night!* It is! The *police* car! Up on the *roof!* And Harry and Shirley, Lew and Jo, are all over the car! With *guns!* The *cop's* guns! Oh, my god, *they did it!* They put the cop's car up on the *roof!* Oh, *bless* you, Harry and Shirley, Lew and Jo! . . . The tow truck is slowing . . . stopping. Now it's swinging around on the bridge, getting into position to back up to the camper. The screen goes dark, and . . . *oh, Jesus.*" The voice suddenly choked. "Ladies and gentlemen, all I can do is report the facts. And the fact is that up there on the screen is good old Harry, Lew, Shirley and Jo . . . stark naked. They're standing before a fireplace, looks like—*dancing.* Harry, modest Harry, is wearing a baseball cap and cigar. But Lew and the girls—bless you, girls, bless you!—are wearing only big wide smiles. Their thumbs are at their noses, all four of them, fingers spread, and the caption across the top says, 'So long, Short Pants,' and across the bottom, 'And so long, California.' One of the men from the truck is down on the pavement now signaling the driver . . . truck's backing toward the camper . . . up on the screen the slide is still there . . . it doesn't go off. The truck's lowering its sling . . . slide is still there, our four naked friends thumbing their noses down at the whole length of Golden Gate Bridge at all of us. . . . The front of the camper is lifting now, and Lew and Jo, Harry and Shirley are slowly sliding off the screen—and *listen* to those horns blast! *Protesting*, I do believe! . . . Screen's dark, the beam of the projector shining off toward the ocean—and the show is over. Well, farewell to you, too, Lew and Jo, Harry and Shirley. Never knew you, but we're gonna miss you now, believe me! I know I will! The first of the stalled cars is edging around the camper. . . . Now here come the others, the tow truck leaving, the beam still shining out the camper window. Traffic flow resuming on the Golden Gate Bridge. Guess I better go report on the Nimitz now, but, oh man, it's gonna be a letdown."

Lew reached out, turned off the radio, and they were silent for some seconds. Off to the right and below, Strawberry Point appeared, and their heads turned for a farewell look. They faced front, Jo sighing slightly, and she said, "Well. That's that. Now on to Santa Fe, is that the idea?"

"Right." Lew nodded, then glanced at her. "But you almost didn't come this time."

"You knew that, did you?"

"Well, it occurred to me."

"Well, you were right. I was going to help through tonight: leave a note in the VW for you when I parked it, go help drag the screen down, then just walk on across the bridge to the city and a motel. I very nearly didn't come along when we moved from San Francisco."

"I know."

"You know a lot, don't you."

"Not too much."

"Well, I still might not! I might just get out at the next bus stop and go back to the city."

"Right. But you might not, too."

"Maybe."

"Jo, how come? How come you stick around? I want you to, but—why do you?"

After a moment she shrugged slightly. "Same old reason, I suppose; the reason I came with you in the first place."

"And what's that?"

"Who knows!" she said as though about to be angry. But then she looked at him, and smiled. "Maybe just to see what happens next."

F

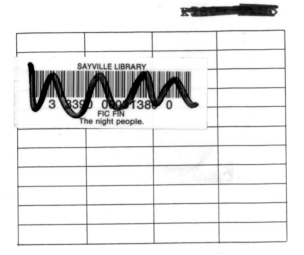